VALERIUS THE KING
The Valerian Chronicles – Volume 2

I0666001

T. R. Rankin

VALERIUS THE KING
The Valerian Chronicles – Volume 2

DOUBLE DRAGON

A DOUBLE DRAGON PAPERBACK

© Copyright 2011
T. R. Rankin

The right of T. R. Rankin to be identified as author of
this work has been asserted in accordance with the
Copyright, Designs and Patents Act 1988

All Rights Reserved

No reproduction, copy or transmission of the publication
may be made without written permission. No paragraph
of this publication may be reproduced, copied or
transmitted save with the written permission of the
publisher, or in accordance with the provisions of the
Copyright Act 1956 (as amended).

Any person who does any unauthorised act in relation to
this publication may be liable to criminal prosecution
and civil claims for damages.

ISBN 978-1-78695-633-0

Double Dragon
is an imprint of
Fiction4All

This Edition Published 2021
Fiction4All
www.fiction4all.com

Cover art by Deron Douglas
www.derondouglas.ca

THE VALERIAN EMPIRE

PROLOGUE

Amid the coarse babble of voices, music filled the hall with a soft murmur of strings. As the girl moved out onto the floor, a flute joined in. Then a drum took up a slow, languid beat. Voices stilled as, one by one, the bearded faces turned towards the girl. And as she began her dance, their eyes fastened onto her form.

Dressed in the merest wisps of silk, her dark hair loose about her shoulders and brushing the mounds of her breasts, she moved slowly at first, like a willow stirred by a soft summer breeze. In the shimmering torch and candle light, her lithe body drifted across the floor, her arms weaving delicate patterns in the air. Then, gradually, the tempo of the music began to build and her movements hardened. Her pelvis picked up the rhythm and began to pulse with the beat. And the eyes of the men grew shiny.

None watched with more fervor than the large, unkempt-looking figure seated on a raised dais at the head of the room. He was a huge man whose once massive frame had gone to flab and whose wild black beard and mane were streaked with grey. His eye—for he had only one, the other being covered by a black scarf tied diagonally around his head—glistened hard and was glued to the girl's every move. Pounding out the rhythm with a meat-filled fist, he fed himself from a platter by his left hand, and drank from a flagon in his right.

Intermittently, between swallows, or at some particularly provocative move by the girl, he would grunt, low and deep in the back of his throat.

As the girl reached the climax of her dance, the silence among the men in the smoky stone hall was profound. The girl was lovely, it was true, and a good deal of her body was enticingly visible through the thin gauze of her shirt and pantaloons, but it was the dance itself, the grace and fluidity of her movements—the way her body seemed to create the very music she danced to—that kept them entranced. Even the servants stopped to watch, standing between tables or at the edges of the hall, their trays held level before them. Only the musicians moved to create their sound, and even these watched enthralled, taking their cues from the girl's moves as if her elaborate acrobatics were a form of conducting.

Suddenly, the one-eyed one let out a roar and leapt at the girl. Catching her by the arm, he dragged her back to his chair, kicked away the small table beside it, and laid her face down over the arm. Quickly, he ripped away the flimsy cloth of her pants and undergarments and began fumbling with his own. No one moved to prevent him. Neither did the girl protest—she had been warned that this was a possibility when performing before the high king, and that any struggle would be futile. As she had no choice but to perform, so she had no choice in this. Rather, she lay quietly, propped on her elbows, and awaited his thrust.

But the one-eyed king was drunker than he realized. He swayed on the dais, fumbling with his small clothes, then tearing at them furiously. And when his manhood finally did emerge, it was plainly unequal to the task. Here and there, a stifled titter escaped in the hall and the king's face turned purple with rage.

Just then, the great double doors at the far end of the hall banged open and a troop of men barged in clamoring excitedly. "Majesty!" the first of them called out. "Your Majesty! They have struck again!" This was an elderly man, but one whose angry stride belied his grey beard and merchant's robes. Unmindful of the revelers around him, and ignoring the distasteful tableau of the king and his prey, he strode directly to the dais. "I've lost another two ships, Majesty! That's five this year alone! If this keeps up, I'll be ruined. And I'm not the only one!"

Sweeping the girl to the floor like a sack, the king sat down heavily, and with effort, focused his attention on the merchant. "Where?"

"The same spot, Majesty. Two days out, south of Zagorbia. Angmar here tells me they appeared out of nowhere, just like before. Five long galleys. Three swept in and engaged him while the other two took my ships and made off."

"And you, Angmar—you who were to protect these ships—you did nothing?"

"I did all I could, Majesty. But truly, it was little. Their galleys are small, but very fast and more maneuverable than mine. I could not ram, for they spun away quicker than I could turn. Neither could I board. And every time I got near one, the others closed in and rained murderous arrow fire on me."

"Did you not give chase? Why didn't you overtake our merchantmen and get them back?"

"I did give chase, my lord. But again, their arrows kept me off. And they headed straight inshore, right in under the cliffs where I dared not follow. Then they disappeared."

The king scowled and tugged at his beard. "Disappeared, eh? You slunk away with your tail between your legs, is what you mean!"

"Majesty," said the merchant, "if you please, Angmar is not to blame here. I am convinced he did all that could be done. But we can't let this situation continue... All trade between Zagorbia and Dulcai is at risk. You have to do something."

"Yes!" came a voice from the back of the hall, "Is the Great Fantar UP to that challenge?" And the laughter was not stifled this time.

"Who spoke? Who said that?" raged the king.

"That's not all, Fantar!" came another voice. "This pirate claims to be the son of Valerius and rightful High King... What are you going to do about that?"

"Seize that man!" Fantar pointed. "Bring him here." And when the man had been brought forward, Fantar had him bound to a post, then leaned close and leered in his face. "So, you would mock your king with a pretender in his own hall, would you?"

"Majesty," the man quailed, "I only repeat what I heard!"

"Heard where, from whom?"

"In town, Majesty. It is the talk in all the taverns. This man claims to be Valerius, Valerian that was and son of the former High King."

"Bah! I took that boy's head when we found him cowering with the women after Valeria fell."

"I repeat only what I heard, Majesty."

"Well, maybe we can fix that," Fantar growled, and pulling a short dagger from his waist, brutally sawed off the man's right ear. "Next time," he said, "maybe you'll think twice before you listen to any more such tales?"

"Yes, Majesty," the man gasped, blood spilling down his neck and shoulder.

"And as for pirates and pretenders," Fantar shouted to the hall at large, "I am the only rightful king here. I, Fantar of Valeria! And any who think differently can join this 'Valerius' when I stuff his testicles down his throat and watch him choke to death on them!"

The hall was silent as Fantar glared out over the crowd. Then he turned to the merchant.

"And you! How dare you barge in here and interrupt my feast? Do you think I cannot make good your filthy losses? Here," he said, tossing the man the severed ear, "Take this as my token and get out of here: We'll deal with this pirate tomorrow. Now," he yelled, "Bring more wine! More meat! Here girl," he said, tossing her the dagger, "cut that

11

one down and have him thrown into the sea... Perhaps his pirate friend will come to rescue him."

Later that night, the girl lay beside the snoring king and watched as a knife-edged sliver of moon sliced its way across the window frame. The king had been no more successful with her in his bed than he had on his throne. Hardly able to stand by the end of his feast, he had dragged her from the hall amid much fanfare and raucous cheering. But there was no possibility of his accomplishing anything, and after ripping away the remains of her flimsy dancing costume and tumbling with her onto the bed, he had promptly rolled over onto his back and started to snore.

She listened now as that snoring grew louder and more rhythmical, and as the edge of the moon touched the window frame, she slowly eased herself out of bed, found her pack that her servant had tucked into a corner, and quietly pulled on her clothes. Then she pulled from the pack the dagger Fantar had given her, and with this gripped firmly in her right hand, stole back to the edge of the bed.

Fantar lay on his back, his arms flung wide, his face turned slightly towards the window so that his neck was exposed and defenseless beneath his matted beard. He snored again, long and ragged, and as he exhaled, his fetid, wine soured breath hit her in the face. Bracing her knee on the edge of the bed, the girl gripped the knife with both hands and raised it high. But then, as men who snore will often do, Fantar snorted violently and just as the knife plunged downwards, his good eye snapped open and his right arm shot up, blocking the blow and knocking the girl back.

"Arrgh!" he growled as the blade bit into his forearm and cut across it. Rearing up like a maddened bull, he grabbed for the girl, catching, then losing her wrist, then her ankle as she tumbled backwards. Cat-like, she sliced at him again as she went, cutting his shoulder. But then she was on the floor, scuttling backwards and he, like a great ape of the forest, vaulted from the bed, his one eye red in the darkness and glowing with rage. But his feet tangled in the bed clothes and he fell heavily, smashing his head onto cold stone of the floor. Again, the girl started in for the kill but as Fantar began to push himself up from the floor, she lost her nerve and fled, leaving behind her bag and her shoes. She did not even notice that after this single effort, Fantar simply grunted and collapsed back onto the floor, unconscious.

Meanwhile, many hundreds of miles away, in a snug, well-furnished cave deep in the fastness of the mountains south of Zagorbia, an ancient mage sat huddled over the embers of his fire and stirred some herbs into a pot that hung simmering from a tripod. Motioning for his servant to add another stick to the fire, the mage stirred until the broth came to a slow boil and began giving off a cloud of sweet, earthy-smelling steam. Into this, he thrust his grey and wrinkled face, inhaling deeply time after time.

Finally, he flopped back into his chair, his arms limp and his eyes glassy.

Entranced, he stared into the depths of the slowly bubbling broth until its surface opened before him and visions emerged, spiraling towards the ceiling. There was a dancing girl, slim and raven haired, twirling in the flickering fire light. There was a monstrous king, bloated and vile with a twitching, evil eye. There was a palace bedroom, the flash of moonlight on an upraised blade, a struggle in a swirl of smoke, then the girl in flight, running wild and barefoot through the moonlit night.

Closing his eyes, the mage let his chin drop to his chest and sighed heavily. "She is the one," he muttered. "She must be the one." And he drifted off into a deep sleep.

Chapter 1
THE PEDDLER

For two days, the girl, Vahla, fled through the hills, knowing neither where she went nor who followed. At first, she ran blindly, heedless of the branches that tore at her, or the stones that cut her feet. So wild was her panic that she lost all sense of direction or place. All she could see in her mind were Fantar's men thundering in pursuit, their horses lathered, nostrils flared, the riders crouched over their necks, faces leering. And she ran. When she fell, she jumped up and ran again. Deep into the hills north of Valeria she fled all through that night, and when she finally collapsed and fell into an exhausted sleep, it was in a small, well protected dell which had not felt human footfall since Fantar himself had camped there some seventeen years before, when his armies had descended from these very hills to attack the city.

In this dell, Vahla cowered all through the following day. She had no food or water, no idea where she was, and dared not make any move to find out. She was sure Fantar's men were just over this hill or the next and would be searching out her dell at any moment. In truth, the pursuit was sadly deficient. Fantar had not been discovered until early morning, and had been able to give no coherent account of the attack for some time after that. And when his troopers did thunder from the

15

gates and spread out across the plain surrounding the city, they found no clues whatsoever and, not daring to return without news, repaired to the nearest taverns where they spent the day.

Vahla could not know this, of course, and as darkness settled over the hills, she set forth again, hoping she was still moving away from the city and not back towards it. A stream slaked her thirst and some berries served for food, but she dared not tarry long at either spot. The rising moon showed her an approximation of east, and in that direction she moved, keeping the shadows of the great mountains to her left. At daylight, she hid in another dell—this one by a small stream—and slept through much of the day, buried under a moldering pile of last year's leaves.

As darkness fell, she moved on again, but by now hunger was becoming a serious concern. Her shrunken stomach screamed at her, and her legs felt weak and spongy. She knew she had to find sustenance of some sort, and soon. Also, she knew she was not the only hungry creature prowling these hills. Wolves were not uncommon, and great cats sometimes came down from the high mountains to hunt among the verdant hills and forests along the coast. In need of a meal herself, she had no desire to become one, and as the waxing moon rose again, she bent her course southward in hopes of finding some habitation.

After some hours, she topped a small hill and was startled to see a fire flickering among the trees in a glade by the side of a small river in the valley below. Summoning all her stealth, she crept down the hill and into the wood, sliding silently from tree to tree and carefully placing every step. As a small clearing opened before her, she could see a single man huddled in his cloak before a dying fire. Behind him, and off to her left, a horse and donkey were tethered to a bush. To the right, on the far side of the fire from him, was a pile of what appeared to be peddler's goods. And suspended from the branch of a tree was a food bag.

Food! Her stomach screamed at the sight of it. But what to do? The answer was 'nothing,' obviously, until this fellow was soundly asleep. She knew not from whence he came or what news might be abroad of her. But what then? The safest thing, she thought, would be to simply slit his throat. She still had the dagger. And perhaps he was not a peddler at all. Perhaps he, too, was a criminal. Perhaps she could claim it was he who attacked Fantar and then carried her off. Fantar was so drunk, he might not know. But then she thought, this was fear talking, not her mind, and the injustice of the idea repelled her. This man had done nothing so far as she knew, and to murder him without cause would make her as bad as Fantar.

So, what then? Steal his horse? Could she do that quietly enough? What if he awoke? Steal his food bag? That could be done quietly. But food and a horse! The thought was as luxurious as a bath. Making herself as comfortable as she could, Vahla settled in to wait.

The peddler heard the approaching footsteps before the girl even reached the trees. He didn't know who it was, of course, but he knew no animal would approach that way, and no warrior worth his salt would make half so much noise. So as Vahla surveyed him from the brush, he feigned somnolence and huddled under his cloak, his long sword stretched comfortably by his side. When some time had passed and the intruder made no move to either approach or retreat, the man stretched and yawned, then pulled his bedding roll from his gear, spread it out before the fire, and settled himself down to sleep.

Soon, Vahla heard the reassuring sounds of snoring, and after waiting another few minutes to be sure, slipped quietly from her hiding place and tiptoed across the clearing. The food bag was hung quite high, and as she stretched up to cut the cord, the man grabbed her from behind, one hand gripping her knife hand, the other arm wrapping tight around her waist. Starting like some wild creature caught in a snare, she fought viciously—twisting, jerking, kicking, biting, scratching—but the fellow was simply too powerful. As he crushed her to him, she could feel the rock hard muscles of his arms and chest flexing about her and she knew she was helpless. Still, she struggled, but as he pinned her to the ground like a kitten, her fear and frustration overwhelmed her and she broke down, sobbing.

"So!" said the man, leaning back to let the light from the fire fall on her face, "it's a filly we've snagged... I thought you were some run-away apprentice boy."

He relaxed his grip then, and she yanked her arm free and slashed at his throat with Fantar's dagger. But he was too quick. Twisting his body away in an instant, he countered with a heavy backhanded blow that knocked her back and stunned her.

"Vixen bitch!" he yelled, and jumped to his bed roll to pull out a great long sword. "You'll not play those female tricks on me again!" Raising the blade high, he brought it down in a swift, flashing stroke aimed right at her neck.

Vahla had only time to recognize—with a startling clarity deep in some primordial recess of her brain—that this was Death. Then the blade stopped inches from her throat.

"Now, your life is mine, Lady," the man said, and his bearded face broke into a grin.

"Bastard!" she spat, the fear turning to fire in her eyes. "You're no peddler... Not wielding a sword like that."

"Sure I am," he said. "I traded for it. But you're no runaway handmaiden either—not with a dagger like that."

"I traded for it."

"Oh, I'll bet you did. Stole it, more likely. Did you slit the previous owner's throat like you tried to do mine?"

"Hey, you grabbed me! If I'd wanted to murder you, I'd have stabbed you in your sleep."

"Yup, just like you were able to steal my food bag without my even knowing about it."

The girl had no answer for this, but countered on a different tack. "Well, if you are a peddler, how about we make a trade?"

"Such as?" he said, returning the sword to his blanket roll.

"This dagger for some food... and your horse."

The man laughed. "I can see you're quite a negotiator! Tell you what: if you promise not to try and slit my throat again, I'll give you some food and you can keep your dagger. After all, if your life is mine, I should take care of it."

"And the horse?"

"Don't press your luck. Now," he said untying the sack, "what might be your pleasure? Bread, not too moldy? Mutton, not too rancid? Wine, not too sour? That should do it: a feast fit for a foraging filly!"

Sitting cross-legged by the fire, Vahla ate ravenously, bread mold and old mutton not bothering her in the least. "What's your name?" the man asked, stretching his length on his bed.

"Vahla," she said, chewing.

"Well, Vahla, I'm Thorngere. I won't ask what you're doing running around out here with no food and bare feet, but if you're headed east and want to tag along, I may let you ride for a while tomorrow... At least until we get to the next town."

"And then?" Suspicion was strong in her voice.

"Then I sell some pots, I hope. I don't know what you do."

"I thought you said my life was yours?"

"Well, I did." he said loftily, "But now that I've saved it, and fed it, I've decided to be magnanimous and allow you to do with it what you will. Right now, though, I'd like to get some sleep. If you rummage in that pack over there, I think you'll find another blanket."

Vahla did as she was told and for the first time in days, soon found herself curled up in relative comfort and contentment. Compared to moldering leaves, the old blanket was like a down quilt, and compared to the chill blackness of the night and the imagined eyes of wolves, the warm glow of the dying fire was like hearth and home itself. All that troubled her—and it was quite silly, she knew, but still it would not leave—was a nagging fear that he would leave her to do 'what she would'. But it was only because she was exhausted and had been through so much.

When Vahla awoke, it was already light and the man, Thorngere, was nowhere to be seen. Quickly, she glanced at the food bag hanging from its branch, and at the dappled grey and donkey quietly grazing on their tethers, then got up and went to the river. He was there, wading waist deep in the swirling stream, long golden hair loose about his naked shoulders, and a small barbed spear poised in his right hand. Vahla sat on the bank, cooling her bruised feet in the stream, and watched the morning light play across the broad muscles of his back. He was a large, powerful man, not as young as he had sounded the night before, but far from old, either. Seasoned rather, she thought, and as he turned back towards her and smiled in greeting, obviously in the prime of his strength. Hard muscle rippled across his chest and abdomen. Nor was he any peddler either; not judging by those scars on his arms and shoulders.

Suddenly, his spear arm flashed out and he dove down in to the water after it, coming up with a larger silver fish wriggling on the point. As he waded ashore, she caught her breath to see he was completely nude, and as he stood before her, grinning broadly and unabashed in his nakedness, her eyes could not help but fall to his pendulous manhood.

"Thought you'd like something a little better than rancid mutton for breakfast."

"Yes, wonderful," she said, tearing her eyes away. She was surprised at the way her heart was pounding.

"Why don't you take a swim while I get this fellow cooking," he said, scooping up his clothes. "The water's great! Besides, you smell like an old compost heap."

When she returned to camp, he was squatting by the cooking fire, wearing a simple loin cloth and frying his catch. But as he looked up, and saw her standing close beside him, it was his turn to gasp. "I washed my clothes, too," she said, the dripping garments slung over her arm. "Do you have some line I could hang them on to dry?"

Thorngere's voice caught in his throat and he nodded towards his pack. He had not expected this. Even with her wet hair plastered to her skull, the girl—the woman—was lovely. Better than lovely. She was incredible. Full swaying breasts, large, deep brown nipples, a slim sinewy body, full hips, that dark patch of pubic hair—he had seen many women, but this one made his head swim.

"I think you'll also find something you can put on in there," he said thickly. He really had no time for this.

"I don't mind," she said. "The sun is nice."

Reaching for the handle of the pan, Thorngere grabbed a coal instead. "Damn it, woman! If you want me to be able to cook this fish, you'll have to put something on."

Grinning in victory, Vahla found a loose fitting shift in one of Thorngere's packs and pulled it over her head. "We wouldn't want anything else to get burned," she said.

Later, the two walked down a dusty, winding, cart track of a road, he leading the horse, she the loaded donkey. They had followed the stream south along an even rougher track, then forded it to intersect this path. Thorngere, it seemed, had been trading deep in the hills to the north.

Now he walked with his hood pulled low over his forehead to shield his eyes from the bright morning sun, but under that cover, his gaze kept straying to the girl beside him. Who was this woman, he thought? And why this coincidence of her showing up in the middle of the night like that? It was too easy, her offering herself like that... Not that it wasn't tempting. But who would have sent her? He could not afford this kind of risk, not now, not even if she was legitimate. But what if she was legitimate?

For her part, Vahla was sullen. She had fully expected him to make a move after they had eaten. In fact, she had been anticipating it. But not the move he made. Not to pack up like the woods were on fire and march out with hardly a word! He wanted her, she knew. She had won that round— that was plain by the way his loin cloth stretched when he stood up to serve the fish, even if he didn't say anything. And he was not exactly unattractive. In her line of work, she got a lot of offers—and an occasional obligation. Most, she rejected. But if he rejected her, what would she do when they got to the next town? It was one thing to be Vahla the dancer with her servants and luggage and money to command the finest rooms. But Vahla the fugitive, totally alone? She had tasted a little of that and did not like it one bit.

Thorngere was also irritated with himself. Why had he bolted out of camp like that? So what if she might be a spy? Why would that have stopped him? He could still have taken her. Gods knew he wanted to! (and at that thought, a quick vision of her naked body set his pulse throbbing so that he inhaled sharply) She had been willing, too—that was plain. And he was usually far from shy in advancing his interests in such matters—in fact, he had even intended to. So what was it with this girl?

He glanced again at the pensive form beside him, at the thick dark hair—dry now and cascading loose over her shoulders and breast—at the delicately etched face, at that magnificent frame, and noticed she was limping. Not used to being barefoot, she wasn't; not used to a hard life at all. Look at those hands, he thought. They've never scrubbed paving stones. And that skin: it's been bathed and pampered. No, this one's definitely not your average serving wench.

"You'd better ride for a while," he said

"I'm all right," she said, not looking up.

"Nonsense. You'll do neither of us any favors by going lame. Here," he said, "let me help you up," and lifted the girl easily onto his horse. "Besides, I've got to prove I'm a man of my word."

"I never doubted you were," she said and their eyes locked briefly, she astride the grey, he standing tall beside it. Then, with something like violence, they each looked away.

"How ever did you manage to leave the house without your shoes?" he quipped awkwardly, inspecting the cuts and bruises on her left foot.

"I was in a hurry," she said, and left the words hanging there.

"I might have an old pair of sandals somewhere in one of my bags."

"Oh, I wouldn't trouble...," she started, then reversed herself. "No, you're right, I don't need to be lame. If you do have a pair, I'd appreciate it, though I don't know how I'll pay you. I left 'home' without any money either."

"But you remembered your dagger," said Thorngere, and their eyes locked again, his probing, hers proud, fearful. She had a wide face, he noted, with prominent cheek bones and large, dark brown eyes. Deep eyes. "You probably could get the price of a horse for it, if not more. Would you like me to help you sell it?"

"I don't think it would do to go flashing that about just now," she said. Her eyes were level, speaking louder than words.

"I see." So whatever trouble she was in involved blood. And the dagger would be recognized. And she herself? Such a face would not be forgotten by any man with teeth enough to chew. Nor by many with only gums to smack! So she was not exactly an advisable companion for one such as himself. Especially not this close to Valeria. Whatever her story—and at this point, he was not even sure he wanted to know what it was— he would be wise to get rid of her as quickly as possible. And he would be definitely unwise to incur any obligations.

"You know," he said, assuming a casual air, "skin as fair as yours could suffer badly from all this sun. Would you like a cloak or something?"

"How far is it before we reach the next town?"

"I think an hour or two. But I wouldn't be surprised if we started running into locals any time now."

"I see. Yes, that sun is awfully bright. If you had some sort of cloak with a hood, I think that would be good. My face is very sensitive."

It was past noon when the two cloaked figures made their way into a small fishing village along the coast, southeast of the great walled city of Valeria. It was a roughhewn place, a collection of flat-roofed, white stone hovels scattered among half a dozen streets surrounding a small harbor lined with brightly painted boats. The two were not much remarked. It was not uncommon for strangers to pass through town these days, nor was it wise to appear too curious about their business. Word of the attempt on Fantar's life had reached the town, of course, and some of his troopers spent a day at the tavern. They asked a few questions, but nobody knew anything. So, they mostly got drunk and grabbed at the plump buttocks of Baena, the serving girl (who pocketed several gold coins for grabbing back).

Fantar was not a popular ruler. Since usurping the throne of the High King, the land he ruled had not prospered. Rather, his reign was marked by so much crime and corruption it had become a cruel joke. Taxes were double what they had been under old Valerius, yet services were nearly non-existent. And what did exist were so corrupt as to be useless. If your house were robbed by brigands, or you were held up on the highway (and miraculously not killed), and you went to make a complaint to the sheriff, you would more than likely find yourself facing the very miscreants who robbed you. And if you could not pay your taxes? In the reign of Fantar, you did not even think about not paying your taxes. Better to sell your children than not pay your taxes.

So, if someone tried to stick Fantar, he was only getting as good as he gave. Besides, it was bound to happen sometime. And that a strange peddler should wander into town was not an event to excite undue remark. And that he was trailing a beautiful wench—the menfolk in town were not so indifferent as to let beauty such as Vahla's pass unremarked, cloak it though she would—caused comment only of the coarser kind.

"If I had a wench like that, I'd cover her up, too," said one wag as the pair passed the tavern.

"Aye," said another, "And I know just what I'd cover her up with! Har har."

"You'd best shut your yap," said a third. "He looks like a big 'un."

"Oh, I'll bet he's big," said the first. "I'll bet he's hung like a stud horse to make one like that follow him."

"Who should know better?" returned the second. "Look at the scrawny little bitch follows you around! Har har."

Through the afternoon, Thorngere wandered the jumbled streets, doing a bit of business here and there, calling softly into open doors and windows, "Peddled wares here. Peddled wares." Mostly, he sold pots, of which he seemed to have quite a number, nested in sacks on his donkey. In return,

28

he took a few coins, but also trade items; leather goods, and candles, bread, bits of clothing, a lovely smoked ham in one instance, more sandals. From one house he was rewarded with a large, misshapen pearl on a leather thong which he presented to Vahla with mock solemnity.

She accepted the bauble graciously, and with as much mock ceremony as it was offered, but did not tie it on That would have required her to remove her hood and while the town seemed bucolic enough, her heart still hammered whenever they rounded a new corner. For the rest, she quietly followed Thorngere, helped him display his wares, and packed up the goods he took in trade. She said little—indeed, barely even looked up—but was secretly amused at the friendly, affable way Thorngere went about his business: he had kind words for all, smiled at the wives, joked with the men, tussled the heads of the children, and behaved rather as if he were on a gift giving spree than a business mission. He never quibbled over prices, but gratefully accepted what was offered, assuring his customers they were more than generous, so that once again Vahla thought, this one was no peddler.

And another curious thing: several times, when his back was towards her, or when she was at some distance packing the donkey, she heard him lower his voice and ask about someone or something—just what she could not make out. The first couple times, she thought it simply a part of his usual banter, but after the third or fourth time—by which point she was actively listening—it sounded like he was asking about some sort of game: Game Lark, or something.

At dusk, they made their way back to the tavern. Thorngere ordered up bowls of steaming fish chowder and mugs of ale for them both and ate his hungrily. "Ah, good day's work," he said, wiping his yellow beard with the back of his hand."

"You looked like you were having fun," she said, smiling warmly at him.

"I was! I enjoy my trade. But listen," he said, lowering his voice and leaning across the table, "are you sure you don't want to do something with that dagger? I could get you a good price for it."

"No, I don't think that would be a good idea."

"Well, how about I buy it from you?"

"Why do you want my dagger?" Vahla demanded, suspicion tingling the hair on the back of her neck.

"Well, I don't, really. But you need money."

Vahla was offended. "I'll find a way to pay you back—surely you can trust me for a bowl of soup and some ale!"

"No, I don't mean that," Thorngere waved dismissively. "I mean you need money because I've got to leave. Now."

"Oh." Vahla was stunned at this sudden resurgence of reality.

"I mean," said Thorngere awkwardly, "it's not that I want to leave you in distress or anything. In fact, I... But I have some very pressing business, you see, and..."

"You don't need to explain," she said stiffly. "I'm quite capable of taking care of myself."

"I have no doubt you're very capable," he said, "but I have no choice. Here, at least take this," and he slid a small purse across the table and pushed it into her hand. Then he patted her hand and—really before she could say or do anything more, or even try to think of a reason to keep him—he was gone. And Vahla was once again alone.

For a few moments she sat still, clutching the small purse and staring at the empty bowl by his place. Then she, too, left the tavern and melted into the darkness outside, oblivious of the four figures who slipped silently out in her wake.

Chapter 2
A DEADLY GAME

Thorngere rode back along the main road until he reached the edge of town, then turned south onto a small cart track that skirted the edge of the harbor and meandered off into the hills backing the cliffs along the coast. He rode slowly, a soft evening breeze cool at his back and the rising quarter moon lighting his path. He felt badly about leaving the girl behind and her image floated before him. Plainly, she had not wanted to be left like that, and plainly, she would have been a delightful companion. But there was no option. Even if she hadn't been a risk herself, it would not have been fair of him to put her at risk. Especially now. No, it was better as it was. She would be able to fend for herself.

At the end of the track, tucked in between a pair of hills some three miles from the town, and commanding a lovely view out over the Inland Sea, was a small farm cottage and several outbuildings. Here Thorngere dismounted and tapped softly at the door. An old woman pulled it open, spilling yellow light into the courtyard and onto the peddler.

"Is this the house of Gamlarch?" he asked.

"It is," the woman replied, squinting at him fiercely. "Who wants to know?"

"My name is Thorngere and I bring messages from Valerius Everreigning, High King of Valeria and all the Inland Sea."

"What?" came a gruff voice from within. "Who is that, woman? Bring him in and close the damned door before the guards are upon us!" Thorngere was shown into a small room with a fire at one end and a ceiling so low he had to duck beneath its beams. At a table, amidst a few high backed chairs, sat a small, wiry man, grizzled with age yet sharp in eye and movement. A crutch stood in the corner behind him, and as he rose, thrusting his chin towards his visitor, Thorngere could see he was lame in the left leg.

"You must be Gamlarch," he said, holding out his hand.

"Aye! It's not easy to hide with an old sword cut like this," he said. "And who might you be? And what is this you speak of King Valerius that could put both our heads on pikes?"

"I speak the truth, General. Valerius lives. He that was Valerian. And he's mustering his forces even now to return and crush this regicide, Fantar, and restore the glory that was of old."

"So the stories are true, you say?" the old man said, flopping back into his chair.

"Aye, they're true."

"Well, you'll have to tell me how. For I was there, you know, commanding the center. I myself saw young Valerian go off with the women, and I was with the King when he fell—it's how I got this little prize!" And he slapped his left thigh. "But

33

where are my manners. Etta! Bring our guest some ale. And throw another log on—the night grows chill. Now," he said, turning his attention back to Thorngere, "start from the beginning. How did you find me?"

"Well, it wasn't easy. And if I had known you were this close to the sea, I wouldn't have trekked all the way over the northern mountains. Why have you stayed so close to Valeria?"

"A cat can't see what's right under its nose. Besides, how would I have managed on the run, crippled as I am? Here there are people who know me and value the service I gave. With their help we get along, Etta and I... Don't we old girl?"

"You're an old fool to be talking with such a one as this," the old woman spat as she shuffled past. "How do you know who he is? Blathering on like you're at a fair. He might be Fantar's brother for all you know!"

"Go on with you, woman! Leave us in peace. Never marry an old woman, Thorngere—orneriest critters the Gods ever conceived. Ain't that right Etta?"

"Don't talk to me," she yelled, "I'm in the other room."

"She does have a point," said Thorngere. "You don't know I'm who I say I am."

"And what does that matter? Fantar doesn't care about the likes of me. If he did, I'd have been dead long ago... And he wouldn't have needed to send some young bucko like you in here to fool me: he'd have just had me killed. That's his way... No subtleties, no bothering with proof of guilt. Just gut you if it suits him, that's Fantar. As for who you are... Well, I'm sure you're a fine fellow, and I mean no offence, but I don't give a damn who you are. What I'm interested in is what you have to say!"

"Good!" said Thorngere, a great smile lighting up his face. "Valerius said you were a spitfire."

"Well, I'm near seventy years old. Spitting is about all I can do."

"I don't believe that. By your own admission, you're still a man of influence around here, and that's why we need you. But don't let me get ahead of myself. You wanted to know how Valerius— Valerian that was—survived the battle. Like you, I heard young Valerian was found with the women, and that Fantar had his head taken and impaled on a pike next to his father's—I myself saw the skulls there years later, before Fantar started to rebuild the city. But the one skull was not the boy's. Valerian did not go with the women: he disobeyed his father and went to battle dressed in another's armor. It was his young friend, Balazar, who went with the women."

"Young Balazar! Why I knew him and his father. Young Balazar marched in the ranks with the Royal Guard."

"Well, that wasn't Balazar. That was Valerian. He went down early in the fighting with a blow to the head, and when he came to, the battle was lost and Fantar was burning the city. He slipped away in the darkness..."

35

"Aye, many of us did."

"After that, he fought for years with the resistance as Fantar conquered city after city, all around the Inland Sea. I myself fought beside him for years, never knowing who he was, for he always went by the name of Balazar."

"But why? If he was Valerian, he would have become Valerius upon the death of his father. He would have been the King Everreigning! Why did he not gather an army then and rid the world of this Fantar?"

"As Volkmir says, the time was not ripe then."

"Volkmir? That old blow-hard is still in the world?"

"He was within the year..."

"Why, he was old in my time! But if you know Volkmir, that adds credence to your tale. But why now? If his Majesty lived in hiding all these years, why come out now?"

"Because now he has gotten back the Eye."

"The Eye! The vision stone of the Kings Everreigning of Valeria? I heard Fantar threw it in the sea after it burned out his eye."

"So I heard as well... But Volkmir got it back somehow, and now Valerius has judged the time is ripe for his return."

"You astound me, young man. Never more in this life did I expect to hear such words as these! Forgive me," he said, wiping at his eyes with his sleeve. "I am a foolish old man and you have affected me greatly. Valerius Everreigning was my liege lord and King since I first suckled teat—as he was my father's and his father's before him back seven generations. If what you say is true, then I am yours to command. Etta!" he called. "Bring me my sword! I am going to war!"

"Not so fast, Gamlarch! Not so fast," Thorngere laughed. "We're not quite ready to form a line of battle yet. It's for other purposes we need your help right now."

"You're not after doing something underhanded, are you? Was it you involved with that assassination attempt the other day?"

"Assassination attempt?"

"Well, I can see from your face you weren't. Good thing, too. I don't hold with that kind of thing... Cutting a man's throat in his bed. Cowardly stuff, I say. If you're going to kill a man like Fantar, do it to his face! Cut his balls off and spit in his eye while he chokes on them. Then put his head on the gates for all to see! That's how to deal with the likes of him."

"What was this attempt? I've been in the hills and have heard nothing."

"Oh, Fantar took some dancing girl to his bed, and I guess she wasn't too pleased with the entertainment—tried to stick him with his own dagger during the night."

"When was this?"

"Oh, three, four nights ago. My people tell me Fantar's troopers were all drunk as lords down at the tavern—looking for her supposedly."

"But she didn't kill him?"

"No, apparently he woke up just in time. He tried to grab her but then—and get this," the old man laughed, "the great warrior king Fantar One-Eye tripped getting out of bed and knocked himself cold! Can you imagine? I even heard his troopers were saying his new nick-name is 'Fantar Flat-Face!' He'll be awhile living that one down."

"And the girl?"

"Got clean away. But I don't hold with this murder in the night business."

"Nor do we," said Thorngere, forcing his thoughts back to business. Suddenly, he wanted to wrap this meeting up and get out of there. "No, when Valerius resumes the throne, it will be with honor. He is a good man, Gamlarch, and a wise leader. He will be marked as one of the best in his line, believe me."

"Well, what do you want of me?"

Quickly, Thorngere sketched out the situation: Valerius had discovered a perfect hideaway along the coast in the outer ocean between Zagorbia and Dulcai. There, he was building his forces and preying on Fantar's shipping until the time was right for him to attack directly. In the meantime, he needed two things, both of which Gamlarch could help supply: men and information. Thorngere's mission was to circle the Inland Sea, searching out the surviving leaders from the old regimes, and set up an active network of loyal men. Their job would be to spread the word that Valerius Everreigning lived and was planning a return, and to feed both information and recruits to him.

"What about fomenting a general rising?" Gamlarch wanted to know. He had been one of the leading generals in old Valeria and was quick to grasp strategy.

"Too early to tell. That would be an ideal solution, but a very complex one to organize. That's why we need information. We know Fantar has put the worst of men into the highest places, but we don't know how that translates into military strength—numbers of troops in the various cities, their supply situation, how effective a force they are likely to be, that sort of thing..."

"I can tell you that right now...," Gamlarch began, but Thorngere cut him off with a warning hand. Slipping quietly to the door, he yanked it open, and a figure that had been huddled there, obviously listening, tumbled into the room.

"You just aren't very good at sneaking up on people, are you?" he said, grinning down at the prostrate form of Vahla.

"And I knew you were no peddler," she snapped, indignant but not without irony.

"I believe this is the girl you were just talking about, Gamlarch—the one responsible for that 'cowardly' attack on Fantar? That is the case, isn't it Vahla? That dagger belongs to Fantar?"

"Well now, hold on there, Thorngere," said Gamlarch. "Don't be so hasty in your accusations. Come over here, girl, and let me get a better look at you: my eyes aren't what they used to be. Nope, nope," he said when Vahla stood before him, " I see nothing cowardly in this face, Thorngere."

"It was you who characterized the attack on Fantar as 'cowardly,' Gamlarch, not I."

"That was before I saw this girl. A beautiful woman, you know, may do in all honor what it is base for a man to try."

"Yes," said Vahla, glaring at Thorngere now, "like defending her honor!"

"And a homely woman, I suppose, has no honor?" Thorngere shot back. "Is that how it works? Or is theirs just not worth defending?"

"And speaking of defense," said Gamlarch, "how come you to know this girl if, as you say, you had nothing to do with the attack?"

"She sneaked into my camp last night and tried to make off with my food bag. I saw she was on the run and took pity on the poor thing. As you've just seen, she's quite inept..."

"Oh, I'm sure that could be disproven quite easily," chirped Gamlarch.

"In any event, I just left her at the tavern in town." Then to Vahla, "Did anyone follow you here, do you know?"

"Yes, someone did," said a voice from the door. Thorngere spun to face a large, dark visaged man in a shaggy cloak, armed with a short sword. He was grinning broadly in impending triumph and baring yellow, rotted teeth. "And I've no doubt Fantar will pay very handsomely when I drop you three before him."

"I hope for your sake that you're not alone in making such threats," growled Thorngere, backing from the door and instinctively moving between the man and Vahla. Quickly, she pushed the handle of Fantar's dagger into his hand.

"No, not alone," said the man. "There are more than enough of us to handle the likes of you." And he nodded towards the windows to his right and across the room beside Gamlarch where the curtains were yanked aside and two other grinning ruffians began to climb in.

"Well," said Thorngere, "since you have us so firmly cornered, I think you're entitled to a little something from Fantar right now." And before the fellow's perplexed look even had a chance to resolve itself into words, Thorngere flung the dagger, and buried it haft deep in the man's throat. Blood gushed from his mouth and his startled eyes went mad with panic as he toppled backwards, kicking and gurgling in his death agony, onto the yellow lighted paving stones outside the door.

But Thorngere did not notice these throes. Yanking aside his peddler's robe, he pulled out his long sword, and before the second thug had even gotten his foot disentangled from the window sill, killed him with a straight thrust in the chest.

The third fellow made it into the room, though, and advanced on Gamlarch, swinging a short sword. Gamlarch held his crutch before him like a stave and blocked the first blow, but the force of it knocked him back onto his bad leg which almost collapsed beneath him. "Etta!" he yelled, as Thorngere lunged past him, "Where's that sword!"

"Just a minute, just a minute!" came her voice from the other room, and just as Thorngere finished

41

the third intruder, she shuffled in, Gamlarch's blade held out before her: both the sword and her sturdy arms were splattered with blood. "I wasn't done with it," she said surveying the grim scene. "Another of those creatures tried to climb in the back."

At Gamlarch's direction, Thorngere found a wheel barrow in one of the sheds and quickly dumped the bodies over the cliff and into the sea. Vahla helped Etta mop up the blood, then sluiced a bucket of water over the barrow and followed Thorngere while he put it away. They stood in the door to the shed in awkward silence, moon shadows flickering over their faces.

"Valerius really is alive, then?" Vahla asked finally. "And you really come from him?" She was standing close, looking up at him.

"Yes," he said, but his eyes were caught by the delicate shell of her ear and the line of her jaw; by the wispy strands of hair that caressed her neck. "And you really did try to do in Fantar?"

"Yes." "If I had known it was Fantar you were running from, I never would have left you, you know." And without conscious volition, his fingers traced her jaw line and she lifted her face.

"I know," she whispered, and he kissed her. It was a soft, slow kiss, but as their tongues mingled, his passion soared. Wrapping her in his arms, Thorngere carried the girl into the shed, and on a pile of fresh hay, made love to her with a fire and intensity he had never known before.

42

It was not that he did anything different than he had done before (though it seemed so) or that she was so much more beautiful than any woman he had known before (though she was), or even that he was more attracted to her than to any other (though he was). It was that their passions matched. She wanted him as much as he wanted her. In the same way. At the same time. He could feel her response rising to meet his own and it drove him even further.

And there was no awkwardness, no unanticipated movement. When he unbuttoned the top of her blouse, she was unbuttoning the bottom. When he moved to suckle her breast, she fed it to him like a babe. When his tongue strayed down across the soft firmness of her belly and thighs, she arched and spread her legs to accommodate him. And when he rolled to his back, she mounted him swiftly and grasped his member like the hilt of a sword. "I hope you don't have your dagger," he whispered. "No," she said, "but I have a wonderful sheath," and she plunged it deeply, effortlessly inside herself.

It was as if each knew what the other wanted the instant it was wanted. Their bodies and their lovemaking flowed together as easily as spring flows into summer. And their climax was as rich and full as the scent of honeysuckle.

Thorngere was breathless when it was done, and for some time could not move or speak. She lay across his chest, equally spent, her cheek against his shoulder and his receding member still snuggled up inside her. He stroked her hair lightly and let his hand rest on her back.

"You're very beautiful," he said

"So are you."

"Ha! Thank you, but no, I'm afraid I'm just a scarred old war horse who has seen better days."

"Oh no, you're not," she said, looking at him earnestly. "You're very beautiful. When I saw you in the river this morning, I couldn't believe it. Your body is like a thing of light, and yet it's so hard and strong. You seemed like a diamond to me."

Thorngere was embarrassed and tried to make light of it. "Well," he said, wriggling his hips so that his shrunken penis dropped from her vagina, "if that's true, then you've just melted stone."

"I'm serious," she laughed. "I've never seen anyone like you."

"Do you see a lot of men?"

"I'm a dancer," she said. "I see men all the time."

"Oh."

"But I'm not a courtesan, if that's what you mean." There was an edge to her voice.

"What about Fantar?"

"What about him?"

"No," said Thorngere, "you're right. It's none of my business. I was wrong to ask."

"I'd much rather you ask than imagine," she said.

"Did you try to kill him before, or after...?"

Vahla sat up angrily. "So you want to know if you were in another fox's den? Pah!" she spat

44

without waiting for him to answer. "Fantar is a pig! And an impotent pig at that: I danced for him in his hall, and the bastard tried to rape me before his entire court. In fact, he tried twice to take me, but could do nothing. Not that I would have had any choice in the matter! But that had nothing to do with why I tried to kill him."

"Why then?"

"Why? Why do you and Valerius fight against him? Why is Gamlarch willing to fight against him? Can I not fight also, just because I am a woman? And for the same reasons? That pig killed my entire family!"

"That puts you in a very large group," he said. "But very few would be willing to risk what you did."

"I am not others," she said and even in the semi-darkness of the reflected moon, Thorngere could see the fire leap in her eyes. "I am Vahla the Dancer! I do as I will. I avenge my own wrongs!" And as she spoke, she threw her shoulders back proudly and Thorngere's eye was drawn to the jutting symmetry of her breasts, and he smiled up at her warmly.

"Well, you are like no others, that is one thing sure. But tell me, Vahla the Dancer, how do you take to the sea?"

"Why, I don't know. How do you mean?"

"Well, it seems to me you have struck a mightier blow against Fantar than all of us warriors. Now, that not only puts you in danger, I think it puts us in your debt. So what I'd like to do is take you with me to the Hidden Valley. Besides, we may have further use for your services."

"As a dancer?"

"Oh, I would love to see you dance, my lady. But something tells me there is more to you than that."

"I have studied all the movements," she said archly.

"Oh, I'll bet you have," Thorngere grinned. "I'll bet you have."

Chapter 3
THE HIDDEN VALLEY

Thorngere was awakened in the early dawn by a change in the ship's motion. For several days they had been running south, parallel to the swells, and the ship had been rolling slowly, side to side. Now they must have made their mark and turned east, heading in-shore, for he could feel the ship begin to pitch as she crossed the waves. From the deck overhead he could hear the footfalls of the crew as they moved about securing lines, and around him, the gentle creek of the ship's timbers as she worked in the sea. From the skylight, the first glimmers of dawn filtered down into the tiny cabin, and he lay with his arms behind his head, contemplating the day.

Thorngere loved mornings like this at sea, when the whole world seemed bounded by the swaying rhythm of the ship. Soon, the watch below would tumble on deck to begin the age-old ritual of swabbing down: the boatswain would yell, buckets would bump, twirling braids of water would sluice from the scuppers, and the day would begin. But for now, in that last hush of the night, all was still and peaceful, and the rocking of the ship was like a cradle. Thorngere watched as the square of gray in the skylight became tinted with blue and listened to Vahla's heavy breathing as she slept on beside him.

It had been just two weeks since they left the house of Gamlarch—six days since they had taken ship at the little town of Balac, and four since they passed into the outer ocean just north of Zagorbia and headed south along the coast—yet he marvelled at how different things seemed with her, at how much younger he felt, and at how much sex they had been having!

Thorngere was not a contemplative man. Blessed with a native cheerfulness and spontaneous wit, he was much more inclined to action than philosophy. In his mind's eye, he had always seen himself as a lone mountain wolf, ravening about the world, snatching prey where he would, then trotting on. He was lean and craggy, this imagined Thorngere, hard bitten and gaunt, and always driven by a restless hunger. He was not without compassion, of course, and enjoyed a good joke as much as the next fellow, but he had always thought of himself essentially as a lone creature, a singular entity motivated by his own will.

But something in that equation, or in the mix of elements that defined it, had changed now. Oh, he was still the wolf all right—those jaws could still snap, those teeth still tear flesh; he was still a figure to excite terror and awe—but he no longer felt alone. As he trotted along the dusty mountain trails in his mind, this fearsome wolf, this ragged creature with the baleful eye, would often stop now and look back; look to make sure that another was trotting along behind, to make sure she was all right, that she was still with him. Because suddenly, it would not be at all all right if she were not. Because suddenly, this wolf no longer wanted to be alone.

But it was a puzzle, this change. Though he felt it, he could not define it, and though he acted upon it, he did so without the consciousness that something fundamental had altered in his life. He did not joke about himself, as he would surely have joked about another—and as more than one wiseacre in the crew had already joked about him—that he was "a poor besotted bastard, drunk with the black brew of a vixen's raven hair." But he was.

He was infatuated with this girl, this lithe dancing girl with the opalescent eyes and skin as soft as soap. The sight of her excited him, the sweet scent of her skin and hair made him drunk with desire, and the touch of her flesh drove him to a passion he had never known before. There had been women in his life, many women. Some he had even found companionable. And sex with them had been fine. There had been little to complain of (except once or twice!). But it had been a solitary act: two bodies had been involved, but at least from his side, only one mind. There had been no joining. With Vahla, there was a total union—body, mind, and spirit—and it was vastly more potent. It was like comparing ripples on a pond to the roaring crash of the sea.

Not only that, the sex itself was an adventure. This Vahla was hot! She was ready anytime and almost anywhere. (Twice on the trek to Balac they had darted off into the bushes right in the middle of the day, and once lay joined and stifling giggles

49

within feet of a travelling family who happened to pick that particular spot for their lunch. Fortunately, they were in a hurry and ate fast!) But it was not just that. It was the openness in their relations that he found so intoxicating. Perhaps it was because she was so used to public performance, but she loved showing him her body. And she seemed to love exploring his. There was a mischievous quality to their love-making, a playfulness. They dallied to delight. And she was as vivid as he.

Even now these thoughts began to stir him (even though they had exercised late into the night before) and he rolled onto his side and traced his finger down the curve of her shoulder. Vahla stirred and opened her eyes.

"Good morning," she smiled and stretched luxuriously.

"Good morning," he smiled back.

"You seem quite chipper this morning."

"I was just thinking about last night."

"Oh...?" There was a glint in her eye

"Well, we didn't quite finish the wine, if I recall. Would you like some?"

"Pretty heady stuff for this time of day, isn't it?"

"Well, we've headed inshore," he said, handing her a mug, "and we'll probably land in Kantar by mid-afternoon—so I thought we might want to celebrate."

"Why, whatever did you have in mind?" she said, sliding the covers down to reveal her breasts and belly.

Thorngere caught his breath—as he always did—at the sight of her, and felt his manhood begin to respond. But at that instant, the small door to the cabin banged open and the mate thrust his head in. "Cap'ns respects, m'Lord... Oh, beggin' your pardon, ma'am," he blurted, eyeing Vahla greedily as she yanked the covers back up over herself, spilling her wine in the process. "Cap'ns respects, m'Lord, but we're close inshore and would you please to come on deck?"

"Very well," Thorngere sighed, stifling an impulse to throttle the man. "Tell him I'll be along in a minute." Then, with a shrug to Vahla as he pulled on his clothes, "I guess we're closer in than I thought."

It was full daylight when Thorngere emerged from the tiny cabin under the poop, but the sun was not yet visible. Nor would it appear for some time, as looming directly across their path and soaring up thousands of feet so that it blocked the entire eastern sky, was a solid wall of rock. So high was this wall, and so tiny did the ship seem in comparison, that to the untrained eye it would appear they must strike at any moment, though they were still a good half-mile from the shore.

Extending to the horizon on either hand, this escarpment was part of the great barrier range which lay between Zagorbia in the north and Dulcai in the south. All along this coast, high cliffs rose abruptly from the sea, offering no refuge for the imperiled mariner, and behind them, according to the conventional wisdom of the day, lay an impassable, and uninhabitable range of mountains. Only a few knew differently, and as Thorngere stood on the foredeck, his eyes strained to pierce the gloom which still clung under the base of the cliffs, until he suddenly spied a small, black hole and shouted back to the captain.

"There she is, Boltar, dead ahead! Bear to port a bit—the current has a slight southerly set here."

"Can you tell the state of the tide yet?" the captain yelled back.

"Not yet," Thorngere said, scanning the sea about the ship. It was only slightly brown. "But I think it's in our favor."

As they drew in closer, the black hole grew before them even as the cliffs reared ever more threateningly overhead. Around the ship, the turbidity of the water increased and Thorngere watched it closely to note the set of the current. "It's just past flood," he called when he was satisfied.

"Very well, m'Lord," said the captain. "Man the sweeps!" and the crew surged about the decks, pulling ungainly poles from racks along the bulwarks and sliding their bladed ends through holes let into the rail.

Ever closer came the ship to the yawning black cavern mouth under the cliffs. On either hand, the sullen ocean swells reared up as they neared the rocks, and as if enraged at the unwarranted interruption of their progress, broke in fury upon them, sending up plumes of spray so that the air was wet with mist and fresh with the scent of salt. But before them, and on into the cavern until it disappeared in the depths of the darkness, the water was smooth and brown, swirling only here and there into muddier patches as the slack tide danced with the outflowing current.

It was at this point that Vahla joined Thorngere on deck. "My God!" she said, taking in the scene at a glance. "Are we all right?"

"Oh, yes," said Thorngere. "This is the hidden cavern I was telling you about."

"But surely it's not high enough to get the ship under. Won't the mast hit?"

"Nah," he scoffed, wrapping his arm about her shoulder. "It only looks that way. It's not high enough for a big war galley, but for a small trader like this, no problem. Trust me."

"Like I have a choice!" she said and snuggled in closer under his heavy arm.

"Out oars!" Boltar called as the ship lost way against the current and the sail hung limp from its yard. Two men to an oar, the crew slid the long poles out and on the command "Pull!" began rowing the ship into the mouth of the cave.

Inside, the light quickly fell away, and they rowed on into a damp, solid, echoing darkness. To con the ship, a crewman came forward with a signal lantern, and by opening a single shutter, was able to shine a beam of light onto the right hand wall of the cavern. On and on they went, the blackness growing so thick Vahla could not see the mast from the bow.

"This is creepy," she said, shivering as occasional drops of water fell on her from overhead. "Who made this?"

"Mostly, I think nature did," said Thorngere, whispering in the eerie, echoing stillness. "The Kantarans cut a cart track in along the wall, as you can see over there, but I think the cavern has always been here. Good thing, too. Otherwise, I think the entire valley up ahead would be one huge lake."

"But how did you find this place?"

"Well, Valerius did, actually. It's a long story, but he was marooned here, oh, about four years ago now, I guess. He was still going under the name of Balazar then. His ship broke up in a gale at sea, and he was several days adrift, clinging to a spar and thinking he was about to be dashed to death on the rocks out there when the flood tide swept him into the cavern. He made his way inland and was taken by the locals—the Iblis—and pressed into service for them as a mercenary in their war against another tribe in the valley, the Kantaran. We all thought he was dead."

"How did you find him?"

"Well, that was strange. Volkmir sent me to find him."

"Volkmir!"

He could feel her start at the mention of the name. "Do you know him?"

"No, no," she said. "I've just... just heard the name."

"Well, he's a mage who advised the former King Valerius and tutored our Valerius, who was then Valerian... As I say, it's a complicated story."

"I've got time... I hope!"

"All right then, I'll give you a history lesson. As you know, Valerius Evereigning has been rightful King of Valeria and High King Over all the Inland Sea for time out of mind—the sons succeeding to the throne and the name for generation upon generation. Well, by the time of Valerius' father, administration of the Empire had become rather lax, and while the cities around the Inland Sea remained loyal to the High King, it was a loyalty in name only: all the affairs of government were administered locally. There were no Valerian officials overseeing anything. There was no need. Everyone was at peace and trade was healthy. Each town paid an annual tribute to the High King, but as this was very modest to begin with, and as it was used only to maintain the navy that protected everyone's trade, there was no complaint. About the only thing the High King did, other than rule Valeria, of course, was make a ceremonial tour every year.

"I was just a boy then, but I can still remember when the High King came. I come from the north, in Thuringia, and we're not on the Inland Sea, but we were still allied with the Empire, and every now and then the High King would come to visit. Wow! It was like we were being visited by the Gods themselves. I mean, we just about rebuilt the town in preparation. People came from everywhere to

55

see him—it was quite a spectacle. Anyway, I can still remember him riding in on a huge white horse, surrounded by his honor guard. He was just covered in gold and purple and had this huge red gem—the Eye—hanging from his chest! It was awesome.

"Anyway, when Fantar rose up, he took Valeria first—you heard me tell Gamlarch how Valerian escaped—and with the head gone, the rest of the Empire just couldn't seem to mount a concerted defense. Fantar took town after town, and all the while kept promising peace. He'd send emissaries out to all the surrounding towns saying he did not want war, that everything would be as it was. Then he'd find some pretext to attack the next town, and the next until, eventually, his armies had completely encircled the Inland Sea.

"But there were many of us—young Valerius included, though we didn't know who he was then—who never believed Fantar from the start. We fought him for years, in city after city, all around the Inland Sea. But there was never enough of us to make a difference and we were beaten, time after time, until finally, when he took Zagorbia, we were pushed right out to sea. We set up in Dulcai then, in the south, and to a lesser degree in Thuringia to the north, and tried to fight Fantar by ship. But it was a losing cause.

"Why didn't Valerius just say who he was and rally support around him then as he's trying to do now?"

56

"I'm coming to that. One day, while my ship was in Dulcai—this was about two years after Balazar disappeared—I was summoned (that's the only way I can describe it) by a series of dreams, and following their instructions, made my way to Volkmir's lair high in the mountains south of Zagorbia. It was he who told me who Balazar really was. He also explained that he, Volkmir, had recovered the great Eye of Valeria, vision stone and symbol of the High King's power, and that the time was ripe now to do exactly what you suggested. He has a very complicated explanation as to why it wouldn't work before, but the point was, it would now, and it was my job to fetch the king. Actually, to rescue him.

"So you were the big hero," Vahla teased and poked Thorngere in the ribs.

"Oh, yes," he laughed, the sound echoing metallically in the dark. "Such a hero! Truth to tell, we both had to be rescued. But in the end, we did manage to settle the war here and get the place back under its rightful rulers. And, in return, they are allowing us to use their valley as a staging area for the war against Fantar.

"Well, it sounds very exotic with mages, and magic stones, and hidden kingdoms, and all, but what I've never been able to understand is how a beast like Fantar managed to grab power in the first place. I mean, you say you were never able to muster enough strength to beat him—but how was he able to muster the strength to beat you?"

"Good question. There's two things, I think made it possible. One is that Fantar appealed to the lower elements, and he promised them the world. And while everything looked good around the Inland Sea—everyone was at peace, trade was flourishing, learning and the arts flourished, there was rule of law—the social order was still very rigid and stratified. If you were born noble, all well and good; if you were born to a merchant family, not so bad either; but if you were born common, well, common you stayed. Because there was peace and stability, there was no opportunity and that, I think, made Fantar's appeals all the more inviting.

"The other thing, of course, is that Fantar's claim was not totally without legitimacy and that, I think..."

"What do you mean?"

"Well, you know, his backstairs relationship to the king..."

"Back stairs?"

"Yes, you know... He was the king's bastard son."

"No!"

"You never knew that?"

"Never."

"Well, if he's stopped touting that claim, then I wouldn't spread it around. Look there, we've rounded the curve. We've still a mile or more to go, but you can see the end of the tunnel."

"Ah yes," said Vahla. "A tiny light beckons."

They emerged into blinding sunlight, and after the blackness of the cavern, it was some minutes before Vahla's eyes could adjust. When they did, she was astounded by what she saw. Spreading out before her was a vast and fertile plain extending for miles before disappearing among distant hills. Through the middle of this, and backed by checkered fields, the great river meandered like a diamond necklace. In the near distance on her right, rose the crenelated walls of a large city. Beyond, a mile or so upriver, was another habitation, a military encampment by the looks of it. Directly across the river, was a third site, a small, ramshackle village, around which she could make out large herds of grazing cattle.

She had not really tried to imagine the place Thorngere was taking her to, but the name, "Hidden Valley," had somehow conjured up the picture of a smallish, confined place, with a rude fishing village and a couple bands of sleepy tribesmen. The king's court she had pictured as somehow hanging precipitously from the side of a mountain. But the reality was not at all like that. This valley could have held the city of Valeria, and obviously supported a population of many thousands. Moreover, the place was an absolute beehive of activity. Dozens of ships were lined up along the quays before the city, and more were being built just up river. Military units were drilling around the encampment, and the city itself seemed to be one huge spiderweb of scaffolding, with cranes lifting huge blocks of stone and workers crawling over the walls like ants.

"Thorngere," she said, "this is incredible!"

"Nice little hideaway, eh?"

"I had no idea!"

"And this isn't all. About a day's march beyond those hills lies another, smaller valley and a second city almost as grand as this one."

"And nobody knows this is here?"

"Nope. The folks who were running this place—the Iblis—had no notion of the sea and no idea there even was an outside world. The Kantaran did—those are the folks we helped put back in power—and they apparently used to trade all over, but that was several generations ago. When the Iblis drove them out of the city, they blockaded the river, and burned all the Kantaran ships.

As the ship pulled clear of the cavern, Thorngere's private pennant was hoisted to the masthead. Several trumpets blared in response, and as they neared the dock, Vahla watched a troop of brightly armed guardsmen leave the city gates and march towards them. There was something very peculiar about them, but it did not really register in her mind until the ship was docked and the leader— brilliantly armed with silver and gold inlay, and sporting a bright red cloak and a red plume on his helm—mounted the gangway and slapped his chest in formal salute to Thorngere. It was only then that it dawned on her—and with such shock that she sat right down on the hatch cover—that this man was only slightly taller than Thorngere's waist.

"Hail Lord Thorngere!" the little man cried. "I bring you greetings from the High King, from Queen Salonis, the lords and ladies, and all the people of Kantar. We bid you welcome, and praise the Gods for your safe return. I am sent to escort you to the King just as soon as you are able to disembark."

"My thanks and greetings to you, Commander Colinus," returned Thorngere, his face breaking into a huge grin at Vahla's shocked expression. "It's good to be home."

Chapter 4
THE FACE OF THE KING

As they threaded their way to the palace—the honor guard surrounding them like a troop of school children dressed for a parade—Vahla's impression of a beehive city intensified. Not only were the walls being rebuilt, but inside the gates, tiny workmen were everywhere, reroofing houses, repaving streets, clearing rubble, digging foundations, setting rafters: so hectic and pervasive was the activity that it was a while before she noticed, in between the many buildings undergoing reconstruction, that a good many more had already been reconstructed. These were neatly plastered, white, single story buildings for the most part, lined up along the streets as neat and fastidious as doll houses. And now, as they approached the center of town, she saw that entire side streets had been completed.

"My God, Thorngere," she said. "Did you have to knock this whole town down to take it?"

"No, actually, we took it without much of a fight at all. But the previous tenants were somewhat neglectful of the property, and as you can see, the Kantaran have been rather busy tidying up."

"Incredible." A few more streets were passed in silence when Vahla noticed something odd. "Thorngere," she said, lowering her voice, "I don't see any women or children. Is anyone living in these houses?"

"Well, a few of them. But that's another story. Look," he said, pointedly changing the subject. "We're almost to the palace. You can see it rising over those roofs there."

Set off from the surrounding buildings by a large courtyard, and approached by a broad avenue, the palace was an imposing structure of several stories, with sweeping stone steps leading up to a columned portico. It had obviously gotten primary attention from the builders. The stone facade gleamed as if brushed, the window casements were all neatly dressed, the roof tiles were new: it looked as if an old building had been physically mingled with a new one.

Vahla had seen more impressive buildings in her time, but as they approached and as she thought about who she would soon be meeting in this one, her pulse began to quicken, and she held tightly to Thorngere's arm. Up the steps they marched with their pint-sized honor guard, and through huge double doors into a great hall, at the end of which, on a raised dais, sat a pair of empty thrones.

"His Majesty will receive you in his private chambers," said Colinus. Dismissing the guard, he led the way up a staircase to the left, down a hall, and into a small antechamber where two full-sized guards stood before an inner door. Word was sent in and Vahla found herself actually twitching with nervousness. How often had she thought of this moment? What would she say? Then the inner doors swung open and they were ushered into the King's private audience chamber. Her heart jumped into her throat as Valerius himself entered the room.

But for the eye patch, a few pounds, and ten years difference in age, he could have been Fantar, so striking was the resemblance. A huge, black-maned, bear of a man with massive arms and shoulders, Valerius had the same square face as his half-brother, the same jet black hair and beard—though his was cleaner, more neatly trimmed and not nearly so grey—and the same commanding presence. But there were differences, too, not the least of which was the large red gem Valerius wore on a chain about his neck. But where Fantar had gone to seed, Valerius was obviously in the prime of his strength. And where Fantar had a dissipated, wasted, almost desultory air, Valerius was clear-eyed, vigorous, and energetic. Where Fantar seemed dark, Valerius was light. And as he rushed forward now to grasp Thorngere's hand, his face was all aglow.

"Thorngere!" he said, slapping him on the shoulder. "Welcome back! Welcome back. You don't know how glad I am to see the likes of you!"

"And I you, Sire. It's good to be home."

"But who's this?" said Valerius, turning a great, smiling face towards Vahla.

"Her name is Vahla, Your Majesty, and I brought her along because she has the particular distinction of having come closer than any of us to actually removing Fantar from power."

"Is that so?"

64

"Yes, she very nearly succeeded in gutting him one night with his own knife."

"Did she really! Well done, young lady. But, I hope it was a fair fight."

For an instant Vahla stood, staring up at this huge man before her, this King, and her mind went completely blank. He was making polite conversation. He was being humorous. She should respond in kind. This was her chance! But then something snapped in her brain and she shot back with surprising venom. "As fair as it can be when one is drunk and disgusting and backed by armed guards and the other is dragged off by the hair! Your Majesty."

Valerius' face went sober in an instant. "I see. But you didn't kill him?"

"No, your majesty, though I think I wounded him."

"Well, I am sorry for your ordeal and did not mean to make light of it. You are welcome here, and we will be happy to provide you with any assistance we can. Now, Commander Colinus, perhaps you would be so kind as to entertain the lady for a time while Thorngere and I discuss some business."

"It would be my pleasure, Your Majesty," said Colinus with a bow, and before she knew it, Vahla found herself back in the antechamber with the tiny commander and the doors closed behind her.

"It's nice to know some things haven't changed, my friend," said Valerius, eyeing the departing

Vahla and smiling at Thorngere. "She's about the healthiest specimen you've turned up in a long time... And a real spitfire as well!"

"Well, I couldn't just leave her... Not with Fantar's guard combing the country for her."

Valerius raised an eyebrow. "I see. And just what did happen?"

"Well, Vahla is a dancer—apparently one with some reputation—and she was summoned to perform before Fantar. He got drunk and tried to have his way with her—though she swears he passed out before he made any way at all—and she tried to get even. She was lucky to get away."

"With your help, no doubt."

"Well, no, not immediately. I had nothing to do with that. She happened on my camp a few days later, and as I said, I couldn't just leave her."

"Oh, of course not... and I'm sure the fact that she's a delicious looking morsel had absolutely nothing to do with it."

"Nothing whatsoever," said Thorngere, a twinkle playing about his eyes. "It was purely a matter of military necessity!"

"Ah yes," laughed Valerius, "I've seen your 'necessity' in action before! But come. I've something to show you and I'm most anxious to hear your report."

Vahla was not pleased at having been dismissed so summarily by His Majesty, High King Valerius Everreigning. Fair fight indeed! How could it be a fair fight between a man and a woman? Nothing was fair between men and women. Men had it all and women were chattel. He had actually been amused that she had almost been killed by Fantar! And to send her packing like that... 'Perhaps commander Colinus would entertain the lady while we men talk serious business!' That was not the way Vahla was used to being treated by men. Why, he had hardly cast a glance at her!

But then, perhaps she should not have taken such offense. He was the king, after all, and he had only been making polite conversation. And they did have serious business to discuss. What had made her snap like that? His resemblance to Fantar? Even so, this was no way to start. What if she had seriously offended him? What would become of her then? She would have to be much nicer to him next time, she thought. Still, his presence had troubled her deeply. He had been very condescending, and as she sat in the antechamber, she seethed with resentment.

Across the room, tiny Commander Colinus stood uneasily, casting about for something to say to this creature. She was the first outland woman he had ever seen, and while he did not want to be rude, he found it hard to keep his eyes off her. He was no judge, of course—and never would be—but if she was typical of her kind, it was no wonder His Majesty and the other outlanders wanted so badly to win back their homes. Not that winning wasn't an enviable goal in itself, of course. But if such as this was to be part of the reward,... Well, it was difficult for him to imagine.

"Did you find the sea voyage discomforting?" he asked, although fearing it was a stupid question.

"What? Oh, the trip. No, not really. But Thorngere said the weather was unusually kind. Can I ask you a question?"

"Why, certainly, ma'am. I am yours to command." And here Colinus gave his best courtly bow and brought an actual smile to the face of this huge goddess.

"His Majesty,... is he usually so,... so imperious?"

"Imperious, ma'am?"

"Well, unfriendly. Overbearing."

"His Majesty? Oh, no, ma'am! Valerius is a very warm and caring man. In fact, he has a tremendous heart. All of our people love him. He has freed us and returned us to our home. He is,... well, he is a very great man, ma'am. Very great. But you must understand that he is under tremendous strain. He has been working without cessation for many months and he is very tired, very tired."

"Oh, of course, that must be it. I didn't realize. The war does not go well, then?"

"Oh, I wouldn't know about that, ma'am. I am only commander of the Queen's Guard. She allows me to attend His Majesty and Lord Thorngere on occasion out of, well, gratitude for how they have helped our people."

"The Queen, then, is not Valerius' consort?"

"Salonis!" Colinus could not help but laugh, though he controlled himself quickly. "Oh, no,

68

ma'am. They are not King and Queen... together. Queen Salonis is of Kantar."

"Oh, I see! Then she is...," Vahla hesitated, not wanting to offend. "She is of your size?"

"Well, smaller, actually. She is pure bred, of course."

"Oh. Of course." Vahla found herself intrigued by this little man, so small and childlike on the one hand with his open face and beardless chin, yet so grave and formal on the other. He was obviously not a child, but something about him made her want to sit him on her lap and pat his cheek. "May I ask you another question?"

"Surely."

"How old are you?"

"I have thirty-eight years, ma'am."

Thirty-eight! By the Gods, he was almost old enough to be her father. Surely the lap sitting would not do! "And how many children have you?"

"No children, ma'am. I am a soldier."

"Soldiers here don't have children?"

"Uh. Well, we... I mean, no, not many ma'am. We have been at war for a long time and now there is so much work in rebuilding the city."

"I see. Yes, Thorngere told me a little about what happened here, and I can see the incredible work going on. But why was the city so ruined?"

"Well, it was the Iblis, ma'am," said Colinus, relieved to be on firmer ground. "They are a very lazy and slothful people... But did Lord Thorngere tell you anything of our history?"

"Very little. But I'd love to hear more," she said, patting the seat beside her to indicate that the Commander should sit. He did so with an amazing show of dignity, even though his feet came nowhere near touching the floor.

Valerius had led the way into another room where, on two large tables set at right angles to each other, a map had been built in relief, showing the coast of the outer ocean from Dulcai north to Thuringia, and all the cities around the Inland Sea. Another Kantaran, this one even tinier than Colinus, stood on a stool by the intersection of the tables, arranging tiny ship models around the port of Zagorbia. Around the perimeter of the room, more tables held piles of parchment reports, and hanging on the walls above them were rows of slate tablets containing neatly printed columns of figures showing the garrison size, number of ships, names of commanders, and other particulars for each town. Thorngere was astonished and circled the room, taking it all in.

"This is incredible!" he said at last. "I've never seen anything like this in my life. Who came up with this idea? And how did you build it? How did you get the cliffs to look so real?"

"Well," said Valerius, beaming modestly, "it was mostly Koltar's idea here..."

"Oh, yes, Koltar, forgive me," said Thorngere, shaking the tiny man's hand. "How are you?"

"Fine, Thorngere, fine. And from what I was able to see in the other room, you're doing fine, as well!" The two men grinned at each other.

"Anyway," Valerius continued , "Koltar found an old map among the Kantaran archives, and his artisans built this for me. They modeled the cliffs out of clay and then baked them in an oven. But it's quite the thing, isn't it? We kept getting swamped in stacks of reports and could never quite get a clear picture of the overall dispositions. This shows the situation at a glance and, as reports come in, why we just update our wall charts and move pieces around on the board."

"Amazing! But where do you find the time, Koltar? It looks like the whole bloody town is being taken apart and put back together stone by stone. And I know you have *other* duties," he added, giving him a broad wink.

"Well, most of the architectural work for the city is already done, so I've been able to break away a bit and work on a couple other projects...."

"Yes," said Valerius, "wait till you see what he's been up to down at the shipyard!"

"And as for my *other* duties, as you so delicately put it, things are actually quite well in hand. The male/female ratio is holding steady now that we're back in the old city, and the conjugal duties aren't nearly as exhausting as they were initially. As I think I told you last time you were here, we've divided the female population up now, so rather than have every pure-bred male trying to impregnate every breedable female, we're each now responsible for a specific number. I've only eleven myself and as most of them are either pregnant or nursing, it's not too taxing. However, I'm sure his majesty would rather discuss other things, though I *do* thank you for your kind solicitation, Thorngere!"

Valerius laughed. "As interesting as this is, I do have to tell you that, as a man who has not had any woman for far longer than I care to recall, I would much rather discuss other things!"

"There are still the Iblian women," Thorngere cracked.

"Oh, now you are getting cruel! But come, let's hear what you were able to turn up. Were you able to find Gamlarch?"

"Oh, aye, I found him! He's still quite the fighting cock, that one is! Though if I'd known where he was living, I could have saved myself three weeks of tramping around in the mountains."

"Is he solid?"

"Well, he's willing, that's sure. But he's old. Well beyond any active campaigning, I should think. But he's got a lot of contacts and he's agreed to send reports. And he's perfectly positioned: right on the coast about a day and a half east of Valeria itself."

"Great! I had many fond memories of Gamlarch from when I was a boy and was delighted to hear he had survived. But were you able to get into the city at all?"

"No, I was going there next, but by then I had Vahla. I'm told, however, that Fantar's rebuilding project is not exactly going like a house afire."

"Well, he's the one who started the fire that required it. It's strange, though," said Valerius, gazing at the map as if he were looking down onto the land itself, "how active he is in some areas, and how lethargic in others. He'll pour all sorts of energy into building ships and machines of war, but does little to even rebuild cities after taking them. Valeria's not the only one. Look here," he said, pointing out two cities near the eastern end of the Inland Sea, "both Bangorum and Durumkae were razed, what, a dozen years ago? Yet, I'm told the people there are still shifting scorched timbers to keep out the rain. And those are his main shipbuilding centers."

"Yes," said Thorngere, "and he's building some damned huge galleys there, too. We saw a three-decker on the way here."

"Yes, I know... And he's building them a lot faster than we're building them here. That's part of the bad news. But what of Grumwald? Were you able to find him?"

"No. Either dead or gone to the benches is what I heard. It was just as we suspected. That amnesty Fantar declared three years ago was simply a trap. Ragnar told me of several of our old comrades who were either killed outright or sent to the galleys as soon as they turned themselves in."

"Aye," said Valerius, shaking his head and circling his map. "I'm not surprised. But come, fill us in on what details you have, then Koltar has a little something he wants to show off down at the shipyard."

73

Thorngere went on with his report then, filling in some items not already listed, and noting where new contacts had been set up. It was his handiwork, this network of informants throughout the Inland Sea. For the past two years he had been making the rounds, looking up old comrades, carefully screening new ones, and arranging for them to send reports to Valerius by ship. They had set up an interesting trade arrangement from their Hidden Valley, sending ships under Fantar's flag south to Dulcai, and using Dulcai's flag to trade north among Inland Sea ports. It not only gave them information, but a growing base of men and material.

But both men feared it was not enough. Their original scheme, once the war had been settled in Kantar and they were able to re-establish contact with the outside world, was to use the Hidden Valley as a staging area for their operations. Starting with the clandestine support of King Reuters of Dulcai—one of the few monarchs in the civilized world not under Fantar's thumb—and by incurring a debt to him he had yet to fully repay, Valerius had intended to use this surreptitious scheme of trade and their continuing raids against Fantar's ships to build his forces—especially his own navy of fast galleys—until he could virtually control the Inland Sea. That way, according to the plan, he would be able to pick key strategic spots as his targets, and by concentrating his smaller number of troops, take them before Fantar could reinforce. From that point, it was hoped they could raise enough popular support to turn the tide.

It was a good plan. With Thorngere's network of informants, they would always know what they were up against, and by operating out of the hidden valley, they were virtually immune from counterattack.

But the plan reckoned without Fantar. It's always easy to win a chess match if the opponent doesn't move his pieces. And Fantar was not content to sit and wait to be beaten. Dissolute though he might be, his one dominant passion was war, and the very threat of a new Valerius attempting to take back what he, Fantar, had taken from the old was enough to give meaning and purpose to his life. And he directed that purpose with all the native genius he could muster.

If he was being threatened from the sea, then he would fight at sea. And if that required ships, then ships he would build: many ships, bigger and more powerful ships, and he would man them with the boldest, most blood-thirsty men he could find. He would rout out this pretender Valerius and send him to hell with the rest of his kin.

In short, after an initial string of successes, the odds were beginning to turn steadily against Valerius and his fledgling force, and nowhere was it more apparent than on the large relief map before them. "Look," Valerius said, pointing out their own locale, safely hidden behind its baked clay cliffs, "we have one shipyard; Fantar has at least a dozen. He has a standing army of over one-hundred thousand and can call up reserves from any town around the Inland Sea. We sneak men in by twos and threes—when we can trust 'em—and have a total force, right now, of just over two thousand, not counting the Kantaran. So, even if we had more ships, we couldn't man them.

"And that's not all. Reuters in Dulcai has turned decidedly cool of late and is pressing for full repayment. I think Fantar is getting to him, somehow. In his last letter, he said he was onto our trading scheme and didn't like it one bit—said I had violated his trust and quote, 'put the brave people of Dulcai at risk.' I think he's seen a couple of those three-decker galleys, too, and is starting to quiver in his boots."

"Why don't we see if we can take one or two of them? If Fantar's got all these shipyards, we might as well make use of them."

"That's another problem. We don't think they'll fit through the cavern, even with their masts unstepped."

"What about the plan to enlarge it?"

"Well," said Valerius, "you tell him, Koltar."

"We looked at it very closely," the tiny man said, "but we're afraid it will collapse if we try any serious excavations. I don't know if you're aware of this, but I checked the archives and found we never did anything with the main cavern, even in the old days—all we did was angle back one side to make a tow road. But there are several sections where the roof consists of huge slabs of rock— like lintels— and other sections where there are already large cracks and veins of very crystalline stuff. If we go chipping away at those, or remove too much from

76

the big slabs,... Well, suffice it to say we could end up turning this valley into a huge lake."

"With us at the bottom," added Valerius. "So we're like rats in a granary, here, slipping out to fill our bellies, then scurrying back into our hole. And meanwhile, Fantar's swinging away at us with a club! It's just frustrating—for me, and the men. A lot of them have been cooped up here for going on two years now, don't forget. And it's also frustrating for Queen Salonis. We've been imposing on her hospitality, too."

"I beg your pardon, Majesty," said Koltar, "But I can assure you the Queen has no such resentments. She is only too well aware—as are we all—that she would not even have the hospitality to offer were it not for your efforts."

"Well, thank you Koltar. You are most kind. And I am sure you are right. Queen Salonis has been most gracious. But having someone else's army camped in your backyard has got to be a strain."

As he listened to this litany of woes, Thorngere watched the face of Valerius—his King and his old friend—and unlike Vahla, saw the lines of strain and worry there. After the initial excitement of their reunion, Valerius' robust face had settled into a somber mask. Bags were apparent under his eyes, and lines now etched their way across his forehead and radiated from the corners of his eyes. His cheeks had a hollowness about them, and even in the dim candlelight, Thorngere could see that his old friend did not have good color. His body, too, had lost tone and added weight. He stood slouched as he surveyed his would-be realm, so imposingly arrayed against him there on the table, and shook his head sadly. There were even, Thorngere saw reflected in the light of an overhead candle, strands of grey in Valerius' regal mane. His King looked tired and worn.

"Well, it's not like we're having no effect," said Thorngere, eager now to paint a brighter picture. "We may not have Fantar on the run yet, but we've certainly got his attention. And he's in a lot worse shape than it seems. I mean, things may look pretty daunting on your map here, but I see the real thing, and believe me, the empire is a sick thing. It's bloated and rotten, and I think ripe for the taking. I mean, two years ago I could barely get anybody to talk to me. Now, look at the network we've established. And for every contact out there, there's a whole organization forming, ready to rise when we give the word."

"You're right, of course, Thorngere," said Valerius, brightening. "And this is no way to welcome you home after a six month trek—dumping all my troubles on you. We should have a party!"

"That's right! You could use a break."

"All right, that's what we'll do. We'll have a banquet! And you can be the keynote speaker!"

"Oh no," said Thorngere, "I don't give speeches!"

"Sure you do! You blather at me all the time. And I'll tell you what: it would do everyone a lot of good to hear about what you see out there. You know, we're blind hidden away in here and I think we worry too much about what's left to do and tend to forget how much we've already done. I think you'd do a lot of good to remind us! But first, come with me down to the shipyard. I want to show you Koltar's latest invention." And before Thorngere could protest again, Valerius led the way out into the anteroom where Commander Colinus snapped to attention and Vahla, having just begun to adjust to Colinus' stature, was again astounded to meet the pure-bred Lord Koltar, who was at least another head shorter.

"Well, what do you think of her?" Valerius asked, a broad grin spreading across his face. They were at the dock in the shipyard, a whole crowd of them; Valerius, Thorngere, Koltar, Vahla, Commander Colinus and his honor guard, the shipyard workers, large and small, breaking away from their tasks and gathering around at the appearance of the King, plus a large miscellaneous contingent of such other people as will always gather whenever it appears something is going on. Before them, gleaming in the bright sun and snugged to the dock with taut, fresh lines, was a brand new war galley. She was a sleek looking creature, long and lean with a raised prow and pointed stern. She was decked over fore and aft to provide fighting platforms, but her midsection was open with rows of benches and neatly stacked oars. Forward of the open section and braced against the after end of the deck beams, rose a tall mast. It was hinged just above the deck between a pair of strong bits so it could be quickly lowered for the cavern, but what was different, and what Valerius was pointing out to Thorngere, were two long poles stretching straight aft from the mast and resting on a crutch-like assembly on the after deck. Between these two poles, the upper of which was considerably shorter than the lower, was what appeared to be a furled sail.

Thorngere gave Valerius a blank look. "Is she not rigged yet, or are those supposed to be her yards?"

Valerius laughed. "It's Koltar's new rig. He invented it. Says it will give us the advantage over Fantar's big galleys. But here, let him show you. Koltar?"

At Koltar's signal, several dock workers jumped aboard and after removing the gaskets securing the rig, hauled away on a pair of halyards. Up rose the upper pole straight to the masthead and between the two, taut now and luffing softly in the breeze, stretched a large linen sail. Thorngere looked even more confused.

"How can a sail work that way?" he wanted to know.

"Well, it sort of can't," said Koltar, plainly delighted at the effect his new contraption was having. "In order to sail, we swing the boom— that's what I call the long yard on the bottom—out over the side and the sail fills with air. But what's different with this rig is that where your standard square rig can only sail off the wind, this can sail very close into the wind."

"Into the wind?" said Thorngere, giving the strange rig a distrustful look.

"Think about it ," said Koltar. "So far, we've had two advantages over Fantar's galleys: first, because we're smaller, we've been more maneuverable. Second, our archers have been able to wreak havoc with his crews. But lately he's started putting archers aboard, too, and because his ships are bigger, he can carry more of them. That puts us at a disadvantage. However, with this rig we'll be able to outmaneuver him under sail, so we'll be able to arm all our rowers. That should even the odds and maybe even put them in our favor."

Suddenly the concept clicked in Thorngere's mind and his face grew fierce with a hawk-like interest. "This thing will sail up wind, you say?"

"Very nearly."

"Gods," he said. "I want to see that! When can we take her out?"

"Whenever you want," said Koltar. "She's all ready to sail."

"Tomorrow?"

"If his Majesty has no objection."

"I have no objection," said Valerius.

"Good," said Thorngere. "As soon as the tide turns in the morning, then."

Chapter 5
PUBLIC APPEARANCES

All the talk of rigs and wind meant little to Vahla, and she was relieved when they started back to the city. She was bored and tired. Besides, she was still smarting from the king's reception, which had not warmed during their excursion to the shipyard. There had been no opportunity for her to speak to him, and other than the necessary forms of politeness, he had apparently ignored her. But she was pleased to hear that both she and Thorngere were to sit with him at the banquet that evening, and resolved to improve the situation then.

She was also surprised and delighted by what she found waiting for her in the palace chambers she and Thorngere were to share: a hot bath and two serving women to attend her. Obviously, the Kantaran shared the Valerian upper class custom of frequent bathing (how often in her travels had she wished it extended to the Valerian common classes as well!) and as she soaked in the deep tub of hot sudsy water, the stress and tensions of the day began to slip away.

She let her thoughts drift, and with half closed eyes, watched the tiny serving women bustle about the room, arranging fresh clothes and towels, fetching more hot water. They were as tiny as dolls, raven haired, and exquisitely formed. But for the obvious fact that both were with child, Vahla would have thought them children themselves, perhaps as young as six or seven.

"You are happy to be off ship?" asked one. She had said her name was Wetanis.

"Yes, very, thank you... it is Wetanis, isn't it?"

"Yes, Wetanis," said the one and they both gathered around, smiling shyly, and obviously eager for a chance at conversation.

"You know," said Vahla, "You're the only other women I've seen since I got here. Do they hide you all away?"

"Hide us away?" Wetanis laughed, a high, easy sound like water pouring into a narrow glass. "Oh, no. We're not hidden away. We're just very busy— and you haven't been here very long."

"That's true."

"You're the first outland pure bred woman we've ever seen, too."

"Pure bred?"

"Yes... Like to be with Lord Thorngere."

"Oh, you mean noble? When is your baby due?" she asked, turning the conversation.

The woman cocked her head to one side, counting. "Four moons now," she said.

"Is it your first?"

"Oh, no! This will by my fifth."

"My fourth," said the other.

"Why, you look so young. I can't imagine! And they are all healthy, I hope?

"One died," said Wetanis. "My girl, of course. But the others are strong boys. Two will go to the army, but the other baby is a pure bred. This one is

83

pure, too." she said, patting her round tummy and smiling proudly.

"Then you must be pure bred, right?"

"Oh, yes. All the women are."

"But your first husband wasn't?"

"Husband?"

"Well, yes. If you're first two children weren't pure bred, then..."

'Oh, no, you don't understand. Since the war ended, there are no more breeder slaves, you see. No more problems. So we're all pregnant with pure breds now. And many, many boys."

"I see," said Vahla, but she plainly didn't. When she climbed out of the tub, Wetanis wrapped a large towel around her and the other held up a new toga for her to put on. "Oh no," said Vahla, "that won't do at all. Not for tonight." And she pulled from her bag a dress she had gotten in Balac before they sailed. She had used the purse Thorngere had given her and had been saving it for him.

"Oh!" Wetanis gasped when Vahla was dressed and her dark hair all combed and arranged, "You're so beautiful! We never thought anyone so,... so large could be so beautiful."

Now Vahla laughed. "Thank you," she said. "Though I'm not sure 'large' is the best compliment I've ever had!"

Thorngere was already dressed and waiting when she emerged from the bath chamber. He was pacing about, irritated, and worrying that they would be late. He turned to snap at her, but the

84

rebuke died on his lips. Dressed in a low cut, white gown that highlighted every line of her body, and with her thick hair piled high on her head, accentuating the delicate line of her neck, the sight of her ignited him.

"Gods, you're beautiful!" he breathed. "I could strip you naked right here."

"I just was naked," she teased, raising an eyebrow. "Where were you then?"

"Ah, you vixen bitch," he laughed, "you'll drive me crazy."

"Thorngere, what's all this talk about 'pure breds' and 'breeder slaves'? And how can all the women be pregnant if the soldiers have no wives?"

"Surely you know how women get pregnant?" he quipped, sliding his hand along her flank.

"I'm serious."

"Oh, Vahla, I can't get into that now. We're late already." Taking her arm, he hurried them out of their suite and down the stairs to the second floor landing where the royal party was to assemble before making its grand entrance. But, far from awaiting them, neither king nor queen had yet appeared. The hall below was filled to capacity, however, and at the bottom of the first floor stairs, Colinus and his guard were stiffly arranged. Thorngere pulled Vahla back away from the railing so they would be out of sight—as a member of the royal party, he felt it would be unseemly to be seen standing about gawking.

"What are you so nervous about?" Vahla snapped, shaking off his arm.

"Me? I'm not nervous. I just thought we'd be late."

"Well, we're not late, and yes, you are nervous. I've never seen you so fidgety."

"I'm not fidgety."

"Yes, you are. Now tell me what's going on."

Thorngere was silent, looking abashed. Then, finally he said, "Valerius wants me to give a speech."

Vahla laughed aloud, then covered her mouth with her hand, the mirth bubbling up through her eyes. "A speech? Oh, you silly man, that's no trouble! You give orders all the time."

"That's different. I hate this. I get all tongue-tied and feel like a buffoon."

"You'll do fine. And if you do get nervous, just think of what I'm going to do to you later and that will take your mind off it," she said, slipping her arm through his and pulling him close.

"That might work," he smiled. "But what about you? Aren't you nervous to go in front of all these people?"

"Well, I've never been in such high company before—at least, not willingly!—but I perform in front of people all the time, remember?"

"Oh, yeah, that's right. I don't know what I'm thinking. This is just different for me. It's all different. Every time I come back here now it seems different."

"How do you mean?"

"Well, bigger, I guess. There's more people, more ships, more going on. There's more stuff like

86

this—you know, fanfare and official stuff—and I know that's the way it's supposed to go—I mean we're trying to raise an army and build a fleet, and all—but it's just hard for me to get used to."

"From what I can see, my dear, you're one of the main reasons it is getting bigger."

"Well, that's true. I do my job. And maybe that's part of it... I'm usually off, wandering around the countryside, pretty much on my own, and then I get back here and... I don't know, things seem to change so fast. But here comes the queen."

Salonis, Queen of Kantar, was a tiny, very round woman of immense regal bearing. Though the outland couple towered over her and Koltar—on whose arm she relied, still frail from a recent illness—she made it seem as though it was she who was looking down upon them. "Your majesty," said Thorngere, bowing deeply as Vahla curtsied, "It's very good to see you again."

"And you, Thorngere," Salonis nodded. "It's too long you've been away from us. But who is this?"

"Allow me to present Vahla, your majesty, a lady of Valeria."

"And a very beautiful lady, too," said Salonis, holding out her hand for Vahla to kiss. "No wonder you have stayed away so long, my dear Thorngere! —though I suppose it was vain of me to think my charms could hold you."

"Alas," Thorngere parried, "that my blood is too base for you, my queen!"

"Ha!" Salonis laughed. "At least this creature has not totally addled your wit! But you are most welcome in Kantar, my dear Vahla. Do not mind if I kid with Thorngere. He and I are old friends"

"He has told me of his admiration for your majesty," Vahla smiled. "And I thank you for your welcome. You have a most beautiful city, and from what I have seen so far, a most noble people."

"Well, I thank you for that. We are on our way back, aren't we Koltar? But it is a long road, and will be longer still before we regain the glory that was ours of old. But listen, Vahla, you must come and visit with me. We have been locked away here in this valley for generations, and I long to hear of the outside world—and you know, you can't rely on men to tell of such things."

"I would be most honored, ma'am."

Valerius appeared then, looking to Thorngere even more tired and worn than he had earlier. Nevertheless, he was most courteous to Queen Salonis, bending to kiss her hand and expressing his delight that she was on the mend, then suggesting they go down directly so she would not tire. To Vahla, he gave a warm smile as, quickly, they formed their group and descended the stair. Salonis and Koltar went foremost with native rights of precedence. Then came Valerius, looking regal in a pure white tunic and purple mantle, and wearing a simple gold circlet for a crown. He had his beard braided in double forks, as was the custom in Valeria, and on his chest, suspended from its golden chain, hung the huge red gem. Last came Vahla and Thorngere, she clinging to his arm, radiant, and he resplendent also in a red mantle, and with his golden mane neatly combed back in a pony tail.

As he saw them descend, Colinus signalled the trumpeters. Flourishes were blown and in the sudden silence that followed, they paraded into the hall.

At Valerius' orders, the great throne room in the center of the palace had been readied for a formal banquet. Banners were hung throughout the hall and the dais at the end was extended to support a long table before the two thrones. Other tables, enough to seat more than two hundred, were ranged in rows up and down the hall, and from all over the city, chairs were gathered and placed behind them. High chairs for the smaller Kantaran guests were placed under the left hand tables, and lower chairs for outland guests were placed to the right.

These were packed now with the leaders of both races, dressed in their finest, though to Thorngere's nervous eyes, it was all a giddy kaleidoscope of color, with shapes and faces coming into and going out of focus as he made his way towards the dais. His heart was hammering in his chest and his stomach churned. Far rather would he have faced battle, even the near certainty of death, than stand before a roomful of people like this and actually speak. But the fact that he would have to do just that became more inevitable now with every step he took. A tactical discussion before a room full of soldiers he would not have

thought twice about. But this 'public' speaking...
This was torture.

Vahla, too, was giddy, but for very different reasons. Though she had been the center of attention in many a crowded hall, never in her life had she been part of this kind of procession, walking in state and flanked by royalty. She walked proudly, her head held high, and tried not to gawk like some rude country girl. Still, she could not keep her eyes from straying and found not a few eyes focused on her in return.

Thorngere saw nothing, and nearly tripped when he reached the dais. Vahla's hands on his arm steadied him, guiding him up. Then he was in his chair, a large one on the right hand of the king. Salonis rose and said something to bid the crowd welcome—he could not follow just what—and introduced Valerius.

Then Valerius rose. It was a signal honor, Thorngere knew, to have a person as august as a king introduce one. And he knew, too, that Valerius' remarks would provide him with an excellent cue for his own. But so nervous was he that the King's words were like water over rocks, splashing and pattering, but making only sound, and no sense. Until the end, when suddenly, in a clear and ringing voice, Valerius said, "But don't just let me tell you how our fortunes fare in the outside world. Let Thorngere himself tell you, who has just come from there."

The crowd yelled and applauded, and as Thorngere pushed himself up from his chair, there was one terrible instant where he thought he would either vomit or disgrace himself—or perhaps both, to his eternal shame—and then everything stopped and he stood there alone, without even the sound of his heart to comfort him.

"Ah...," said a harsh, metallic voice, which he realized was his own, though it actually sounded as if it came from some distance, "thank you, your Majesty—your Majesties," he corrected, turning and bowing just as if he had control over his limbs—though who actually provided that control he could not say, as he, himself, seemed to have retreated some distance to the corner of the dais where he stood, detached, watching himself speak with that stranger's croaking voice. "It's good to be home—though it still seems hard to believe I actually think of this leaky lake bottom as home." There was some smiles, a few titters, and even a single laugh from the far end of the room. Thorngere felt his stomach muscles relax a bit, and his phantom self edged a bit closer along the dais.

"His majesty, Valerius, has asked me to give you my assessment of the effect our activities are having on Fantar and his cronies. I know we are very few here in a very small place, and that the empire is huge, and that if Fantar could reach us, he would crush us like bugs. It's been two years now, and I know that many of you are feeling a little frustrated that we have not made more progress—I have even heard it said that, in his first two years, Fantar took half a dozen towns while we've not even broken out of this valley.

"Well, that's not quite true. In the two years after he took Valeria, Fantar may well have taken half a dozen towns, but before that, he was ten years in the mountains, building up his forces. Ten years to our two!" Back inside himself again, Thorngere began to feel blood circulating to his limbs as he warmed to his topic. And suddenly, he knew there was something he wanted to say.

"But what's more important than how many we are—or that we are still here—is the effect our two short years of work have had on Fantar, and why I believe it's not going to be anything close to ten years—or even five—before we drive that bastard out of Valeria and clean up the Inland Sea!" Thorngere was on a roll now. Nervousness gone, his words began tumbling out. He didn't know whether he was speaking too fast, or too loud, or not loud enough, or even if he was making any sense. He was just driving his words as he would drive men to battle; minding his alignment, watching his flanks, and pushing hard on the salient points.

These were three and as he made them, he backed them up with information and impressions gleaned from all his travels. The first was that Fantar was scared and off balance. Their threat to him was not large—as yet—but it was an unknown. It struck from nowhere and went back to nowhere. He couldn't find it to fight, so it assumed an even larger menace in his mind. And this threat carried the name of an old and very potent enemy, one he thought had been vanquished years before, but was now back from the grave to haunt him. Nor was it only to Fantar that this name had meaning. The name of Valerius was being whispered throughout the empire, and wherever it was spoken, light and hope appeared. This frightened Fantar badly, said Thorngere: to him it was like the rumble of an impending earthquake.

Second was the state of the empire itself: it was rotten with corruption and teetering on the brink of self-destruction. This, said Thorngere, was the fruit of its own planting. Fantar had always been a renegade and a scoundrel, and this was the type of crony he attracted. He promised plunder and spoil and filled his ranks with the most degenerate of men. And now that he was in power, it was this same scum that ran his empire. Incompetent to govern in the first place, their interests were not in furthering his aims, but in feathering their own nests. You couldn't do any kind of business in the empire without paying rounds of bribes, and when something was done, it was with the worst materials and the shoddiest labor. So while the empire looked large and imposing, it was on very shaky footings.

"But number three is the most important reason of all," said Thorngere, pacing the dais and orating now like an impassioned politician. "If Fantar has got the worst of men, we've got the best. And I've seen them! All over the empire, wherever I go, good men are standing up and joining with us. They are not here, that's true, but they will be there when we need them. They will rise with us and throw off this oppression. And they will do it because we've got the right. Because we follow the

Gods' path to justice and law, because we want a good world to raise our children in. Because we want to be free. And I tell you, we will be free! Valerius, High King of Valeria and all the Inland Sea will make us free."

Finally, he was done and the applause was so loud and sustained, Thorngere felt as if he had just broken an enemy battle line—or been broken himself. He could not quite tell which.

"Well, my friend," said Valerius as Iblian servants began setting out dishes heaped with food, and in the corner, a group of musicians started to play, "little did I know you were such an orator! We shall have to keep that talent in mind."

"Your Majesty," Thorngere retorted, a spoonful of mashed tarot root poised, "how many battles have we been in together?"

"Too many."

"Well, when we've been through that many again, then will I consider giving another speech!" and he stuffed the spoonful into his face.

"Ha! I hope we don't have to go through that many again. But don't underestimate yourself: I think you've had a tremendous effect on morale."

"Yes, and I thought you were wonderful," said Vahla, squeezing his arm. Seated on Thorngere's right, she was too far from the king to make casual conversation. Nor was conversation on his mind, or Thorngere's either, for that matter. Being men, they leaned over their plates and shovelled in their food with single-minded intensity. Only when their plates were emptied and their wine mugs refilled did they lean back in their chairs, and with sighs of contentment, reawaken to the world about them.

Still, Vahla felt awkward and eyed Valerius covertly, waiting for an opportunity. How did one speak to a king when protocol required that you merely answer? Though she had been in the presence of many petty kings in her travels, she had never before felt the need to actually speak to one. And neither had they been interested in speaking to her, beyond a certain point. Usually, it was enough for her to be demure and alluring, to snare her prey with a look or two while keeping the cloak of mystery securely wrapped about her. And it usually worked: most of the time she was able to leave her patrons swooning, and get away without actually having to deliver on any of those hinted promises.

But she couldn't do that here: especially not with Thorngere sitting there. And there was no opportunity anyway, because Koltar rose then to introduce the main entertainment of the evening, an old, blind singer named Teukonis, who was led in by a boy, and sang a long poem about the history of the Kantaran people and their war with the Iblis. Most of the story was what Colinus had told her that afternoon and she sat, content to let the music drift past her. But a couple points snagged her attention. There was something about Iblian "abominations" that was not specified but sounded peculiar, and several other references about "the seed of the people dying in their loins."

95

Several times, she sensed the king looking her way, and tried to catch his eye, but each time he looked quickly away and she began to sense that he felt awkward, too. Then, by the end of the performance—at the point where new verses had been added lauding Valerius' part in the drama—he had settled into his wine, and while not actually drowsing, gave every impression of serious contemplation. At the applause, he started up with a surprised look, and when Thorngere was called away to speak with some of his friends, Vahla finally threw protocol to the wind and tried the direct approach.

"I'm amazed at how much you've accomplished here, your Majesty." She said it quickly, as if the speed of the words would lessen their offense. And maybe it did, for Valerius visibly brightened. He, too, had been awaiting an opportunity.

"Well, we have a tremendous amount yet to do, but thank you. And I hope you do not feel too out of place here," he went on quickly. "There are very few outland women—and fewer, I think, whom you'd want to associate with—and the customs of the Kantaran people are somewhat strange."

"You've already made me feel very welcome, your majesty," she said with her warmest smile. "And I do thank you. Without your help—through Thorngere, I mean—well, I'd probably be dead by now. I just hope I can find some way to repay your kindness."

Valerius was suddenly conscious of the wine he had drunk, and of the tremendous warmth of her

96

smile. As she leaned closer to him, the top of her gown opened to reveal a goodly portion of her right breast, and he felt a surge of dizziness. It had been a very long time since he had seen anything remotely as enticing. But he was also conscious they had gotten off to a bad start, and was anxious to make amends. He had even prepared a little speech of his own which he launched now, precipitously.

"Oh, no, young lady," he said, "it is we who are in your debt. It took a great deal of courage to strike out as you did—more courage than most possess who come under Fantar's thumb—and I believe you've set an example for others. It's not that I encourage assassination, mind, but I think your actions have spoken loudly that oppression need not be tolerated. You made Fantar a laughing stock, and I'm sure you wounded his pride much more than his flesh. It will be a long while, I think, before he drags another such as you to his bed! And I believe a lot of men will say—and I mean no disrespect by this—'if a dancing girl can do this, what might I accomplish?' That may be of more help to our cause than anything we've done. So no, Vahla, you need not think of repaying a kindness, but of accepting our gratitude."

Vahla was sincerely flattered by this little speech, though it sounded rehearsed. It was nice to know he had been thinking of her. But before she could respond, Thorngere rejoined them, and that was all the conversation they had. The King colored brightly and turned immediately to him.

"Well," he said, "it grows late and I know you want to get an early start in the morning."

"Me?"

"Why, yes. You're going out to test Koltar's new rig, aren't you?"

"Well, yeah, but I thought it was 'we.' Aren't you coming along?"

"Oh, Gods, no. I've too much to do here. I couldn't possibly."

"Nonsense—Your Majesty. A day or so won't hurt. And it will do you a world of good. Clear your mind and your thoughts."

Valerius considered, then shook his head. "I can't. I've too much to do."

"Reading more reports? That's no work for a warrior."

"Well, a man who would be king cannot be just a warrior."

"Nor can he cease to be one."

"True. True." There was a wistful sound to this last remark, and Thorngere studied his old friend hard for a few moments.

"You know what, Valerius? I think you could use a bit of warrioring. I think you've been too much the king. You've been cooped up here too long, making maps and reading reports—and having me make speeches! You don't need any more speeches. You need to feel a few bones crunching under your blade, see a little blood that's not in your own eyes!"

Valerius laughed and nodded. "You're probably right. But what do you suggest I do, go chasing off right now and challenge Fantar to single combat?"

"No, I think you should come along sailing with Koltar and me in the morning. Why, a day of fresh ocean air and you'll want to go chasing after Fantar!'"

Suddenly, Valerius stopped and looked back at his friend. Something of Thorngere's enthusiasm had taken hold and his eyes began to sparkle. "All right," he said. "I will go. Perhaps we'll stumble on a merchantman and have a bit of fun!"

Later, in their chambers, Thorngere was trying to implant a little of his enthusiasm in Vahla, but she wanted no part of it. There were too many other things on her mind. "I thought you were going to reward me for my speech," he complained.

"I'm too wrought up," she said, pushing him away. Then, thinking better of her remark, she sat up and stroked his chest and belly. "I just couldn't do justice to a 'reward' right now," she cooed. "But I'll make up for it later."

"Deal," he said. "What did you think of Valerius?"

Vahla cocked her head and considered, conjuring the image of the King's face. "Large," she said. "Large and powerful. At first I thought he was very imperious, but now I think he's very warmhearted. And very different from Fantar. Fantar frightened me terribly, you know— he was like a snake. But with Valerius I felt... I don't know,... protected, I guess."

"And the Kantarans?"

"That's what bugs me," she said. "What's going on here? You've got different sized people, soldiers with no wives, houses full of pregnant women, 'pure breds' and 'breeder slaves,' 'Iblian abominations,' seeds 'dying in people's loins,' Valerius the great 'bringer of beef'... What in the world happened here?"

"What did Colinus tell you about the Iblis?"

"That they appeared from the north several generations ago, and that they drove the Kantarans out of their own city, which started the war you and Valerius helped win."

"Did he tell you about their beef?"

"He said they accused the Kantarans of stealing it. That's what the song said, too."

"Well, the truth is, they didn't have any cattle with them when they arrived, and there were none here. So they not only accused the Kantaran of stealing their cattle, they started to cannibalize them."

"Cannibalize?"

"Eat them."

"Ugh."

"Right. They're not very pleasant folks. And that's what their part of the 'war' was all about— they'd go out, capture a bunch of Kantarans, and eat them. But that's only part of the story. In the meantime, the Kantarans built a new city way to the east of here, but they started having problems of their own. I can't tell you exactly what happened— they thought it was a curse from the God, but Koltar

100

figured it was something in their diet—but for some reason, they stopped having male children, or at least, had very few of them. So, in order to defend themselves, and to protect the pure bred men who were left, they started capturing Iblis and using them as breeder slaves with lower class Kantaran women. Their male offspring, like Colinus, were castrated and put into the army. The females were killed at birth."

"That's horrible!"

"Well, yeah, but they had no choice. It was either that or die off themselves."

"It's still horrible."

"I know, but it's over now. We brought in beef and helped subjugate the Iblis. And now that they're back in their old city, the Kantarans have started having male children again. That's why all the women are pregnant. Purebreds like Koltar have been working overtime to repopulate their race. Want me to show you what they've been doing?" he asked, sliding closer.

"Oh, God, Thorngere!" she said, turning away. "How could you even think of it!"

Chapter 6
SEA TRIALS

The tide was ebbing strongly, and the early sun glowing gold on the river when Valerius and Thorngere reached the dock, trailed by Commander Colinus and his diminutive honor guard. Koltar was already aboard the galley, checking last minute details and pestering the outland crew to make sure this, that and the other lines were all well secured. They endured him as they would a difficult child, and did his bidding with tolerant grins. Valerius was about to mount the gangplank when Colinus stepped forward and saluted sharply.

"Request permission to come along, Your Majesty."

"You, Colinus?"

"Well, us, Sire. Yes sir."

"Do you think I'll be needing an honor guard at sea?"

"No sire. But there's no telling what you could run into out there, and you might need some extra hands. Our archery is very good, and... well, we'd like to come along, Sire."

"Archery, eh? Do you think a couple of you could climb that?" he said, pointing to the tall mast.

"Oh, certainly, sir."

"What do you think, Thorngere? Could we use a few more men at arms."

"Well, we may have to haul them aloft with a halyard, but we can always use doughty fighters."

"Very well, Commander. Aboard with you, but keep your men out from under foot as we get underway. And take off that armor. If you go overboard with all that on you'll sink like stones."

Quickly, the hinged mast was lowered by the forestay, and the dock lines let go. The sleek galley dropped downstream on the current, and in the bright morning sun, shot like a golden arrow into the black maw of the tunnel. Again, a man went forward with a lantern to light their way, and forty strong hands stood by at the oars. But they were not needed. The steering board bit well in the racing current and in a very short time, they were through the tunnel and shot out into the open sea.

It was foggy and dank outside. The mists had rolled up against the walled cliffs like carpets at a party, and were as yet untouched by morning breeze or the rising sun. As the river current dissipated, the ship lost way, and the men took to their oars and pulled clear of the treacherous shore. Valerius stood by the port taffrail, feeling the ship rising to the gentle swell and took huge lungfuls of the wet, salt-pungent air.

"Ahhh!" he breathed. "This smells better than the finest perfume. You were right to talk me into this, Thorngere. It's been over a year and a half since I've even been out of that stinking valley."

"Well, if you think this muck smells better than perfume, you're in worse shape than I thought.

103

Shall we step the mast? Once we clear the fog banks we should start picking up some breeze."

"Step away! Lively now, lads," Valerius yelled, and the hands rushed to the braces. The tall mast rose on its tabernacle. Stays and shrouds were secured and Koltar's crew made ready to hoist sail. The ship began to pull clear of the mists and a slanting sun cut down, warming the backs of Thorngere and Valerius on the quarterdeck, and glinting off a patch of ripples that heralded the first morning breeze. "How shall we stand to hoist sail, Lord Koltar?" Valerius called. "Shall I bear away?"

"No, your majesty, keep her head to the wind. I want the sail to luff until we've all the halyards secured and can man the braces."

"Very well, then. Haul away!" Quickly, the smaller of the two yards, the gaff, rose up the mast and the large quadrilateral sail spilled out below it. Valerius kept the men rowing and kept the ship's head directly into the wind, which at that hour was straight out to sea, while Koltar directed adjustments to the peak halyard, which was a line attached mid-way along the gaff that controlled the tightness of the sail. When he was satisfied with his arrangements, he made his way aft between the benches of rowers and joined Valerius on the quarterdeck. "All set, then?"

"As ready as we can be, Your Majesty."

"You want to run a lookout aloft?" asked Thorngere.

"Yes, we'd better... just for safety's sake. Colinus!" he yelled forward to where the commander was crouched with his men in the bow—as 'out of the way' a place as he could find— "don't I recall you volunteering to go aloft?"

Colinus looked up at the towering mast, and swallowed hard. It seemed much taller and thinner out here than it had from the dock, and it was also moving. "Yes, your majesty," he replied. Very quickly, two brawny, outland seamen lashed a halyard end about his waist, and with as little trouble as they would have had hoisting a boy, ran him up the mast. There, he made himself as comfortable as possible, standing on the gaff and clinging to the masthead, while the halyard was made fast below.

"Are you all right?"

"Yes, your majesty." And he was, too. The view was spectacular.

"Very well, then. Take command, Lord Koltar, and let's see what this contraption will do."

Aware of the grandeur of the moment, and assuming a look of suitable importance, Lord Koltar strode to both sides of the ship, checking wind and weather one more time. The morning breeze was beginning to freshen, but was still so light as to only ruffle his hair, and the large linen sail flapped lazily between its stretched booms. The sky overhead was clear and cloudless. Before them stretched limitless leagues of open sea and behind, the cliff-bound coast looked soft and unthreatening as it faded in the distance.

"In oars!" he shouted, his voice surprisingly deep and commanding coming from such a small frame. And as the ship coasted, "Port your helm." In an easy arc, the ship's bow swung off towards the south and the eye of the wind began passing around the starboard bow. The great sail stirred and filled and the boom gently swung out to port, tightening the block and tackle sheet that controlled it, and tugging at the men who held its bitter end. As it felt the pressure, the ship heeled slightly to port and began to gather way. "Steady as she goes," said Koltar when the wind was just forward of the beam. "Ease that sheet a bit. That's good, now belay!" The ship steadied on its course, and as the angle of the sail to the wind was increased, she righted a bit and picked up more speed.

"Hey, it works!" yelled Thorngere. "We're moving." Everyone aboard watched with broad grins as a small wave began curling at the bow, and a wake bubbled astern. "We're easily making three knots."

"Well, it's still very calm" said Koltar, studying rig and wind critically, "and the wind is still pretty much abeam. Let's head her up and see how close she'll sail." Gradually, the ship's bow was inched towards the west, the sail trimmed at every step, and her progress evaluated. In that light morning air, she sailed quite well up to an angle of about seventy degrees off the wind. Closer than that and she lost way until, at an angle of between sixty and sixty-five degrees, she stalled altogether, and the sail began to luff. Koltar had been hoping for better.

"Hey," Thorngere consoled him, "this is fantastic! It's a whole lot closer than any square rigger can sail. But let's see how she handles off the wind." Over the next hour they experimented with various points of sail and found that the rig did very well, pushing the ship faster and faster as the wind rounded further and further aft until she was headed directly downwind with the boom swung way out over the port side, when performance fell off again. "Boy," said Thorngere. "This is exactly the point where a square rig sails best!"

"Yes," said Koltar, "but there's something else I think we can do with this rig that a square rigger can't."

"What's that?"

"Well, let's try and see." Koltar headed the ship back up wind until she was sailing as close as she could get without stalling. Suddenly, Koltar ordered the helm thrown hard over and the ship's bow swung sharply up into the wind and then through it. The great sail shivered and flapped and the boom swung right across the deck—nearly catching Valerius and Thorngere who ducked it just in time—then slammed against its restraining sheets on the other side. The sail filled, the ship heeled, resumed speed, and sprinted off as close to the wind as before, but with it blowing over the port side instead of the starboard.

"I call it tacking," said Koltar, a delighted grin spreading over his face.

"Yes, and I know why you call that thing a 'boom', too! Warn us next time or the throne of Valeria will be headless again."

107

"Warn me, too!" yelled Colinus from aloft. "If I hadn't been tied on, that little move would have flung me half-a-league!"

They practiced this maneuver several more times and found they could move the ship quite well to windward by sailing a zig-zag pattern. They also practiced an opposite maneuver, bringing the ship's stern through the wind so they could change tacks quickly sailing off the wind. This was the livelier of the two operations, as the wind caught the sail full force from behind, and tended to slam the boom over even harder. As the morning breeze continued to freshen, and now began kicking up small whitecaps, they found they could control this by having the men on the main sheet haul the boom inboard as they jibed, then let it out again quickly on the opposite tack.

They had, by this time, worked their way some dozen miles south of the cavern entrance, and as their last jibing exercise had brought them quite close inshore, they decided to head north and beat their way off shore. This is when they noticed another problem with the rig design, one that could be potentially serious.

Koltar had a native genius for invention, and had been responsible for a number of technical innovations both in their former habitation of New Kantar, and in the rebuilding of the old city once they had taken it back. His ball valve design, for instance, provided a system of pressurized water in the palace, utilizing a reservoir on the roof. It was also he who had diagnosed the dietary basis of the

108

fertility problem with pure-bred males which had nearly extinguished his race. But despite this mental acuity, he had no practical experience with sailing, and the need for some form of counterbalancing weight to offset the wind pressure on the sail had not occurred to him. In short, while he had modified the galley's rig, he had left untouched the basic canoe shape of her hull. This was fine in lighter air and when sailing off the wind, but now, trying to claw their way off a lee shore in the face of a stiffening breeze, they noticed two things.

The first was that the boat was increasingly tender. Where earlier she had heeled nicely to the breeze as she scooted along, now she began to lean way over in the gusts, and threatened to dip her rail—not a good thing in an open boat, and not a very comforting prospect for poor Colinus who clung desperately to his perch and felt like he was attached to the business end of a whip staff. They fixed this problem for the moment by moving more and more hands to windward (actually, the hands moved pretty much on their own accord, and with some alacrity as the rail dipped, evidencing a kind of mass intuition, and inventing on the spot the concept of movable ballast).

But the more serious problem was leeway. Part of what gave the galley hull form its speed was its shallow draft. But this also meant that there was very little underwater profile to resist the lateral pressure of the wind, and Thorngere noticed now by taking a bearing on the shore, that even though they were headed up wind at the same sharp degree angle as before, and even though they were now slicing along at a good seven or eight knots, they were also sliding sideways at some four knots. "I'm glad we're not trying to clear a headland," he said.

"Me, too," said Valerius. "What do you think, Koltar? Can anything be done about this? This is only a moderate breeze—I wouldn't want to try and sail this thing in a blow."

"No, I wouldn't either. But I think we can fix things... We seem to need weight and additional hull form underwater. I'm thinking we might rig a pair of rudder-like assemblies ..."

"Ho, deck there!" came a cry from Colinus at the masthead. "I see three ships, heading our way."

"What kind of ships?" Valerius yelled up.

"Looks like two war galleys and a merchantman."

"Two galley's guarding a single merchantman?" Valerius and Thorngere looked at each other, their eyes glinting. "What do you say, Lord Koltar? Shall we put this contraption of yours to a real test?"

"Well, if you think you can manage with something less than perfect performance, then have at it, your majesty."

"What could be in that ship they'd want to guard with two galleys?" Thorngere wanted to know as the two climbed onto the rail by the weather shrouds and looked seaward. There, to the west and south they could just see them, two long, sleek galleys and a stubby merchantman, heading north at about two leagues distance.

"I don't know," said Valerius. "But I damn sure intend to find out."

Just then, the lead galley spotted them as well, and altered course to intercept. In moments, a large square sail spilled from its yard and quickly steadied into a hard, billowing engine as the crew trimmed it to the wind. Accelerating visibly, the ship pulled away from its fellows and began bearing down on its smaller opponent. Valerius studied the two ships' courses intently. His own was laboring upwind towards the northwest on the port tack, the other running easily downwind on a broad reach towards the northeast. "Looks like he's got the weather gauge on us," he said.

"Aye," said Thorngere. "But I'm thinking we might be able to give him the surprise of his life."

"Aye," said Valerius, "hopefully, the last surprise of his life. Can you bear up any more, Lord Koltar? I want him to think he's got us nailed dead amidships."

"We can, your majesty, though we may ship a bit of water."

"Well, ship away, then. Thorngere, set some of the hands to bailing—it'll warm them up for the work to come. Colinus!" he yelled, "can your men function without you?"

"Certainly, your majesty!"

"Good. I want you to stay up there and keep an eye on the other two ships. You men," he yelled to the Guard, "pull some bows out from under the forepeak there, but keep yourselves out of sight until my signal."

"Send a bow up for me, too," yelled Colinus.

The two ships converged with increasing speed, and with the advantage, apparently, all to Fantar's ship. Larger, faster in the water, and with the wind on its stern quarter, it could control the action: no matter how Valerius headed his galley, it appeared the other ship could move to cover, and in a very few moments, would ram and sink them.

Appearances, however, reckoned without Koltar's new rig. Just at the point where ramming seemed inevitable, Valerius yelled for the helm to be thrown over. His little ship spun neatly over onto the starboard tack, and slipped so quickly past the larger ship, that its captain had no time to react. Once past, Valerius ordered another tack and, as he crossed his opponent's stern, yelled for his Guardsmen to loose their arrows. That their effect was felt could be seen as three oars in the port bank suddenly dropped and fouled their fellows, and the steering oar was momentarily left unattended.

The other captain quickly got matters under control, however, and turned his ship to the left to follow, and hopefully ram Valerius. This left the two running on near parallel courses towards the north west. Valerius now had the weather gauge, and was sailing as close to the wind as he could. But the other ship was now heading upwind, in a direction it could not sail at all, and its great square sail—so powerful an aide only moments before— was now backed against the mast and actually working counter to the efforts of the rowers.

112

Quickly, the captain sent a dozen men to furl the monster while the galley slaves pulled for all they were worth.

Still, the ship momentarily slowed, and sensing his opportunity, Valerius struck. Ordering the helm over hard to starboard, and letting the boom swing out as she turned, he bore directly down on the other ship, archers firing as fast as they could draw their bows, and rammed her hard in the port quarter. There was a sickening screech and crunch of splitting timbers as the iron shod ram ripped into its opponent's vitals.

The force of the collision drove the larger ship's stern to leeward and, aided by the still drawing sail of Valerius, the two ships, locked at right angles, neatly pirouetted around until the larger was upwind with its bow pointed now southwest, and Valerius was downwind pointing northwest and with his sail luffing. Backing oars, his ship disengaged, leaving a gaping, sea-sucking hole in the other ship. Letting his bow fall off to leeward to fill his sail, he quickly bore off northwards with all aboard cheering wildly. Not an arrow had they taken and not a scratch had anyone aboard sustained while, behind them, the other ship quickly settled, then rolled to port and sank.

"That," said Thorngere, pummeling Valerius on the back and shaking his hand, "was about the neatest bit of nautical execution I've ever seen!"

"Aye," said Valerius, "but I'll bet there were some old friends of ours chained to her benches."

"Deck there!" yelled Colinus. "The other galley is making sail."

"Ah!" said Thorngere, "looks like we get to play another round!"

"Oh, most certainly. But, now that this fellow's seen the game I doubt he'll be quite so obliging," said Valerius. "Bear up northwest if you please, Lord Koltar, and put us as close to the wind as you can. Let's see if we can get the weather gauge first this time."

The two sleek warships began to race then, Valerius in the lead and the apparent quarry, angling upwind towards the northwest, and the other, her square yard twisted around as far as it would draw and with her oars pulling at ten strokes a minute, plowing on due north and quickly making up much of the distance between them. Left alone on the broad blue sea, the slow, bluff-bowed merchantman had no option but to slog along on her course.

The wind continued to freshen as the sun neared its zenith, and Valerius' ship heeled more and more under its pressure. Oars were useless at this angle, and as many crew as could be spared lined the weather rail for ballast. The sea was also kicking up. White caps danced along the wave tops, and as the bow plunged into them, sheets of spray were tossed aft like rain showers, dousing king and crew alike. More and more frequently, too, did capping waves slop over the leeward gunwale, flooding the bilge and keeping several men busy with bailers. On his perch atop the mast, Commander Colinus rode with his heart in his mouth, for no longer was he suspended over the deck, but was angled far out over the tossing sea, and with every gust, took a sickening lurch closer to it.

On and on the ships raced, though it soon became apparent that while Valerius was gaining distance to windward and had crossed the other's bow, the pursuing ship was gaining ground.

"He's trying to get between us and our hole," yelled Thorngere, his yellow beard streaming with water. "He must think we're running."

"Let him think so!" Valerius yelled back, his eyes glistening. "Let's let those slaves of his pull till the blood spurts from their ears! Lord Koltar, ease off to northward, if you will, and let's see if we can't make more of a race of it."

With the wind more on the beam and the boom angled further out, the ship lifted her rail and picked up speed perceptibly. Back over solid deck once more, Colinus hugged his mast and felt like he'd come home. Now they were running parallel with Fantar's ship between them and the distant land, and it was even more apparent that the enemy was gaining ground. Then she altered course to intercept, furling her great square sail as it lost the wind, and trusting to her oars alone.

"Now we've got her!" yelled Valerius. "She's committed to the chase. Head her back up to windward, Koltar... I want those bastards to die at their oars!"

Closer and closer ranged the other ship, a long, powerful galley, half again the length and breadth of

115

Valerius' and carrying at least twice as many men. Valerius and Thorngere stood at their rail and watched as the oars of the other ship rose and fell, rose and fell. So close was she now that they could hear their splash, and over the tossing sea, hear the mallets of the master, beating out the stroke. Bang bang, bang bang. Forty strokes a minute now she pulled, as fast as men could pull. But for how long? And still she angled westward, threatening to regain the weather gauge.

"Bear up, Lord Koltar. Bear up. This is the dicey part."

"Shall we put our men to the oars?" asked Thorngere. "We might outrun them yet."

Valerius gave Thorngere a strange look. "No, I want our men as fresh as possible. Besides, I don't want to outrun him. I want to sink him."

Closer and closer Valerius headed his ship into the wind, and farther and farther did Colinus dangle out over the sea. Again the crew climbed to the weather rail, and again the bailers took up their buckets. But now it was with one of Fantar's larger and more powerful galleys bearing down on their port quarter. Looks of concern began to pass among the crew.

"All right," said Valerius, oblivious to all but the relative movements of the two ships. "We're almost there. Now, Koltar, here's what I want you to do. This fellow has seen us tack and he knows that if we try to cross his bow now he can nail us. So on my signal, I want you to throw the helm over as hard as you can and fall off to starboard. Come around as quick as you can. Get your men ready at the sheets, take her stern right through the wind, and come up heading southwest. That will put her fat beam right under our ram, and we'll rip her open like a pig's gut! Ready? OK,... Now!"

On his perch, Colinus suddenly felt the world start to twirl as the ship beneath him spun on her heel. First, the gaff on which he stood swung way out to starboard as the ship's bow swung in a tight arc towards the east. But they were swinging too fast, and the wind was too strong. The men on the sheets had not got their timing right, and as the wind caught the back of the sail, the gaff was suddenly jolted out from under Colinus' feet and slammed over to port. As he dangled from the halyard tied about his waist and tried to regain a foothold, he heard a sickening crack as the mast shattered at the hinge, and in a swift, swirling second, he was hurled down with the mast and plunged into the cold, salt sea.

Chapter 7
CONTRARY WINDS

In an instant, utter confusion broke out aboard the galley as the mast went by the board. Thorngere, seeing Colinus whiplashed into the sea, leaped to the rail, sword in hand, to cut the halyard that bound him. Other men, at Valerius' orders, sprang to hack away the shrouds and cut loose the now useless stick that threatened to swamp their craft at any instant. Meanwhile, the drag of the mast in the water sloughed the ship around and brought her to a standstill—a tender and easy target for Fantar's great galley which executed a comfortable turn of its own and bore down on them with all the power sixty pairs of oars could generate.

"Cut away that forestay!" Valerius yelled as the last of the shrouds parted and the mast started sliding sideways. "You men, heave it overboard! You others, get to starboard! Counterbalance her." Twenty strong men shoved the mast butt seaward, it and their combined weight dragging the gunnel underwater and nearly upsetting the craft until finally, it floated free and away, the great sail spreading out across the water like a tiny patch on a huge blue quilt.

But it was not quite a smooth patch. There was a lump in the middle, a kicking, flailing lump, and as the ship bobbed upright, Thorngere dove from the rail and dragged Colinus free. Willing hands hauled them aboard and left them gasping in the bilge as they sprang back to their oars.

"Give way all!" yelled Valerius as the sharp prow of the enemy' galley loomed over their starboard quarter. "Left full rudder! Pull! Pull!"

But it was too late. Though they were able to turn the ship enough to avoid a direct hit, the enemy's bronze sheathed beak ripped down their starboard side, snapping oars like match sticks, flinging rowers into the air, and tearing a great gash along the length of the hull just below the water line. In rushed the swirling sea, swamping them in seconds. But not before Thorngere had pulled out the ground tackle. As the ship settled, he and several other men flung grappling irons over the enemy's rail and made them fast to their own, keeping their little ship afloat and tying it securely to the bigger ship's side.

While Colinus' archers kept the enemy clear of the rail and the vital grapnel lines, Valerius and Thorngere quickly organized boarding parties on the fore and aft decks—the only remaining parts of the ship where they could stand dry-shod. With a shout, they mounted the enemy's rail, and with swords flashing, leapt down upon their foe.

Now it came down to vicious hand-to-hand work, bloody hack and slash combat that Valerius revelled in. Thorngere was a more elegant fighter and preferred room to maneuver, but in close, Valerius was a prodigious butcher. He fought with a great, curved falchion, a broad bladed hacking sword not unlike a cleaver, but made extra-long and heavy to his specifications. For defense, he bore a small buckler on his left forearm, and for a large man, was exceptionally fluid and graceful in his movements. But it was his brute power that made him such an awesome foe and few could withstand his blows. If his great cleaver descended on an opponent's shield, it was as like as not to cleave both the shield and the arm that held it: if an opponent caught that blade on his own, it was not unusual for Valerius' blade to drive the other before it and for the opponent to be bloodied by two swords, one of them his own. And the death he wrought upon his foes evoked sheer terror among their ranks.

Seldom in that age were men killed outright in battle. It happened, of course, but the far more usual case was for a death wound not to be immediately fatal. A man would receive a vicious cut, and thinking he had simply been wounded, remove himself from fighting. If he went down, he would crawl away or his friends would drag him clear. Only then, when he was away from the immediate face of his enemy would the reality of his situation begin to dawn. And in most cases, death resulted from loss of blood.

But this was not the case when men faced fighters like Valerius. Valerius did not just slash or stab his opponents: he hewed them. When Valerius swung his great cleaver, arms and heads were severed, torsos were split and blood spewed. There was no question of the outcome to the next man in line: evidence of his predecessor's slaughter was splattered all over his face and on his lips. And that the same fate awaited him was only too clear.

It was not unusual, then, once Valerius' prowess had been demonstrated, for men to do their absolute best to avoid coming to blows with him. In line of battle, there was always a wide circle around him and wherever he advanced on the field—no matter what the general state of the battle—his foes retreated. That was the case now as well, but the fact that this fighting took place on the crowded decks of a war galley nearly proved disastrous.

The two ships were so situated that their bows were together and the stern of Valerius' galley lay about three quarters of the way along the other's port side. So when they boarded, Valerius' party ended up on a narrow catwalk running along the ship's bulwarks, and Thorngere's on the enemy's crowded foredeck. Thorngere and his fellows were immediately engulfed in a furious melee, and it was only with great difficulty that he was able to advance enough to provide room for his men to board behind him.

Valerius, on the other hand, vaulted onto a virtually empty deck, thanks to the efforts of Colinus' archers, and his fellows were easily able to clamber aboard behind him, filling the catwalk forward, and in moments, joining up with Thorngere's men on the foredeck. But in that position, Valerius was most exposed, and of all his men, was the only one able to come to grips with the enemy. Several men immediately charged him along the catwalk from the enemy's stern, the first swinging his sword in a wide right handed blow aimed at Valerius head. He caught this on his bucker, and with an underhand thrust, skewered the fellow through the body, lifted him bodily off the deck and tossed into the ranks of his fellows so that three or four of them—including the dead man—were bowled off the catwalk and clattered down onto the chained rowers on their benches below.

Another attacked, more cautiously than the first, keeping his guard high and feinting with his sword for position. But Valerius was not interested in the niceties of dueling. Besides, his blood was up now and the battle lust raged within him. Screaming like a fiend, he waded into the fellow and with a horrific chopping stroke, cleft his shield and split his skull to the jaw line. Jerking his falchion free with both hands, he kicked the body aside, parried a blow from another and beheaded him with a single, backhand stroke which sent a geyser of blood into the face of the next man in line who began backing into the fellows behind him like he was pushing a wagon.

This left Valerius alone and exposed on the catwalk, and a perfect target for a lone archer who had managed to struggle through the crowds on the opposite catwalk and somehow found room to draw his bow. Valerius saw the movement out of the corner of his eye and spun to catch the shaft on his buckler, but he was a fraction of a second late and the arrow sank deep into the hard muscle of his right shoulder just as the bloodied fellow in front of him found his courage (or was encouraged from behind) and charged along the catwalk, sword raised high.

Now it was Colinus' turn to earn his passage. Loosing an arrow, he caught the fellow in the fleshy tissue under his chin and the sharp barbs drove upwards, cleaving his tongue at the base and plowing deeply into his brain. The man collapsed in a lifeless heap, his eyes shining like wet, white stones, and his corpse hindering those behind. Another of Colinus' archers dispatched the lone enemy archer before he could draw again, but Valerius was incapacitated. He could not raise his sword arm and wisely stepped aside and let his fellows bear the brunt.

The battle now became more general and more vicious. There were casualties on both sides and the air was filled with the horrific din of the dying and the mad. All of Colinus' archers now lined the rail of their own ship, and by firing between the legs of their comrades on the catwalk, did good carnage among the enemy whose screams confused and disheartened their fellows. Still, the man who replaced Valerius on the after end of the walk was soon struck down, as was the fellow who replaced him. Indeed, the enemy began advancing along the walk while on the foredeck, Thorngere found himself even more beset.

As every land general knows, choice of battle ground can make the difference between victory and defeat. On the right field, with the advantage of a hill for defense, for example, or of a swamp to hinder deployment of the enemy's battle line, a smaller army can often overcome a larger one. A wise general knows that it is not overall superiority he requires, but local, tactical superiority. A ten-thousand man advantage does not help an enemy if he cannot bring them to bear on the fighting.

Just so in battles at sea where great fleets maneuver for position, and even more so in fighting of this kind, on the cramped and constricted decks of a single ship. Here position is paramount and the location of a mast or deck house can be a vital strategic element. Just as the catwalk kept the majority of Valerius' men from coming to grips with the enemy, so the deck layout on the galley's bow influenced the fighting there, and not to Thorngere's advantage. He had boarded at the after end of the foredeck, which placed him at the base angle of a triangle with convex sides. This meant that for some time, the enemy was able to put more men in line against him than he was able to put against them. Still, with the help of Valerius' men coming forward along the catwalk, he had managed to advance until roughly half the deck had been taken.

But here he was stalled, for dead center in the foredeck, and filling the entire forepeak were the heavy timber bits, capstan, and coiled hawsers used to moor the ship. These provided a natural defensive barrier his men were unable to surmount. Every time one tried to climb it, he was cut down.

Thorngere moved to his left, thinking that if he could advance on that side, the men at the bits could be isolated and the foredeck battle won. But it was difficult even moving among the packed and pushing troops, to say nothing of the bodies underfoot. "Drive left," he yelled, "Drive left!" and by doing a little pushing and shoving of his own, got his offensive moving. But so tightly packed were the lines, he could not get himself back into the fighting. Edging more to his left, he came up against the rail at the after end of the foredeck and, leaning over this, tried to squeeze his way along to get in a blow or two at the enemy. But he timed it badly: at the instant where he was least balanced, the man he was trying to squeeze around lurched back to avoid a blow and his elbow caught Thorngere right on the ear, toppling him over the rail. He landed on his head and left shoulder on the oar deck below, and for several minutes lay in a crumpled heap between the foremost benches.

"Thorngere! Thorngere!" a voice called to him, seemingly from afar: a single, recognizable sound amid a distant tumult. Then it came louder. "Thorngere!" and somebody was kicking his leg. Opening his eyes he saw the slave on the foremost bench—a rangy grey-beard with a vicious scar down the side of his face and but half a set of teeth—leaning over him urgently.

"Grumwald?" he said lazily. "I thought you were dead?"

"Well, I soon will be if you don't turn us loose, you stupid bastard! Can't you see how it goes?"

Thorngere snapped back to full consciousness then, and a quick glance at the fighting above showed him Grumwald was right. The enemy were pressing along the catwalk and had regained much of the foredeck. "Are these fellows all right?" he asked, indicating the rowers.

"How many slaves have you known who wouldn't fight for their freedom?"

"Good point!" Quickly, Thorngere unhooked the main chains that led along the benches on both sides and fed through the leg irons of the men. Even more quickly, some two-hundred and forty eager hands and arms pulled the chains aft, and the men leapt from their benches to attack their former captors. They pulled them down by the legs from above, and swarmed onto the upper decks from all directions, grabbing up the weapons of the fallen, and even yanking swords from the defenders' hands.

It was over in moments. Seeing themselves suddenly outnumbered three to one, and beset from all sides, the galley's crew quickly threw down their arms. A heavy silence fell over the ship, broken only by the moans of the wounded, as men who had been killing each other only moments before, stood glaring at each other, their breasts heaving. His own shoulder quickly bound by Koltar, Valerius strode onto the quarter deck, the galley's crew backing away before him.

From their midst a grizzled officer hobbled forward, dripping blood from a cut on his left leg. "I am Varga," he said, slapping his chest in salute, "captain of this vessel. May I ask to whom I have the honor of surrendering my ship?"

"Well may you ask," said Valerius, taking the captain's proffered sword and letting his own voice

126

ring out over the still decks, "and let all here know, you have come under the hand of Valerius Everreigning, High King of Valeria and all the Inland Sea. Obey me and you will not be harmed."

"Valerius!" said the captain, his eyes round with surprise. Promptly, he dropped to one knee and bowed his head in submission. Most of his crew followed suit, and all the former slaves but one. That one stepped forward at Thorngere's side.

"So," he said, a crooked grin twisting up his face, "it's Valerius now, is it..., Your Majesty?"

"Grumwald!" said Valerius, laughing and pumping his hand. "I should have known they couldn't tan an old hide like yours."

"Aye, it's me... Though I seem to recall you as someone else! But no matter. I'd rather see you here than my old mother came back from the grave!"

"So, what's the gig with you and Balazar?" Grumwald whispered. "And where'd he get that rock—it makes a powerful impression!" He and Thorngere were seated in the stern sheets of the galley's barge, an eager crew rowing them over the short distance to the merchantman, lying placidly under their lee.

"It's no 'gig', Grumwald," said Thorngere quietly. "It's the truth. And that 'rock' is indeed the Eye of Valeria. With my own eyes I saw that stone strike down the wizard Volkmir and leave him blind for three days."

127

"Gor! Balazar is King Valerius! Who'd a thought it? You're sure you're not having one over on your old mate Grumwald?"

"Look, I'll tell you the whole story later on and you can believe it or not. But in the meantime, if you show any more disrespect to the king, I'll toss your rancid old butt overboard."

"Oh, never fear, me lad. It's 'His Majesty' to me, through and through!"

"Good. So," he said, changing the subject and raising his voice to a conversational pitch, "I take it from your recent employment that Fantar's amnesty did not work out quite as you had expected?" The last time Thorngere had seen him, just over three years before, Grumwald had been on his way north from Dulcai to turn himself in, along with his ship and crew, under an amnesty program promised by Fantar. He had been one of the leaders of that shrinking band of rebels—among whom were Thorngere and the man called Balazar—who had fought Fantar's advance all around the Inland Sea until, with the fall of Zagorbia, some five years before, had been pushed right out into the outer ocean. There, with the covert help of King Reuters of Dulcai, the tiny band had waged a pirate's war on Fantar's commerce. But his amnesty program had effectively ended organized resistance.

"Bah!" said Grumwald. "The only peace that bastard offered was a piece of an oar shank to pull until I died of it, or drowned."

"Don't I seem to recall someone warning you that would be the case?"

128

"Oh, aye, you told me, you bastard! You told me. Go ahead and have your laugh on old Grumwald!"

"Well, I'm not laughing, see? What I told you was the truth then—that Fantar was as faithless as an adder—and what I'm telling you is the truth now, understand?"

For a long moment, Grumwald studied Thorngere's face. "It is true then, the Eye and all?" he whispered.

"Aye, it is true."

Grumwald whistled softly under his breath and was silent all the while they came alongside the merchantman and scrambled up over her rail. Her crew offered no resistance. They knew they were helpless against a war galley and, besides, most of them were simple sailors, engaged to haul a cargo. At Thorngere's orders, the hatch cover was unbattened and partially slid back, and he climbed down below. The hold was surprisingly empty, considering how low she sat in the water. There were only a half dozen small crates in the hold, evenly spaced, and bolted securely to the deck. Using his sword as a pry-bar, Thorngere loosened a board on the center crate, brushed aside a covering of straw, and inhaled sharply at what he saw. Quickly, he resealed the crate, scrambled out of the hold and ordered the cover replaced. Leaving Grumwald and part of his crew on guard, he hurried back to the galley and found Valerius in the former captain's cabin, being attended to by Koltar. His shoulder had been more properly bandaged now, and his arm was nestled in a sling. He seemed quite jolly

"Ah, Thorngere," he said, "you're back quick enough. Koltar and I were just discussing his rig design. Other than that little problem with the mast falling down, I thought she did quite well, didn't you?"

Thorngere closed the door behind him and sat down close by his old friend's side. "You won't believe what I found in that merchantman, Your Majesty," he said urgently. "I'm not sure I'd have believed it either, if I hadn't seen it with my own eyes. But it's gold. Pure, solid gold. In ingots. Tons of 'em!" The three men sat in shocked silence for a few moments, then Valerius ordered the captain, Varga, brought in.

"Yon merchantman has a very interesting cargo," he said when Varga stood before him, his head bowed under the deck beams.

"Your Majesty has been very lucky today," he smiled.

"So it would seem. But tell me captain—there is only one possible source for so much treasure. Has Dulcai been captured?"

"Not captured, no, Your Majesty! This shipment is just..., well, let us say, a token from King Reuters of his esteem for my former master."

"A token, hey? Well, Thorngere, I think you had better get back over there and help sail this little token home with us."

Thorngere headed out, but turned at the door. "Oh by the way, Your Majesty, a very contrite Grumwald sends his most humble regards."

"Him humble? Hah! Tell that old bastard I still haven't forgotten what he did to me on the march from Durumcae."

"Durumcae? What did he do then?"

"Nothing, the old curmudgeon. But he won't remember that, and he'll curdle his milk worrying about it!"

131

Chapter 8
A LOOK IN THE EYE

What could have induced Reuters to pay such a tribute? Valerius knew he should be excited about having it, but the next morning, as he trudged along the road, that question kept nagging at him. He had left the city early and headed east along the river bank towards the hills, trying to think. But it was difficult with so many passers-by whose greetings and salutes he had to acknowledge, and so many others who simply stood aside to watch him pass. It was quite an unusual sight to see the king out like this, alone and unattended. Around him, too, the morning bustled with troops drilling in the fields, workers hammering in the shipyard, and along the road, carts rumbling towards the city, laden with produce and building material.

His shoulder was still painful and tightly bandaged. Having his arm all trussed up in a sling made walking rather awkward, but the wound had started to bleed again when he tried taking it out. Still, the previous day's fight had convinced him Thorngere was right about one thing—he needed to get out more. And it wasn't just to get away from his musty maps and reports in the situation room. He needed exercise! It had been an exhilarating fight with glorious results, but boarding the enemy, he had felt like there was a sack of grain tied to him, and the little fighting he did had left him totally blown and exhausted. He hadn't said anything to anyone else, of course, but if that arrow hadn't taken him out of the fight when it did, he wasn't sure how long he could have continued. And for a man who prided himself on his strength, and who had inured himself to physical hardship and the rigors of battle since early youth, that was a startling occurrence. Worse than that, it was risky!

So wound or no , he had determined to get himself back into shape (how many times before this had he dragged his weary butt long miles with an enemy in hot pursuit, and far worse hurts than a pricked shoulder to bother him?) But he also needed time and space to think. That was another thing the previous day's outing had done: that fresh sea wind had stirred the cobwebs and raised swirling clouds of dust in the attic of his brain, and he realized how stuffy and stale he had become, how much the works up there needed a good airing.

And if there was ever a time when clear thinking was essential, it was now. Reuters' treasure had been immense, tons of pure gold bars—enough, at current mercenary rates, to equip and maintain an army of 12,000 in the field for a year! Reuters' kingdom was far from poor, but how he could have consented to the extortion of such a sum—apparently without a fight—was beyond Valerius, and its ramifications needed to be carefully weighed.

A company of Kantaran cavalry clattered by, and Valerius stopped to acknowledge their salutes. There were too many distractions here. With a more determined stride he headed down to a small rope drawn ferry just below the ford, and with his left arm, quickly pulled himself across the river. It was on this side that he and his fellows had established their first encampment when he returned with the Eye. The crumbling earthworks, now used to pen the army's livestock, were dotted with cattle dung and tufts of long, super-fertilized grass. Valerius circled the camp, watching where he stepped, and headed for the quiet of the forested hills to the northeast.

It had only been two years, he mused, since they built those walls and brought cattle back into the Hidden Valley. It seemed so much longer, sometimes, and at others, like he had only just begun; like there was so much to do he dared not sleep lest it not get done soon enough. Yet two years of not sleeping much can wear on a man. Thorngere was right about that. And much had been accomplished. Where they had returned to this valley with but four ships and a couple hundred men, he now had a fleet of forty ships and nearly twenty-five hundred men, not counting the Kantaran. And there was Thorngere's network: news and recruits were coming steadily in and, just as importantly, the word was going out. 'Valerius lives.' 'Valerius will rise against Fantar.' 'Valerius has the Eye!'

But none of it—not those crumbling earth walls, not the cattle, not the men themselves— would be there now were it not for Reuters. It was his gold that had financed the entire venture, and while Valerius now had enough gold of his own to pay Reuters back (to the victor go the spoils!) what would happen if the port of Dulcai were closed to him, or if he lost the support of such a valuable ally? And what could have made Reuters cave in like that? So much gold had to be half his treasury!

Topping a small rise, Valerius was surprised to come upon a small group of Iblian herders, lounging in the grass. They jumped to their feet when they saw him, startled and frightened. But when they saw he was alone, their posture changed. They were smallish people, larger by a considerable amount than the Kantaran, but foul looking and loutish, easily given to greed and perversity. Among them was their leader, Haradin, the former second citizen of Kantar and its chief butcher. It was he and his minions who processed the flesh of their enemies for their fellow citizens' consumption. After the war, he had been sent here to herd the cattle while the rest of the city's population were kept securely locked away tending the inner fields of the New City. He stepped forward now from among his men, his bald head and portly frame giving him the look of a besotted cleric.

"Balazar!" he said with an insolent smile. "I mean, Your Majesty... It's so hard for me to get used to your new position—and to forget our former intimacy. It appears you have been wounded, Your Majesty. We heard you had won a great sea battle."

"Have you no chores to attend to, Haradin?"

"I was just instructing my men in their morning duties, Sire. But I am surprised to see you out alone

135

like this,... Your Majesty. Especially with that wound—it looks so awfully painful. Why, it looks like you can hardly move your sword arm at all." Haradin nodded and several of his men began fanning out, circling Valerius.

"Do you really want to see whether I can wield my sword, Haradin?" said Valerius, easing his right arm from the sling and resting his hand on the hilt of his great falchion. "I promise you'll be the first to die."

Haradin caught his breath quickly, and held up his hands. "Ah, no demonstrations are necessary, Your Majesty," he said quickly. "And I meant no disrespect, merely concern... And you are absolutely right, Your Majesty, we should be getting to our chores. By your leave, sire." and he started backing away.

Valerius watched the group disappear over the hill, then spat, and gingerly placed his arm back in the sling. Haradin was a hyena, always had been. And it was not that long ago that he, Valerius—then Balazar—had worked for him as a butcher of Kudanim. He had even, in his ignorance—and may the Gods forgive him!—eaten of the flesh of his fellow man. He had no choice at the time, of course. It was either that or die. But it is always easier to accept the inevitable when it confronts you than to forgive yourself for it afterwards. Still, he should have killed Haradin after the war. He would cause trouble if he could.

Resuming his march, he worked his way steadily deeper into the forested hills. It was more shaded and peaceful here, the air sharp with the scent of pine, and the ground covered with a thick carpet of needles. He walked in silence, save the occasional flutter of a startled bird, but his mind would not leave Haradin. Why had he not killed him? He certainly had the opportunity then, and was not without justification. But there had been so much killing, and he had wanted the Iblian people to submit peacefully, which they had, once he gave them beef. He had told himself at the time that Haradin, too, was a victim of circumstance and deserved a chance. But was that a wise decision? Had he been seeking justice, or expiating his own guilt?

If he, Valerius, were captured, would Fantar spare him as a "victim of circumstance" just because he had been born to the throne that Fantar had usurped? Of course not, but then, Fantar made no pretense of being just. That was, supposedly, one of Valerius' weapons against him. Still, it did not seem wise policy to leave a live snake in your bed, justice or no.

And was there not a larger parallel here? He to Fantar as Haradin to him? Here Haradin had escaped with his life and was now essentially free to pursue his daily routine. To be sure, he was constrained by circumstance to do certain things and not to do others, but who in this world was without constraint? And was not he, Valerius, in exactly the same situation—barricaded here in this fortified valley, a king in name and symbol, but unable, really, to strike a significant blow at his enemy or regain that which he claimed?

No, acquiring a shipload of gold was definitely significant. Or was it? Was that what was really bothering him? He had a shipload of gold: now, what could he do with it? Was that the rub? Sure, he could hire ten-thousand men, but where would he put them? What would he do with them? Aye, that was the problem: here he had been laboring night and day to acquire the means to resist Fantar. Now, suddenly, he had the means and had no real idea what to do with it. Especially if Reuters was going over to Fantar. His notion had always been to use the Hidden Valley as a staging area: now the question confronted him, a staging area for what? It was clear that Koltar's scheme for achieving naval superiority with galleys that could fit through the cavern was somewhat less than practical (though he had no doubt Koltar would worry the problem until he came up with a solution!) and other than that, what plan did he have?

Topping a hill, he came to the spot he had been seeking: a high rocky mound surrounded by tall pines. It was a totally secluded spot, one where the bones of the earth broke through the surface to bask in the light of day. Here he rested awhile, stretching his weary legs out on the warm grey stone and squinting up at the sun. It was well overhead, but not yet at its zenith. But perhaps, he thought after a time, it was close enough. Rising up again, he faced carefully into the sun and lifted the large red gem to his eye.

Only once before this had he used the Eye, that when the Mage, Volkmir, returned it to him after Fantar had supposedly cast it into the sea. The stone had been in his family, and been borne by the High King for many generations. It was reputed to be a vision stone. Only the rightful king could use it—which is how Fantar became known as "One-Eye"—and according to legend, with it the king could see into the future, and into the hearts of men. But what its real powers were, or how he was supposed to evoke them, he did not really know. His father had never used it—Valerius could remember him referring to it as a "useless bauble"—and Volkmir's only advice had been to "face into the sun and open yourself to the will of the Gods." When he used it before—outside Volkmir's cave after rising from a sick bed—he believed he saw visions. But even then he was not sure whether they came from the stone or from his own fancy, and as time passed, it seemed more and more likely he had simply nodded off into a very vivid dream.

But dream or no, it had been prescient: acting on it had led to peace here in the Valley, and had allowed him to establish his base and make what little progress he had towards regaining his throne. Another dream as potent, he would gladly accept. Surely there were powers in the universe beyond his poor ken and if, through this stone, they allowed him a glimpse of their purposes, or used the stone to give him a sense of direction, he would accept it and be grateful.

139

But what was there to see? Looking deep into the stone, all he saw were swirling patches of red light, like current eddies on the surface of a brook, and the reflection of clouds moving high overhead. Or were they not clouds? Shapes of some sort? And how moving? There was no wind this day, nor any clouds. For a long time he stood gazing into the stone, focusing his thoughts, opening his mind. The sun reached, and then passed its zenith, and finally, he realized the shadow of his own head was blocking the light. He had seen nothing.

Disheartened, he started back down the hill when a thought struck him: "Fool," said the voice of his mind. "You have just captured a whole ship full of gold. Is that not portent enough?"

At the High King's orders, the following day was declared a holiday. All work was suspended, and the plain around the outland encampment was readied for a day of feasting and celebration. Races and athletic contests were to be held, with rich prizes to the winners. Casks of wine were brought out and set up in stalls around the battlements. Tents were pitched for a bazaar, and on the battlements, a large pavilion was erected for Valerius and his retinue. Orders went out also to Haradin in his ramshackle encampment on the north side of the river; several prime head each of cattle, sheep, and swine were to be slaughtered, dressed and delivered for roasting at the feast site; and one prime bull was to be readied immediately for sacrifice.

This poor creature, a twelve-month bull calf in the first blush of his strength, was led in from the green fields where he had been at play with his fellows. He was washed and brushed, and had the buds of his horns painted with a bright red ocher. Another red symbol was painted on his forehead, in consecration, and a special mark painted on the large artery in his throat. He seemed to enjoy the attention, and did not mind at all when he was lead onto the ferry and drawn across the river.

A large crowd of Kantaran and outland warriors had gathered on the plain around a small stone altar. It was on this spot, or as near to it as the memories of the participants could fix, that Prince Koltar, emboldened by the hope of victory and entering the first battle of his life, had faced the Iblis Lawgiver, Chubar—a man near twice his size—and had killed him in single combat. Afterwards, he had consecrated the spot in honor of the God, Kala Atar, who granted their victory, and as a reminder to his people that greatness could be theirs if only they kept to the God's will.

Valerius stood at this altar now, adorned in his kingly regalia and with the brilliant red gem bright upon his chest. As the bull was lead forward, Valerius lifted a golden cup to the heavens and uttered loud a prayer of thanksgiving.

"Oh Kantaran Kala Atar, and you of Valerian Thunder, Valdator, hear us now, and accept the spirit and flesh of this offering with which we honor and thank you for our great victory, and for the great treasure which thou hast vouchsafed us. Grant honor, as well, to those who compete here today. Give strength to their arms and speed to their legs, that their efforts may better reflect your glory.

"And hear this, too, my plea—Valerius Everreigning, Rightful High King of Valeria and all the Inland Sea. Many long years have we labored in our quest to reclaim our homes and our patrimony. Many of our comrades have gone down to dark death, never to see wives or children more. Many of our cities have you watched go up in flames, our women led off into bondage, our babes dashed upon the rocks. See us here, a pitiful remnant of the glory that was Valeria of old! We are but a few hands where once there were many. Yet still we stand to our arms, and put keen edge to our swords. Still we march to the fight, though the road is long and churned to mud with our blood. Now you have given us the means, grant us also Thy victory, oh Valdator of the Storm! Break over the head of this Fantar, drive him before us like chaff blown from the wheat. Show us the path to win back our homes! Grant that we may rebuild our cities, and do honor to your name."

In the silence that followed, he poured a portion of the wine out onto the ground in honor of the Kantaran God, and the rest over the head and neck of the bull to invoke the Valarian God. The bull did not like the wine stinging his eyes and shook his head and bellowed, and tried to jerk free of his handlers. But sturdy men held his legs and tail, and two others held his head and stretched out his neck. Valerius the king drove a silver handled knife through the marked vein in his throat, and stood back as the bright blood spurted out onto the ground. The bull stopped bucking when he felt the blade. He was not in pain, but he knew his death had come, and he stood very still, rolling his large eyes and snorting softly as his life force gushed out and soaked into the earth. Soon, his strength ebbed and he dropped to his knees, then rolled onto his side. His eyes glazed, and the spirit left him.

Valerius cut tender portions from the thighs, wrapped them in fat, and burned them on the altar so that the smoke would be pleasing to the Gods and lead the bull's spirit home. The carcass was then dragged off to the cooking fires and Valerius, mounting the battlements and taking his seat in the pavilion, signaled for the games to begin.

Vahla's interest in the competition was feigned. Sitting with the royal party and looking out over the massed troops towards the ships clustered in the river, she applauded the winners, gasped at critical moments, "Oh'd" and "Ah'd" with the crowd at particular demonstrations of prowess, but had little real interest. As a dancer, she could appreciate some of the coordination, and conditioning required—in the gymnastics, for example—but without music there seemed nothing to shape and give meaning to the movement. And as a woman, she could certainly appreciate the bodies of some of the men—especially the wrestlers, who competed naked—although the winner, a huge man named Rax, whose face had been hammered nearly flat over the years, was as ugly as a bog and no doubt smelled as bad. But why men took such pleasure from these things, she could not fathom. To her, dance was symbol, poetry. It gave expression and had meaning. Dance was subtle and evocative. This was brute strength, sinew and speed. This was like men themselves, rooted in the rough forces of the earth. Dance, she thought, was a kind of conception. These games forced conclusions.

Still, there were some thrilling moments, and some amusing ones—not the least of which was when Thorngere leapt down from the battlement and snuck in to kneel behind the great wrestler Rax while his back was turned. His opponent, catching the joke, gave Rax a mighty shove and he tumbled head over heels, much to the delight of all but him. He leapt up raging, and took off after Thorngere, who ran as if his life depended on it. The crowd howled as the race continued halfway round the field, but Vahla jumped into Thorngere's seat beside the king and clutched tight to his arm. "He won't be hurt, will he?"

Valerius laughed aloud at the spectacle. "Well," he said, "Rax has been known to crush skulls like eggs – but I doubt he'll have much luck with a blockhead like Thorngere! Besides, as you can see, Thorngere can move rather quickly, given the proper incentive."

Finally, Thorngere circled back into the crowd, and several men tackled Rax and held him down while Thorngere made it safely back to his place. "I see it didn't take you long to move in on my woman!" he gasped, flopping down into Vahla's chair.

"I moved in on him," Vahla smiled, patting the king's arm. "You know how I am with high kings!"

"Yes, I've heard!" said Valerius, pulling away in mock horror. "She's not hiding a dagger anywhere, is she?" and they all laughed.

More wine casks were broken open as the foot races began and the party became more lively. Valerius had thrown off his pensive mood of the day before and joined wholeheartedly in the festive atmosphere, calling often to have his cup filled, and making sure Vahla's and Thorngere's were filled as well. He also seemed to be enjoying the presence of the beautiful woman beside him, and more than once Vahla felt his eyes upon her. She sipped slowly and pretended to enjoy the games, having learned long before that it was not wise to keep pace with drinking kings.

She did find the races interesting, however, for here both outland and Kantaran warriors competed together, though they were scored separately, and it quickly became apparent that bigger was not always better. In the shorter, faster races, the big men had all the advantage, finishing in a pack well ahead of the smaller Kantarans. But as the distance of the events increased, the more the results were mixed, for where the bigger men had strength and speed, the smaller warriors had great endurance. Their legs also had less weight to carry, and when the final race was completed—a long run of several miles which took the contestants right through the

145

city and back—it was the Kantarans who finished in a pack well ahead of the nearest outlander. Not only that, but they still looked fresh and vigorous after their outing, while the outland runners staggered and gasped over the line, some falling flat in a dead faint.

But the most impressive thing—for Vahla had never seen its like—was a demonstration by the Kantaran horse archers. The field was cleared for this and about a hundred targets were set out in a line running across the plain. These were straw-filled bags hung from spears driven into the ground. At a signal from Valerius, several thousand horsemen swept out onto the field from behind the hills by the river. Thundering over the plain, they passed in review before the packed battlements, then swung around and raced back. They lined up by the river then, and in groups of a hundred each, dashed back across the field, knocking and loosing their arrows as they neared their targets. Group after group charged through, firing their bows until the targets looked like porcupines. And from what Vahla could see, there were very few misses.

The little people fascinated her even more now that she understood a bit of their history. The soldiers, like Colinus, seemed so stiff in their military dress, yet looked so much like beardless youths. Then there was the other group, smaller still and obviously aristocratic, gathered on the battlements. Prince Koltar, for example, was so tiny and sharp featured, and so very deft of movement and thought, he was like a young child, except for his perfectly adult proportions and his well-trimmed beard. Stood side by side, the soldiers were a good head taller than their lords, yet were obviously subservient.

Still, the day was long, and after the many contests, and the feasting, and after Valerius awarded prizes to all the winners—with Rax glowering at Thorngere all the while Valerius set the laurel on his head—she was looking forward to a hot bath and a quiet evening, when Valerius invited them to join him for a quiet supper.

They ate in his private quarters in the palace, sitting on pillows around a low table. Valerius and Thorngere were still quite gay from the festivities. They replayed the afternoon's games, discussing the merits of this and that contestant (Thorngere swore he could have taken Rax at any time!), and after they had sampled not a little of Valerius' private wine, they relived the sea battle, blow by blow, laughing again and again at the look on poor Colinus' face as the mast he was riding went by the board. Thorngere was in very high spirits, leaping about the room to reenact his discovery of Grumwald, and talked and laughed in a steady stream. Several times, he even broke into old campaign songs. Vahla sat quietly for the most part, smiling tolerantly at Thorngere's antics, and sipping her wine while the men drank. Several times she glanced up to see the king's eyes, somewhat red and glassy now, feasting upon her. Finally, he interrupted one of Thorngere's comic monologues:

"Thorngere, my friend, I do believe we're boring the young lady here."

"Boring the young lady?" said Thorngere, flopping blearily down beside her and nuzzling her neck. "I should have known... She always loses interest if I don't lavish all my attention on her!"

"Oh, you pig!" squealed Vahla, pushing him violently away. "I'll give you 'attention!'" and she began pummeling Thorngere who rolled away, laughing, and dragged her over on top of him.

"All right," he laughed. "I give up. I give up!" and lifting the girl easily, set her back in her place. "I swear I'll never ignore you again! But listen," he said stopping as if to seriously consider something. "Instead of us trying to entertain you, how about you entertain us? After all, you're supposed to be this great dancer. Let's see you dance."

Vahla was startled, and glanced quickly at the King. "Oh, no!" she said. "Not here!"

"Why not?" Thorngere wanted to know. "You dance all the time."

"I... I don't know. It just doesn't seem appropriate, that's all. Besides, I have no music."

"We can get music."

"No, I don't want to."

"Why not? Come on, you promised to dance for me some time. Why not now?"

"Thorngere," she said quietly, her eyes pleading, "please don't make me."

"My friend," said Valerius sobering, "I think you've been overruled. But it's all right—there's

148

something I need to talk to you about anyway. I've got a little job for you."

"Oh?" said Thorngere sitting back up to the table.

"Yes, I want you to go to Reuters. I need to find out what is going on there. We can take the occasion to pay him the money I owe him, and use it to sniff around. I was going to go myself—I was even thinking of going in force—but I think you'd do a better job of it. Especially after the wonderful job you did giving that speech the other night. You can be my ambassador."

"Oh, thanks again for that! Vahla, would you like to take a trip to Dulcai?"

"Well, I..."

"Actually," said Valerius, "I would prefer it if you went alone."

Chapter 9
MISSION TO DULCAI

Early the following morning, before the sun had climbed above the high cliffs, the trading scow *Elusive* braced her single yard around to pick up the first of the westerly breeze and pointed her bluff bows south towards Dulcai. From her masthead fluttered the yellow and red banner of Zagorbia, and on the afterdeck, her captain, Boltar, manned the long arm of the steering board, while a hand stood by. Leaning against the rail, with his back to them, stood Thorngere, pensively watching the black hole of the cavern mouth slowly fall astern. He had taken too much to drink the night before and now felt its effects: a hollow booming ache in his head, a tremulous feeling in his hands, and a stomach that was not quite queasy, but nonetheless very sensitive to the slow roll of the ship. He pressed his fingertips against his forehead and groaned softly. He should have behaved himself better, he thought. He'd gotten carried away, overexcited. And he'd gotten himself in trouble with Vahla, which he had heard about in no uncertain terms when they got back to their rooms. Whatever happened to fond farewells?

Women, he thought. Pains in the butt, all of them. Here the girl dances in every town and tavern around the Inland Sea—makes her living at it, by the Gods—yet he asks her to dance one time and it's

150

like poking a lion with a stick! What the hell was wrong with asking her to dance? She didn't want to be treated like a tavern wench in front of the king, she said! But who said anything about tavern wenches? She was the one always waxing poetic about dance as an art form. What kind of art is it you can't ask to see? And what's the problem dancing before Valerius? Because he's supposedly the High King? You'd think that would be an honor.

"Wind's piping up nicely," said Boltar. He had turned over the helm and came aft to lean on the rail beside Thorngere. "If it keeps building like this we'll make six knots."

"Oh, she swims like a dolphin, this old girl does... Though, I wager it would take a pretty decent gale to get six knots out of her."

"You wait and see," said Boltar. He was a trim looking fellow, a few years younger than Thorngere, with black hair, a closely cropped beard, and black, snapping eyes. He was a good seaman and had captained Thorngere's ship for two years. "I got her careened down while we were in port and the lads scrubbed her bottom good. She's slick as a baby's butt."

"Well, it's a comfort to be in a seaworthy craft again after that little expedition in Koltar's galley."

"I heard you had quite the ride there—mast going by the board and all."

"That wasn't the half of it. You should have seen her heel... Put her whole rail down, she did, scooping up green water like a bucket. I thought we'd sail her right under several times."

"But did she sail up wind?"

"Very nearly, yes. And off the wind she went like a scalded cat—made Fantar's boys look like proper monkeys!"

"Till the mast went."

"Well, give Koltar a little credit. This was just his first attempt at this new design, and it was blowing pretty hard out here. He told me yesterday he's already working on a couple new ideas."

"For a little fellow, he sure didn't come up short on brains."

"No, that he didn't. You should see the relief map he made for the king—a scale model of the whole coast, harbors, towns, everything. Looks like you could live on it."

"How is Valerius' wound?"

"Ah, a pin prick. I've seen him cut himself worse at dinner."

"Good. Rumor has it that trader you captured was filled with gold."

"Well, you know how rumors are," said Thorngere lifting his face to the wind. "Feels like it's backing northerly. You suppose we could get a bit more offing? I wouldn't want to be caught inshore if we happen on another galley."

Boltar went off to tend the helm and Thorngere went back to his thoughts. It wasn't just the argument that troubled him, or that she didn't want to dance. It was that she didn't want to dance for Valerius. That's what was troubling. Why wouldn't she want to dance in front of him? She'd said he looked like Fantar... Was she afraid he was going to drag her off to his bed? Would he? They had shared women before, but surely Valerius realized Vahla was more to him than just a tavern wench. Or did he? Thorngere hadn't said anything to indicate otherwise. Of course, he was sharing his quarters with her. But there were no ties. Could he trust Valerius? Was it even a question of trust? He was sure that if Valerius knew how he felt about Vahla he would have no reason for concern. But did Valerius know? And perhaps more to the point, could he trust Vahla? She had certainly shown considerable interest in the king. That was not imagination.

No, he was being silly. Other than getting yelled at for being drunk and behaving like a boor the night before, he had no reason to distrust either of them. And such worry would certainly not help him in Dulcai. Abruptly, he spun from the rail and strode to the edge of the quarter deck, yelling as he went. "Is this as high as she'll point? I said I wanted offing! Come on, goddamn your eyes, haul that yard!"

They raised Dulcai early on the fifth day. From a distance, the city was a shimmer of white nestled under the bright morning sun among the hills at the end of a deep bay. Thorngere watched it for hours as the *Elusive* skirted the long protective spit of sand which guarded the mouth of the bay, and entered through the narrow channel along its

153

southern edge. From an early hour, the bay was dotted with brightly colored fishing boats, casting and hauling nets, and contrasting sharply with the sandy brown of the surrounding hillsides. The land was arid and hot this far south, and only in the protected groves of the city and along the river valley, which wound into the hills behind it, was there any appreciable sign of green.

Reuters' people lived by the sea, fishing, trading, or worse when the occasion presented. Legend had it that the land used to be lush and green, and that life in Dulcai was as easy as reaching out your hand to pluck a fruit. But year by year the land got dryer now. The great forests were nearly gone, and hot winds swept down from the desert to the northeast, stinging with swirling sand. There used to be rich fields around Dulcai, said the stories, acres of corn and wheat, and groves of plantain and bananas. Now sheep and cattle scoured the sparse grasses, and what gardens remained were carefully tended plots in and about the city. For survival, the people of Dulcai relied on the sea.

Luckily for Reuters, however, one other thing also kept Dulcai alive: there was gold in the hills around the city. Not a lot of gold, and not gold that could be gotten without considerable effort, but gold just the same. With the product from his mines and a fleet of sturdy trading ships, Reuters was able to buy what he could not grow. Many of those ships could be seen now dotted about the harbor, along with the galleys of Reuters' war fleet, as the *Elusive* dropped her anchor close inshore along the southwestern edge of the basin, and Thorngere was rowed ashore in his gig. In the bilges at his feet was a large strongbox which took two crewmen to lift onto the small, rickety wharf on the edge of town. Then the gig returned to the ship and fetched two more strongboxes of identical size.

Thorngere was dressed in his finest tunic and his armor—a hand-beaten breastplate with gold inlay and a plumed battle cap lined with red leather—had been burnished to a high sheen. At his side, as a deterrent to the curious, hung a great, two-handed battle sword, and on his left forearm, after the fashion of Valerius, was a small round buckler. Behind him, crewmen carried the chests on poles slung between them, and a squad of others marched behind, also well-armed. They were not molested, but drew many stares as they marched straight down the coastal road, then directly up to Reuters' palace. There they were met by the captain of Reuters' guard, one Loquis, a man well known to Thorngere.

"Who are you and what business have you to approach in arms the seat of His Royal Majesty, King Reuters of Dulcai?" he demanded, observing the forms.

"I am Thorngere of Thuringia, a Lord of Valeria and Ambassador from His Majesty Valerius Everreigning, Rightful High King of Valeria and all the Inland Sea. I bring greetings to King Reuters, and would treat with him."

"You are welcome, Lord Thorngere," Loquis saluted. "Come with me and I will send to see if

His Majesty is at leisure. And may I say," he said under his breath as Thorngere fell in beside him and they made their way into the palace, "it's nice to see the likes of you come around *bearing* gifts for a change!"

As luck would have it, Reuters was at leisure, and had been, in fact, since the *Elusive* was first reported entering the harbor and coming to anchor in his port. And when it was further reported that men were disembarking with heavy chests, he decided to take his leisure in his throne room with several of his courtiers in attendance. It was here that Thorngere was escorted and announced with all formality.

"Thorngere!" Reuters said, rising cordially and stepping down from his dais. He was a short, stocky man, no longer young, with an open, jowly face and iron-gray hair which hung straight down to the bottom of his ears and was cropped square. "My people thought it was you, but they weren't sure... They said your arms were all polished and you looked like a prince. How nice to see you looking like a prince, my friend!"

"Thank you, Your Majesty," said Thorngere, kneeling before him and bending over the signet ring on his outstretched hand, "though I'm afraid it will take more than a polished hat to make a prince out of me!"

"Nonsense, my boy. Nonsense. And how is *his* Majesty, Valerius?" said Reuters, resuming his throne.

"Well, Your Majesty, very well. He sends you his warmest regards and bade me deliver this..." Thorngere stepped aside as his crewmen set the chests down before Reuters and opened their lids: they were full to brimming with coins of gold and silver, and with precious gems. Some of the contents spilled out onto the floor and tinkled like bells. Reuters eyes went round with surprise, and he half rose from his chair. Without conscious volition, his hand reached out for the glittering stuff. Thorngere continued, "Your Majesty, my liege, Valerius, bids me say this to you as well: 'Most noble Reuters, King of Dulcai and long friend to our cause, two years ago I stood before you, penniless and with no more claim to my name and throne than the red stone of my ancestors. Yet you took my hand in brotherhood, and sat me down beside you as an equal. You gave succor to our rag-tag band. More, you accepted my bond and on faith alone, financed our venture to the Hidden Valley. Cattle you gave in several hundreds, and supplies for our ships, new arms for our men you provided, and coin for our purse; all this you gave with no terms for return. You relied upon me, you said, to make good my promise.

'Reuters, most noble king and honored friend, the gods have showered favor on that seed you helped plant and it grows to a strong young sapling. Not yet have we claimed our throne, but many thousands have joined our cause. Many are the shields on the rails of our ships. Rich are our fields and forests, and far has the word spread among the peoples of the Inland Sea and among the minions of our enemy, Fantar One-Eye, that Valerius Everreigning is alive and will reign once more. Even now preparations are underway to strike down this usurper and build up again the glory that was Valeria of old.

'You, Reuters, we name First Friend of this new Valeria. And though we can never hope to fully repay that which was freely given in need, we offer this as a token of our faith and as a pledge of greater rewards to follow.' Thus," concluded Thorngere, "was I bidden to say by His Majesty Valerius Everreigning, Rightful High King of Valeria and all the Inland Sea to his First Friend, King Reuters of Dulcai."

Reuters sat quietly on his throne for a time, tapping a finger on his cheek bone and gazing at the splendid treasure before him. "His Majesty is generous," he said finally, looking up at Thorngere. "This is three times, at least, what I gave him."

"He says to tell you, Your Majesty, that ten times will not begin to acquit his debt."

"Hmmm, most generous, indeed. I am impressed. Inform him of my gratitude. But let us speak no more of these things now. It has been long since we have had the pleasure of your company and there is much we need to catch up on. Besides, if I know anything of my old friend Thorngere, delivering such a speech must have made you thirsty."

"Exceedingly so, Your Majesty," said Thorngere. "Exceedingly so."

For three days was Thorngere, as a Lord of Valeria and official Ambassador of King Valerius, lavishly entertained by Reuters, King of Dulcai. Banquets were held with musicians and dancers and entertainers of all kinds. Reuters' best wines were brought from his cellars and served unmixed. Thorngere was given a grand tour of the city and led down into the depths of one of Reuters' many mines. Together they rode on horseback into the desert hunting after wild boar. They flew falcons from their wrists, and watched the fishing fleet race across the bay. Gifts were given him, a silken tunic said to protect like armor, and a hammered gold cup. At night, they drank late and women were proffered—but these Thorngere, surprising even himself, declined. His desire was strong, but his thoughts were elsewhere.

Not till the afternoon of the fourth day, and after sleeping late and then seeing to the readiness of his ship and crew, was Thorngere ushered into the private salon of Reuters to discuss the real business of his journey. Reuters lounged on a couch lined with cushions, and though somewhat red-eyed from their recent festivities and a bit pensive, he appeared to be his usual amiable self. But Thorngere immediately sensed an undercurrent of tension in the man and sat down by him cautiously.

"What shall it be today, Majesty," he joked, "something as tame as a boar hunt? Or shall we try to soar with the eagles?"

"Let us leave off the eagles today, shall we?" Reuters laughed with a wan smile. "I am afraid I am quite done in with soaring. But I did want to have a chance to talk with you. I am delighted, of course, with Valerius' evident success, and I must confess, the extent of his generosity to the people of Dulcai is a most pleasant surprise. Yet I am sensible also of the ways of this world, friend Thorngere, and such gifts do not come without condition."

"There is no condition, Your Majesty. Valerius asks only that you remain what you are, his First Friend and ally."

Reuters pulled at the fleshy folds beneath his chin and furled his brow. "Allies are wonderful things, Thorngere—in time of peace. Allies trade amongst each other, and entertain each other, they speak fine words and admire each other... But in time of war, the word 'ally' has an entirely different connotation. And I sincerely doubt it is an era of peace your Valerius has in mind."

Thorngere suddenly felt he was standing on shifting sand. Reuters was not going to make this easy. "But that is exactly what Valerius has in mind," he countered. "A long era of peace, and trade, of fine words and harmony—an era extending to our children and our children's children. That is the ideal of Valeria."

"Well do I remember the peace and prosperity that was 'the ideal of Valeria,' my friend. I watched it grow soft and opulent and drop like an over-ripened fruit into the hard hand of Fantar One-Eye.

And who is to say there is not now a new prosperity? But listen, Thorngere, I am a man of trade," said Reuters, swinging his feet down from the couch and leaning forward on his elbows. "I understand the language of the marketplace. Tell me what it is Valerius wants of me."

"Your harbor."

Reuters inhaled sharply and sat upright. "My harbor! Indeed. A simple request, that... My harbor. And no doubt a bit of my town?"

Thorngere smiled. "We might welcome a rocky patch in a corner field... Enough to pitch a tent or two."

Reuters got up and began pacing to the window and back. "I see," he said. "You know, Valerius never would tell me where this 'Valley of Kantar' was hidden. I've always supposed it to be somewhere along the coast between here and Zagorbia, but though I've sailed those waters many times myself and have asked my captains many times as well, I confess we have no notion exactly where. But I take it from what you say, that this valley of yours must have some limitations?"

"Limitations? Say, rather, that you can't grow wheat where soldiers sleep."

"You have so many soldiers, then? We don't have much luck growing wheat here, either, you know."

"The more reason we should more actively ally ourselves."

Reuters resumed his seat and Thorngere could see that behind the casual diplomacy of his demeanor, there was conflict, even fear, in his eyes. "It's one thing to offer safe haven and a few cattle to some vagabond ruffians," Reuters said. "It would be quite another to deliberately set up in opposition to Fantar... What would make us different from every other city that tried it?"

"Valerius."

"It's a very nice name."

"It's a power name, Reuters. A name of destiny. You know that as well as I. How many years did we fight Fantar before Valerius? And with how much success? Time after time, we were dispersed like chaff before the wind. Now we have a center. Now we coalesce. Now we grow in power. Can't you see, Reuters, the tide has begun to turn against Fantar? For the past two years I have been traveling the Inland Sea, seeing what Fantar has wrought and talking to the people—the name 'Valerius' brings hope to their eyes. Together we can start to make that hope a reality."

Reuters began to pace again, clenching and unclenching his fists as he went. His face was tight. "Thorngere," he said, resuming his seat and leaning forward confidentially, "I think there is merit in all that you say. But to understand my position, you must understand my situation here, so I will be frank with you. That gold mine I took you into the other day? There was no gold in it. It was a sham—played out years ago. And the other mines? No gold there, either. What gold there was in the hills of Dulcai was mined long ago."

"But I saw hundreds of men working those mines."

"There were more than that. Nearly half the men in Dulcai work in the mines."

"I don't understand..."

"It's not gold they're mining, it's ore... Iron ore."

"But I saw no furnaces."

"Exactly. How could I have furnaces when I have no trees to make charcoal? Do you see? My ships are not going north with gold to buy: they go north loaded with ore to trade. Gold is part of what comes back—or, at least, it was."

"What do you mean?"

Reuters waved his hand dismissively. "It's beside the point. The point is that without the ore trade, the people of Dulcai would starve. And I don't think trading relations would go quite so smoothly with Fantar if your ships were anchored in my harbor and your men camped out on my shore."

Thorngere leaned back in his chair, tugged at the long yellow strands of his beard, and eyed Reuters carefully. This was not all. There was something more. There was one ship of gold that was definitely going north. "Your Majesty," he posed, "you said earlier you were a man of trade, and I certainly understand more clearly now what you meant by that—but it seems to me that trust is the basis of trade. Can you tell me truly that you trust Fantar? That the gold comes back to stay?"

Reuters flashed Thorngere a look of pure rage that collapsed into despair. "Well, it did for a while," he said, rubbing his face, "until he decided he needed a 'tribute!'"

"And you gave in to him?"

"I had to!" Reuters cried, his face twisting. "He has taken my daughter!"

After Thorngere left him, Reuters sat very still, staring through the window into the deep blue of the cloudless sky. He did not even move when the door to an inner chamber, which had been standing slightly ajar, opened fully and another figure entered. He was dark complected, this man, and smooth shaven with dark, curly ringlets cropped close about his head. He did not approach Reuters like a subject, but crossed in front of him with an insolent casualness and flopped down into the chair Thorngere had just vacated.

"You didn't find out anything," he said curtly.

Reuters turned his head slowly and gazed at the man. "Glaucon," he said flatly, "you and your master have my people in thrall, you have most of my gold, and now you have my daughter. But you will, at least, address me properly."

"Noted, your Majesty." said Glaucon, not bothering to hide a smirk. "But you still did not find out anything... My lord."

"I found out there are more of them than you thought."

"How many?"

"Enough to pose a real threat. Enough to begin moving against you."

"Bah, that was bluff. But where are they? That's what I want to know: where?"

"That, my disreputable friend," said Reuters, "Thorngere did not vouchsafe to tell me."

"Well, then, my reputable friend, we'll just have to find out, won't we?"

Chapter 10
THE ESCORT

Thorngere stood on the beach the next morning, anxious to be off, while Reuters delivered an obsequious farewell speech, the brunt of which was that he, Reuters, would consider Thorngere's proposals, and they would discuss them again, but that in the meantime he was glad to see the budding growth of Valerius' movement, was all for continuing improvement in their relations, etc., etc., etc... It was clear to Thorngere that the lavish gift and his slight exaggerations of their naval and military capability had impressed Reuters, but it was also clear that the man had buckled under Fantar's pressure, and that his fine sounding words were meaningless. But he tried not to let his impatience show as Reuters presented him with a small dagger as a parting gift. "Use it on your own meat, friend Thorngere," he said finally, "and remember, should you tend to think harshly of us, or of me, that both food and utensils came from the grace of Dulcai. Remember, too," he said stepping closer so that only the two of them could hear, "that sometimes even kings may not do as they please."

"I will remember, Your Majesty." said Thorngere, bowing and turning to his waiting gig. But Reuters was not quite finished.

"One more thing," he said. "We have had reports of a number of Fantar's galleys cruising off

166

the coast, so as a precaution I have ordered one of my own galleys to escort you part of the way."

"Oh," Thorngere protested, "that is not necessary, Your Majesty."

"Perhaps, but it would make me feel ever so much better to know you were looked after."

"I appreciate that, your majesty, but I do believe we would be safer on our own."

"Nonsense, my boy. Besides, I believe my captain is a man well known to you: Blumholt?"

"Ah, yes, Blumholt," Thorngere acquiesced, "Very well, Your Majesty. And thank you for your concern."

Boltar and his men were still hauling in the anchor when a sleek, oared galley pulled up alongside, and its wild-maned captain yelled across the narrow space between the two ships. "Ahoy Thorngere! We'll wait for you just outside the bar."

"Hello Blumholt!" Thorngere yelled back. "Glad to see you're coming up in the world. Think you can go slow enough to stay with an old tub like this?"

"I'll drag a couple wine casks over the side," Blumholt retorted. "That'll slow me down, and make you try to speed up!" Crew on both ships laughed at this joke, but as the ships parted, Thorngere's eye was caught by a single unsmiling face. It was one of Blumholt's mates, a dark, smooth-shaven fellow with curly hair. He stood, somber-faced, beside the captain, gazing steadily at the *Elusive*. Thorngere met the man's eye for a brief

167

second before he turned away, but in that instant, he knew the escort was a charade.

The wind stood fair from the west throughout the first few days as the *Elusive* made her way steadily northward, her sleek escort following close enough to be in tow. Hardly a sheet was touched as watch succeeded watch and the long miles slowly filled their bubbling wake. Through much of the trip Thorngere paced his quarterdeck, his impatience with the uninvited escort only exceeded by his eagerness to be home. Fore and aft he stalked, his eye falling first on the sharp prow of the galley, slicing through the water behind, and as he turned forward, his thoughts darting over the horizon to Kantar and Vahla.

Indeed, Vahla had hardly been out of his thoughts during the entire journey and he had resolved—though exactly when he was never sure—that as soon as he got back, he would ask her to marry him. It was a rather surprising resolution for him to make—at least, to him—and one that started butterflies in his stomach every time he thought of it. He was not quite sure how the subject had come up in his mind, or precisely what had tripped the conclusion, but there it was and he was incredibly anxious now to put the matter before her and find out if she would have him.

But with this idiot Blumholt loping along in his wake like a ravening wolf, he would never get there! How long was he planning to keep up this game? During the first day or so, he had hoped the galley would give up and turn back. He had even hailed Blumholt and assured him they were fine now, that he could go back in good conscience. But Blumholt had only smiled and yelled across the stretch of blue water between them that his master would never forgive him if he was less than thorough in his duty to his old friend.

So, it was obvious from then on that Blumholt would not turn back until he spotted the entrance to the Hidden Valley. But just as obviously, Thorngere could not let that happen. So what was to be done? Over and over, he ran through the same train of thought. How could a slow, undermanned trading scow hope to outrun a sleek war galley? He couldn't. Nor could he outfight them. The galley carried a crew of at least a hundred. He had twelve. And how could he fight anyway? The ship had done nothing hostile. It was simply an escort, sailing under the flag of Dulcai.

But flag or no, there was very little doubt who was actually giving the orders. Not only was there that shady 'mate' Thorngere had seen, but his own crew had reported seeing some rough looking characters in the bars along the quay in Dulcai— types who looked like they could easily be in Fantar's service. Several of them had even tried to volunteer as crew, but the Innkeeper had given Boltar the high sign and he had sheared off—said he'd return later and pick them up. Another crewman said he had walked inland along the river, and that up beyond the bend he had seen a good dozen of Fantar's galleys moored. And several had heard the rumor of the King's daughter being taken hostage.

So what to do? Up and back, up and back, Thorngere's thoughts traced the same paths as his feet wearied the same planks, with neither end nor resolution in sight. Late that afternoon, however, the wind began backing northerly, as it sometimes did in that season, and he thought he saw a chance. Shaping his course in towards the land—as he had no choice but to do with that wind—he sailed in close under the overarching cliffs and, dropped anchor in the semi-protected lee of a promontory. True to his duty, Blumholt also anchored, a bit further to the south, but within easy bow shot.

As night fell, the two ships rigged anchor lights on their bows. But as soon as it was full dark, Thorngere had his gig carefully lowered over the side, taken forward, and secured to the anchor cable. A mast was rigged in it, and as the two swung together, his anchor light was switched over. In the dead of the night, then, when there were no more sounds coming from the galley, they cut their cable and with muffled oars, rowed the *Elusive* offshore until they picked up the gentle northerly wind. Then, with hardly a sound, they set sail and headed straight out to sea.

"Well," Boltar said, leaning on the rail beside Thorngere and staring back at the two anchor lights bobbing quietly in the growing distance, "we seem to have gotten the jump on them. But won't they just pick us up again in the morning? We aren't going to be able to beat very far north with this wind."

"We aren't going to beat north," said Thorngere, "at least not this night, nor the next neither."

"We're going back south, then?"

"Nope, west."

"West! There's nothing to the west." Even in the darkness, Thorngere could see the fear on Boltar's face. In that age, sailing out of sight of land was not something the prudent mariner chose to do.

"There's sea."

"But we'll lose sight of the land. How will we get back?"

"We'll also lose sight of that fat bastard!" Thorngere said. "And as for getting back, why, how about we head for the rising sun?"

In Kantar, Valerius was growing anxious. He knew how long it took to sail to Dulcai and back, and he knew Thorngere would not simply be able to run in, confer with Reuters and dash back. He knew there would be forms to follow and entertainments to be held (and he knew how well Thorngere liked his entertainments!). But, he did not know how extensively Reuters would play the gracious host. So when the day of Thorngere's expected arrival came and went, he tried not to think about it. And all the next morning, too. That evening, to show himself exactly how unconcerned he was, and because he was sure that by then Thorngere would have appeared, he invited Queen Salonis, Koltar, and Vahla to join him for dinner.

He went all out, too, ordering a fine large roast for Vahla and himself—one large enough for Thorngere, too, should he show up at the last minute—and the best local dishes for Koltar and the Queen, (like all Kantarans, they did not eat the flesh of animals). Musicians were ordered to set up in the small alcove off his dining room, extra candles were set about, and his best plate laid. This was an old set, delicately carved of chalcedony with onyx inlay, which had been made in Kantar before the Iblis took the city. It had been found packed carefully away in a corner of the palace cellars and had been granted him as part of his share for retaking the city.

But Salonis, when she came, was plainly ill. Of all her people, she alone, it seemed, had not thrived on the return to their ancestral city. Whether it was the exhaustive work of rebuilding, which she had thrown herself into with an energy that surprised even her closest advisors, whether it was some mysterious 'humor' that was wasting away her once robust and very rotund frame, or whether it was simply the inevitable ravages of age inflicting their claim, Valerius could not guess. But it was plain when he saw her, stooped and pale, and leaning heavily on the arms of Vahla and her nephew, Koltar, that the specter of death was about her. This wrenched him for he had grown very fond of the lady despite the fact that in former times she had ordered him kidnapped, duped, poisoned, hunted, and executed by turns.

Fortunately, he had survived each of those calamities (and, he might even have said, thrived on them) and now was very solicitous of the Queen. He helped Koltar place her in a chair, poured her wine himself and even helped her hold the cup. If there was anything special she would like, he said, he would have the cooks prepare it instantly. She responded with a wispy good humor, waving off their attentions with a waxy hand and trying to laugh, though she was hoarse and it brought on a fit of coughing.

"Valerius," she wheezed when her breath had returned, "you are a good and kind man, but you make me feel like a perfect invalid with all this attention. Here," she said, indicating Vahla on the other side of the table, "here is what a full blooded man such as you should be fawning over—a beautiful woman!" Vahla blushed deeply at the compliment and Salonis tried again to laugh, but coughed instead. "I am afraid I am not going to be much company for you this evening," she gasped.

"Nonsense, My Lady," said Valerius. "It is a delight to see you, though we are concerned for your health."

"Well, I don't think you need be concerned for too much longer... Which is why I came," she said, straightening in her chair and looking at Valerius with something like her old fire. "I wanted to have a chance to talk with you and, if you will indulge me, I would like to do so now."

"By all means, My Lady," said Valerius, concerned. "Would you like Vahla to withdraw?"

173

"No, no, it is nothing of a particularly confidential nature, and besides, the very sight of her lifts up my heart—there is too much of beauty I have already missed in this world."

Vahla blushed again, and bowed her head to murmur, "You are too kind, Majesty." But she felt the tears start in the backs of her eyes.

"Anyway," Salonis resumed, "I want to speak to you about my people, and about this valley, and about the direction of this path we all seem to be travelling. Koltar here has told me you are concerned about using up our resources here, about overstaying your welcome. And I want to assure you there is no risk of that. This land is yours by right of conquest, King Valerius Everreigning, and if that were not enough, you have captured the hearts of our people as well. You delivered us from a conflict that consumed us for generations—a conflict that would surely have led to our extinction. So you have earned our fealty, and we are yours to command. But...," she said, and held up her hand as Valerius was about to interrupt, "I am also Queen of Kantar. The welfare of this people is my duty and obligation, and well do I know the terrible choices we sometimes face as rulers. Sometimes we must risk destroying a thing in order to save it. I know you have a great quest before you, Valerius, and that your spirit grapples daily with another force. But do not overlook this land that was your beginning."

"What would you have me do, Your Majesty?" he asked.

"Only that you see clearly, Valerius, and that, in looking afar, you do not overlook that which is before you. I cannot be more specific than that. You told me once that men can do Gods' will, but that they often grope blindly for it. Well, I also believe we are tools in the hands of the Gods, but I am not so sure they always impel us towards the light. I think sometimes they trick us and trip us up, set us on blind paths. We are always searching for their greater purpose, but I think sometimes our biggest mistakes lie in small things."

"I am afraid I cannot follow you, Your Majesty. You speak in riddles."

"Yes, I know. And I am sorry Valerius, for that is not my intent. But my intentions are so vague, I hardly know how to put words on them. Yet I am driven to try. Let me try this: I fear there is a danger here for you. A danger for us all."

"You fear the Iblis will rise again?"

"No," Salonis sighed heavily and began to sag in her chair. For a few moments, she was silent, regaining her breath and summoning the little strength she had left. "I do not fear that. Rather, it is the opposite that concerns me. They were vicious enemies to us and now they are safely locked up in the new city. But for how long? I keep wondering, must we keep them in bondage forever? And what if the sterility curse that afflicted us there afflicts them as well? Are their sins so great they must suffer extinction?"

175

"Had the battle gone the other way," Valerius countered, "would they not have exterminated you?"

"No doubt. But does that justify the same treatment of them? Is that the will of the Gods, do you think? Or is there a way we can perhaps move a step closer to the light? Do you remember the Iblis' curse?"

"The one Koltar found in the old archives?" Valerius smiled. "Where they blamed my ancestor and cursed all the generations of my house for driving them from their homes? Do you think that has devolved upon me?"

For one brief moment, Salonis summoned all her old regal powers and shot him a steely glance. "Have you not tasted of their guilt?" she said.

Valerius was visibly stung by this and there was a deep silence in the room while he sat, staring with hard eyes at his plate. Even the servants, hovering by the doorway with cooling platters of food, dared not move, or hardly even to breath. Finally, Valerius nodded his head and made a snicking sound with his tongue. "Yes, Salonis, you are right. I have done that. And old curse or no, it does weigh on me. What would you advise?"

Seeing the pain she had caused him, Salonis' eyes went soft and the fire left her. "I do not know, Valerius. I have too much of my own guilt to even try to say. But you have been a great friend to my people. You are our savior, yet I fear this danger so much I felt I had to warn you."

"Thank you Salonis. You are a noble woman."

"And you are wise and good, King Valerius, and I pray that your heart will guide you to the light. But now, if you don't mind, I would like to excuse myself. I'm afraid I'm quite worn out."

Half carried by a pair of servants and attended by Koltar, Queen Salonis was led away, leaving Valerius and Vahla at table with an awkward silence between them. Vahla sat demurely, hands folded before her. The king seemed to be enveloped in black clouds and she knew not whether she should quietly slip away and leave him to his thoughts, or interrupt him and try to cheer his mood. One thing was certain: she no longer thought of Queen Salonis as small.

Suddenly Valerius shook himself like a great bear waking from some winter slumber. "Well, Vahla," he said, "it looks like this party is down to you and me. I am sorry it has not had a better beginning, but what do you say we have some wine and at least try some of these delicacies Gundar has prepared?"

"I could well do that, your Majesty," she said, forcing a smile.

Valerius signaled the wine steward and when their cups were filled, held his up to Vahla. "Here's to young beauty...," he toasted, "And the solution of old riddles."

"To solutions," said Vahla, and their cups touched.

Valerius drained his at a gulp, then sighed and shuddered as if to dispel the last of the black shadows that lingered in his mind. He had several more cups before their meal was done, and did justice, as well, to a sizeable portion of the roast. The state of his emotions, Vahla noted, did not seem to affect his appetite. But by the end of the meal, the wine had definitely affected the state of his mind, and as he pushed away his plate at last, and leaned back to drain yet another cup, he gave her a decidedly unfocused look.

"So, young lady," he said, holding out his cup for the wine steward, "how do you like our little hide-away now that you've had a chance to settle in a bit?"

"Most interesting, your Majesty. I had no idea there were such people in the world. They look so much like children, yet they are so obviously..."

"Adult?"

"Well, yes," she said, and flushed as she felt his eyes sliding down her neck and resting on the swell of her breasts, quite a bit of which were exposed by the low neck of her white gown.

"Yes, they are definitely adults," said Valerius draining another cup. "Have you heard how they are rebuilding their population? Each pure-bred male has to service about twenty women."

Vahla could not help but smile. "That must be a terrible burden."

"Well, they're quite stoic about it... Going off to their duty night after night like proper soldiers, with their swords thrusting straight out before them."

178

Vahla giggled in spite of herself. The wine had made her a bit heady, too. "Your Majesty sounds envious."

"Not at the moment," he smiled and gave her a look that was startlingly reminiscent of Fantar. "Here, let me get you some more wine." Jumping up unsteadily, he took the jug from the steward and filled her cup with one hand while dismissing the servants with the other. Some of the wine spilled and splattered on the front of her gown. "Ah," he said, "I'm so clumsy. Let me help you," and began dabbing at the front of her gown with a napkin. Vahla felt the pressure of his hand, lingering, and looked up to see his large dark face, looming close. She pulled away and hugged her arms over her breasts.

"Your Majesty," she said, her voice suddenly frightened. "You mustn't..."

"But you're so beautiful," he said, moving closer and sliding a huge hand across her shoulders. "Wouldn't you like to dance for me now?"

"No!" said Vahla, jumping up and moving quickly around to the other side of the table. "I can't!"

"I thought you liked me?" said Valerius, his bleary face was child-like, perplexed.

"I do," she said.

"Well, if it's Thorngere, you don't need to worry," he said, edging around the table. "We've long had an understanding, he and I."

"No, it's not that. It's, it's... There is something you must know."

179

"What then?"

"It's us... It's me, I mean," she stumbled. "I've been trying to tell you since I got here. I'm not just a dancer. And you're not just a man... Oh! I'm not doing this well at all." Suddenly she straightened and looked him in the eye. "What I'm trying to say, your Majesty, is that I am your sister."

Valerius sat down hard on the chair Vahla had just vacated. "My sister?" he said, suddenly sober and sounding like he had just been struck. "How can this be?"

"Oh, Majesty, I'm so sorry if I've upset you!" Vahla, rushed back and knelt by Valerius' chair and clasped his forearm. "I tried to tell you earlier, but there was... There was just never an opportunity. I never meant..."

"Just tell me how this thing can be, child," said the king, and while his eyes were still hard with surprise, she saw there was no meanness in them.

Haltingly at first, but with more confidence as she progressed, Vahla told her story. "I was born of Vauhna," she said, "the daughter of the king of Palemia, who was sent to court as a handmaiden to your mother, Queen Alair. None in the royal house knew of my mother's tryst with the king, or of my birth. At the time of Fantar's attack, I was still an infant in the care of a local nurse, and only know the story from my mother. She was supposed to stay with the Queen's women when the army marched out, but she came instead to fetch me from the nursemaid. There, she decided not to join the other women. She said she was afraid of what the Queen would do when she found out she had a child. She would have known immediately whose child I was, and what then? So we stayed with the nurse.

"The nursemaid's husband was off fighting, of course, and when Fantar's army breached the walls, the three of us hid in his fishing boat. When the city was put to the torch, the nursemaid slipped the dock lines and let the boat drift out with the tide. At dawn, we sailed east to Palemia, and stayed with my grandparents. But even here we were not safe. Early the next year, Fantar's hordes swept over Palemia as well. My grandparents were killed, but my mother and I were again rescued by the nursemaid. We lived with her from then on, but were quite poor, and when my mother died four years ago, I started dancing in order to support myself."

"Well," said Valerius when the tale was done. "You surely have good reason to hate Fantar. And I do remember your mother from when I was a boy. She, too, was very beautiful and not unlike you. But what proof do you have that my father was also yours?"

Vahla shook her head and sighed. "Only what my mother told me, I'm afraid, Sire. I had a broach she said the king gave her, but it was in the bag I left at Fantar's palace. And what a brooch would prove anyway, I do not know. So I would not push any claim on you, your Majesty. I don't even want anything! I just had to tell you and I certainly couldn't... I mean, even if it were not for Thorngere, I couldn't..."

"No, no, I understand. You did right, my dear. I'm glad you told me. As you heard from Salonis, I have enough of guilt on me already. But as for giving you something, I'm afraid you've already got whatever I can offer—as you know, my kingdom is, well, shall we say slightly less than secure?"

Vahla smiled and for a long moment met the king's eye. "You frightened me when I first saw you," she said. "You look so much like Fantar. But you're not like him at all."

"Thank you. I wish I could see a resemblance in you, but other than your raven hair, you seem to have taken after your mother."

"Yes," Vahla nodded. "She did tell me I had the old king's temper, though."

"That I can believe!" and they both laughed.

"There is one thing, Sire. I don't know if it's important, but it might help you believe. It's something my mother said the king told her and that I should not repeat to anyone. It was about that," she said, nodding towards the great red gem on Valerius' chest.

"The Eye?"

"Yes. She said King Valerius told her it was a bauble, that it had no powers at all."

Valerius tugged at his beard and looked hard at the beautiful girl across from him. "Well," he said finally. "The king, my father was wrong. This stone has one power at least: that he would have said such a thing proves your mother was no casual

182

acquaintance, or a mere handmaiden. And that's good enough for me to believe you're my sister."

At this, Vahla's face lit up with joy and she flung herself onto the huge, bear-like man who was suddenly as dear to her as her own blood—indeed was of her blood—and hugged him, and laughed, and cried, and then laughed again. But then, just as suddenly, she reared back, fire in her eye. "And what's this about 'an understanding' between you and Thorngere?" she demanded.

"Oh," said Valerius, "I may have been mistaken about that."

Chapter 11
FORTUNE'S WAY

Thorngere paced the deck throughout the night, and at the first glimmer of grey, sent a lookout aloft. Of course, the man was able to see nothing immediately, and below him, Thorngere began to pace again. It was the only way he could keep his nerves in check, though his legs felt as though he had been marching for days—as in fact, he had. But not as tensely as this. This sailing offshore was a dangerous business and every man in the ship knew it. He could feel it in them. None had said anything, and the watch on deck stood their usual stations, but there was about the whole ship a tension, an alertness that was almost palpable. These were men who, for the most part, had spent years at sea and had faced storms and dangers uncounted. But to deliberately leave the familiar loom of the land—that was to hang from a very thin thread indeed.

And the reason was simple: once the dark shoulder of the cliffs fell astern, and with the overcast sky, they had no absolute way of knowing where they were or whither they were headed. They kept the gentle offshore breeze astern, of course, and if that had held steady, then they were heading west, and with the sun, could find their way north and east. But if the wind had shifted gradually in the night, they could have worked around with it without even knowing. They could even be heading due east by now and with the light, might find themselves right back in their anchorage. Or they could be many miles to the south, or nowhere at all. After all, none really knew what lay beyond the world's rim.

But the grey Thorngere sensed was not the dawn at all. It was fog, a thick, swirling fog, and within minutes, the rigging was dripping with it. Thorngere could not see the man at the masthead from the deck below. Indeed, he could not even see the bow. It was lost behind a black-grey curtain. They were still sailing, still coasting along before a gentle breeze, but where five minutes before he would have sworn that breeze was still pushing them steadily westward, now he was very much less than sure. Whether fog banks wandered the offshore sea, he did not know. But he did know full well that they tended to hug the cliffs. And there were spots along this coast where those cliffs dropped straight into the sea with water so deep a ship could slam right into the face of one without ever touching bottom. Until she sank.

Thorngere ordered sharp lookouts all around, and sent two other men forward to heave the deep sea lead. Then he listened—everyone listened; cocked their heads and strained their ears to listen— for that ominous seething and sucking sound that was the surf surging against the rock. But there was nothing beyond the gentle gurgle of water along the hull and the occasional creak of her rigging. The ship slid along the oily water as silent as a ghost in that ghostly sea.

And when the dawn did come, it came in ghostly fashion, seeping through the fog like milk through gauze, and lighting the white walls around them so gradually that none could agree from whence the light came. It was just there. They had gone from black-grey to white-grey and had no more idea now than before which way they were headed.

"We'll sail out of this soon," Thorngere said, as if saying it aloud would make it true. "We sailed into it quickly enough."

"Aye," said Boltar, "if we don't sail into a cliff first."

"We'd know where we were then, wouldn't we? Anything with that lead?" he called forward.

"No bottom at thirty fathoms," came the reply. Nor was there any bottom an hour later, nor an hour after that, nor any lessening in the thick blanket that covered them. The breeze freshened and they felt the ship stiffen in response. The bow wave gurgled now, and behind them, for a few feet, they could see the wake bubble. That was usually a sign the fog would lift, but for hour after hour they watched that wake quickly slip into a white haze as impenetrable as it was elusive. Once or twice during the morning Thorngere saw a brighter, yellower spot rising overhead that he thought sure must be the sun. But the first time it appeared to starboard, and shortly thereafter, to port. So unless the wind was blowing in circles—which seemed not altogether out of the question in that fog—it had to be an illusion.

Finally, Thorngere admonished the watch to be extra alert and went below with Boltar to try and reason the thing out. "Look," he said around a huge mouthful of bread, for he was also famished, "it does not appear that the wind has changed since last night. So by all apparent signs, we should still be sailing west. And unless we fall off the world or land in the God's lap, all we have to do when the fog does lift is reverse course, right?"

"If the wind has held steady, and if the fog lifts," said Boltar. "But if it hasn't held steady, we have no idea where we are, and if we are way offshore, how do we know the fog isn't perpetual?"

"Well, I've been out pretty far and I've never seen any perpetual fog. Besides, it doesn't make sense—wind blows fog and there's nearly always wind at sea."

"Well, there's been a pretty good wind up there all this watch and it doesn't seem to have moved that fog very much."

"Maybe it's moving with us... Maybe that's it! The wind normally blows out of the west, right? And the fog settles in along the cliffs in the morning, until the wind pipes up and blows it up and away. Well, maybe we've just got a strange east wind for a change and it's blown the fog out to sea with us. If that's true, we should put the wind on our starboard beam... That would head us north and the wind should blow the fog out past us."

"What if the wind is coming from the west?"

"Well, if that's the case, we're heading straight for the rocks now anyway, and turning would just point us south is all. The only way there'd be danger is if the wind has gone southerly. And I've hardly ever seen a southerly wind along this coast."

"All right. Makes sense to me... As much sense as anything in this stuff."

Elusive's bow was turned to the right, then, and her yards braced around to catch the wind from her starboard side. The ship heeled to the wind, which was now blowing a good ten to twelve knots, and there was a definite difference in her motion as she began gliding diagonally over the long, low ground swell. It was a slow, swaying, circular motion, the kind guaranteed to make a novice ill. But if the fog was supposed to leave, no one told it, for it stayed just as thick and just as impenetrable right through the afternoon watch. Then, suddenly, just before the hands were piped to dinner, as if someone had yanked a sheet off a lay-a-bed child, they sailed out of it.

The wind was still rising and the bank rolled quickly away to the west—if west it was—leaving them in the midst of a vast, empty sea, flecked with white caps that shone pale under heavy, leaden skies. There was no sun to be seen, just solid overcast, and dark rumbling clouds that threatened rain. Thorngere hailed the lookouts who scanned the horizon yet again. But there was nothing to be seen in that vast grey realm but sea and sky.

"Well," said Thorngere, forcing a grin, "looks like we lost Blumholt."

"Aye, m'lord," said Boltar. "That we did."

"And we didn't smuck into a cliff."

"Nope. We didn't."

"Or fall off the world, or drift away in a perpetual fog."

"Nope, we didn't do that either."

"Sounds to me like a successful maneuver."

"With one slight exception, my lord...," said Boltar, but he was interrupted by a sudden cry from aloft.

"Land ho!"

"That little exception?" said Thorngere, his face breaking into a real grin this time. "Where away?" he yelled, looking fiercely over the starboard rail.

"Two points off the port bow, and about three leagues distant!"

The port bow? Boltar and Thorngere cast questioning glances at each other as they ran to the other side. If the land was in this direction, it would mean the wind had indeed backed around to the west and that they were now heading south. It would also mean that if they had not turned when they did, they would have smashed into the cliffs. But as they climbed atop the rail, a sight even more unexpected met their eyes. No cliffs were here, nor even a hint of the rock-bound coast between Dulcai and Kantar. What they saw emerging from the swiftly fleeing fog was a high green mountain, forested hills, and a verdant shore. What they saw was an island. And beyond it, another island, and beyond that, a third.

"Well, I'll be damned," said Thorngere.

"Not alone, you won't be," said Boltar, and the two stood there atop the railing, clutching to the backstay that descended to the chainplate between them, and along with most of the crew, gaped.

"Shall we make for it?" asked Thorngere finally. The question was rhetorical.

"You mean, my lord, interrupt this busy afternoon of being totally lost at sea just to discover some knew and unknown world?" Boltar's eyes were dancing at the prospect.

"Well," quipped Thorngere, "I realize it would be an imposition. I mean, it looks like there's a storm coming and I know how much the men would love to ride that out, but we do have a duty, don't you think?"

"It's your ship, my lord. I only help steer it."

"Very well, then. Let's make for that point there. It looks as though there might be a bit of a bay on the other side."

That bit of a bay turned out to be an excellent harbor, and a not unwelcome one either, for by the time they entered it, the wind and sea had kicked up ferociously, and the heavens were threatening to break open at any moment. Their sail had been reefed twice in the two hours it took to reach the island, and as they entered the constrained waters at the mouth of the bay, a fearsome sea had built up behind them. Thorngere had the leads going again at the bow and Boltar had two men on the steering board arm, but if there had been anything to avoid, it is doubtful they would have been able to do anything about it. As it was, the best they could do was to keep the ship from broaching. One by one, huge rollers reared up behind them and came running down onto the ship, snatching her up like a toy, and dashing away with her for a bit until, their speed being greater, they outran her and left her sliding diagonally down their back sides while the men at the helm fought to keep her head. Had they broached in one of these, or had one decided to break over them, it might well have tumbled the *Elusive* like a pair of dice.

As it was, the little ship shot into the bay on the foaming back of one of these monsters and as it subsided, scuttled off into quieter, protected waters in the lee of a shoulder of the great mountain that hid the depths of the bay from the wild sea. Right into a quiet little cove they coasted, while outside the wind screamed and they could hear the surf roar as it smashed upon the beach. It sounded worse in here than it had outside, and seemed, Thorngere thought, as if the Gods were enraged at their escape and were venting their fury on the battlements of their sanctuary. Then, just as their spare anchor splashed down in two fathoms of water off a lovely little beach, and the sail was triced up and furled, the heavens opened with a deluge and all hands headed for cover.

"Well," said Thorngere, as he and Boltar settled back in the tiny cabin, mugs of mulled wine in their hands and the remains of a long delayed supper between them, "I believe we would not be too far amiss to call these The Fortunate Isles."

"Indeed, m'lord," said Boltar, watching a drip start on the underside of a deck beam and making a mental note to repay some of the seams as soon as they had sun enough to soften the pitch. "This isn't the kind of storm I would choose to ride out at sea. What do you suppose chances are our friend Blumholt got caught in it and blown off shore?"

"Hmmm, that would be fortunate indeed, wouldn't it? Unless, of course he blew in here. But I don't know. He was ever a decent seaman."

"Aye, but if he did get caught offshore in that blow, I doubt they'd be able to pull back in against it. And there's plenty of spots along the coast there where there's no holding ground at all— where you're in more danger inshore than off. He could well have got caught between a pig and a poke."

"Well, I'd be content if he just gave up on us and headed home to poke his own pig."

The storm pounded the islands for two days and nights without pause. Rain poured down, creeping through every seam and crack in the *Elusive's* exposed hull, and dripping steadily on the cramped, sodden men, huddling below. Overhead, the wind screamed and howled like an enraged beast, and on the outer shore, the wild surf boomed and roared like the drums of an advancing hoard. Of their escort, they saw and heard no sign. If he had been blown off shore, he had not been fortunate enough to be blown their way.

On the third day, the men awakened to a strange silence: the rain had stopped. Outside their little cove the surf still roared, but when they came on deck, it was to clear blue skies and best of all, a warm, welcoming sun that quickly told them their guesses had been right all along. The breeze had held from the east all through the fog; they had turned north—or at least north northwest—and once they got back in sight of the mainland, they would probably be only a half day or so sail south of the cavern. At least, that's how Thorngere reckoned it. Boltar said he'd see the land when he saw it and in the meantime, was content to see to the condition of his little ship. A party was sent aloft to inspect all the rigging, the hatches were thrown open to dry out down below, and as the morning sun baked steam from the deck, he set another party with a pitch bucket to scrape and pay the leaky seams.

Thorngere inspected the island, first from the deck, then from the masthead. From their little cove, and behind the protective shoulder of hills that separated them from the sea, the land swept back, thickly forested and rising gently for a mile or more until it butted the craggy chin of the mountain's head. This basin extended around the bay to the west, while another arm of the mountain swept around to form the southern boundary of the bay. It was as if, thought Thorngere, some great, green mountain god had lay back on his couch here in the middle of the sea and stretched his two arms out before him. The lush green basin was his chest and the little cove where they were hidden was tucked up under his left arm. Over all the island reigned a profound silence that was somehow unaffected by

193

the cacophony of forest birds, and a deep, richly humid smell of wet earth and wild vegetation. Under the hot rising sun, steam rose from the trees. Nowhere was there any sign of human habitation.

Sliding hand over hand down the backstay, Thorngere dropped nimbly to the deck and ordered the longboat dropped over the side. "Care to do a little exploring?" he asked Boltar.

"Aye," said the captain. "And if we find some good water, I can set the lads to refilling the butts. The way you have us sail, you know, there's no telling when we may get another chance."

"I don't have to take you back, you know."

"Ah, m'lord, you know you'd be lost without me."

"To hear you tell it, I'm lost already. But pick three or four doughty men to attend us and issue full battle gear... I'd rather be safe than sorry."

They found a lovely fresh water stream that dropped conveniently over a small waterfall into a shallow rock basin right at the head of their cove. They were able to row the launch right up alongside the bank, and the stream was so swollen from the rains that all the men had to do to fill the casks was roll them into the basin and stand them upright. This was done with much frolic and laughter as the force of the cascading torrents knocked the men this way and that. Yet the water was so sweet and pure that Boltar ordered all the casks brought up, emptied and refilled. Then, leaving two men on guard while the others worked, he and two other armed men followed Thorngere off down the beach.

They hiked for several miles until the hot sun was well overhead and the sweat streamed from their faces, but were unable to find any sign of human habitation, although several times they heard the far off barking of dogs. Indeed, there were few places where they could even leave the beach, so thick and lush was the vegetation. At several spots they were able to work their way inland for a hundred yards or so—mostly following beaten down animal trails—only to be stopped in their tracks by walls of jungle and flower-clustered vines. Several types of fruit trees were found, and Thorngere nearly broke his neck cutting down a bunch of bananas: fortunately, he landed on the bananas instead of on his head and when they got back to the waterfall he was very glad to shower off the sticky, pulpy mess he had made of himself. The bananas were very good however, and they managed to bring several bundles aboard.

In the afternoon, they hoisted anchor and explored the western end of the bay. The wind had gone around to the west again—though the surf was still strong outside—so they were forced to use their sweeps. All along the shore they pulled, sounding as they went and watching as mile after mile of sandy shore and forest canopy slid gently by. Just at sunset they pulled up and dropped anchor again under the lee of the western arm of the bay, some three leagues distant from where they started. The men had a late supper and lolled about the decks, tired and languorous from the day's labors but feeling, overall, as if they had been on holiday.

As the sun set, Thorngere and Boltar sat on the starboard rail, their feet dangling outboard, and watched the encroaching shadows of darkness fill the basin and work their way, valley by valley, up the slopes to the base of the mountain.

"You know," said Boltar, breaking a long silence, "you were righter than you knew when you called these 'The Fortunate Isles.' I don't think I've ever been to a lovelier spot in all my life."

"I know what you mean," said Thorngere. "All day long I've been thinking, 'Gods, what a place for men to settle.' But then, in the same breath I think, 'my God, what would men do to such a place?'"

At first light, the *Elusive* catted home her anchor, set her square sail before the steady westerly breeze and proudly sailed out of Fortune's Bay. The sun rose straight before her bowsprit and as she left the confines of the bay behind and lifted her head to the first of the ocean swells, she began to race like a pony who knows the barn is at the end of the road. The wind freshened quickly as they gained sea room and the *Elusive* soared over the swells like a gull. For Thorngere and company, it was glorious sailing, with sun, a fresh wind, clear blue skies, and an ocean as blue and deep as the eyes of the most beautiful woman. They were on a ship which had been miraculously transformed from a doughty little scullery maid to the grandest dame of the sea, and all hands stood their watches with broad grins on their faces.

Throughout the morning they held straight on their course, and for an hour after the sun passed the tip of the dancing mast. Then, just about the time Thorngere was thinking 'any time now,' the look-out sang out those most welcome of sea-weary words. "Land Ho!" And this time it was not some strange and mysterious shore, but the old familiar cliffs of home.

As they closed with the land—*Elusive* carrying on so swiftly it hardly seemed any time at all—they fixed their position just a few short leagues south of the cavern, and braced around to head north. There was a good way to sail, still, but if the wind held—and even as the afternoon waned it showed no sign of slacking—they figured to make the cavern just before dark. They were, in fact, just in the process of congratulating themselves on a highly successful voyage—after all, it's not every trip one gets to sail right out to sea and discover a strange and wondrous new land—and Thorngere was thinking of Vahla's welcome, when the man at the masthead sang out again.

"Sail ho!" There, just to their south and pulling strongly out from behind a promontory, was the sleek, low shape of a war galley.

197

Chapter 12
A LONG SHOT

It took Thorngere only a second to recognize the galley as Blumholt's, and only a few seconds more to realize there was no possibility of outrunning him. He swore a great oath.

"So much for your theory of him being blown out to sea," he said to Boltar.

"Aye. I'll bet he holed up in yon nook when it started to blow and has been sitting there ever since, just waiting."

"Patience is ever the fat man's virtue." Sullenly, the two men studied the galley. Due to the angles of their courses, the Elusive could sail while the galley had to row, and Thorngere thought fleetingly of gaining from that by putting his own men to the oars as well. But he quickly realized the advantage would be fleeting. As the galley settled in pursuit, their courses would parallel and she too, would be able to set sail and quickly make up any distance lost. Better, he thought, to keep up the charade. "But I wonder how patient he is. Boltar, keep her well out to sea so he doesn't spy our little rat hole, and let's see just how far he'll follow us."

"How far will you go, m'lord?"

"Have you ever seen Thuringia? It's lovely this time of the year, with the heather spreading on the hillsides and the melt from the high snows rushing down the valleys. I've some friends there as well who'll help us murder this bastard if it comes to that."

"He won't go that far."

"No, but I'm damned if I'll just sally up and show him the front door to Kantar."

For two hours or more, the two ships kept to their course; the smaller, stubbier Elusive in the lead, now stripped of her lofty airs in the eyes of her crew, and become again a slug-like thing; and the swift galley, its mainsail set and drawing, but brailed up to keep her pace down, following closely behind. Were this a more modern era, one would have thought the two were a racing team; a great sailing yacht and her tender making their way back to port after a day of trials. As it was, the scene was more reminiscent of a hawk, hovering above a frozen rabbit.

Thorngere paced the deck as he had days before, but this time there was no change in his thoughts: they were all on his pursuer and what he might do to escape. He weighed impossible odds, schemed fantastic schemes, and even indulged in sheer flights of fancy, but could come up with no better plan than to plod on as they were, hoping their pursuer would give up, though he knew it was a vain hope. On the quarter deck of the galley he could now plainly see the curly haired figure who had stood beside Blumholt as they left Dulcai. But the man was clearly not posing as a mate any longer: he stood alone on the weather side of the deck, austere and authoritative, and even at a distance, Thorngere could see that he was approached with deference, even by Blumholt himself.

As dusk neared, they were nearly abreast the cavern entrance, but too far at sea for it to be visible even from the masthead, when the lookout called down softly. "Deck there. Something's going on. There's a party gathering in the galley's waist... Looks like they're arming themselves."

Thorngere and Boltar shot each other sharp glances. "Looks like Blumholt's patience is running out," said Boltar.

"Aye," said Thorngere, "They're probably afraid we'll give 'em the slip again in the dark, and I'll bet whoever that is over there with the curly hair has decided if we won't show them our little hide-away, he'll show us something less pleasant. What do you suppose our chances are of making a run for it from here?"

"Not good."

"Well, we're in agreement, then. And I wouldn't want to show them the way, anyway. But isn't there a spot a couple miles north of the cavern where we might just be able to beach this old girl and climb the cliffs?"

"I know that spot," said Boltar, "and we can definitely ground the ship there. But scale the cliffs? Only if we had wings."

"Well, do you have any better ideas?"

"Yes," said Boltar, hauling the arm of the Elusive's steering board aft so she did a quick pivot to starboard and came before the wind. "Start growing some!" Sheets were adjusted and tuned to set her square sail drawing full, and the men quickly unlashed the long sweeps from their racks along the bulwarks, and in moments, added human muscle power to that of the wind. But at the same moment they executed their turn, the galley also loosed the constraining brails on her sail, and as she quickly spun to follow in their wake, her long oars came out again as well. Clearly, the charade of ambassador and escort was over. Now they were enemies at war.

Carefully, Thorngere studied the relative positions of the two ships. The galley was plainly gaining but the question was, how long did they have? The Elusive was lightly laden and was at her best sailing before the wind. With the oars adding to her speed, she might make eight knots. No, he thought, make that seven. The galley, with her longer, leaner hull, could easily make ten, more if the men sprinted. Right now, they were just out of bow shot astern, which meant they'd easily close within an hour, probably less. It would be dark by then, but they'd be so close it wouldn't matter.

"Masthead," he called, "can you see the cavern?".

"Just, sir. Two points off the starboard bow."

It was not yet visible from the deck. That would put them about three and a half leagues from their destination: an hour and a half sailing at their present rate. In short, the galley would catch them and they'd die before they got past their own doorstep. Unless he could do something to slow old Blumholt down.

Going below, Thorngere pulled his fancy armor from his chest and quickly donned it. Then, from a special case under his bunk, he pulled a long staff-like object and carefully unwrapped its canvass covering. It was a long bow, oiled and polished to a high sheen. It had been a present from Koltar, the result of one of his experiments. Instead of being made from a single shaft of wood, this bow was made of several slats of different wood, all glued and tightly bound together. It was wondrously powerful, and would carry far beyond any other bow Thorngere had ever tried, but what a single bowman could do against an armed war galley was anybody's guess. Quickly, he tore the canvas cover up into long, thin strips, and with a large quiver of arrows on his shoulder and his long sword at his side, hurried back on deck. Boltar looked at him in surprise, then shrugged as if to say, 'why not?'

The galley had drawn perceptibly closer while he was below. Stringing the bow, he tested its pull, then tried a ranging shot. It went wide, zipping into a wave along the galley's side, but his next went aboard and obviously found a mark, for one port side oar suddenly shot up into the air and then fell afoul of its mates. The galley swerved off course a bit as the oarsmen missed a beat, but then recovered just as quickly.

"Well," said Boltar. "You made the buggers blink, at least."

"Keep watching, my friend," Thorngere grinned, for his blood was starting to rise, "and let's see if I can make them break wind!"

202

"No, you go ahead and fart around," Boltar laughed. "I'll sail this tub."

"You may want to issue arms as well."

"There's time enough for that. Let's keep the lads pulling for a bit."

Thorngere nodded and went back to his archery. It was difficult, firing from one moving deck and aiming at another, but still, a good many of his shots landed aboard the galley, and over the next fifteen or twenty minutes, there were several more indications that they had found marks among the crew. He was not, however, able to land an arrow close to his main target, the curly headed figure standing so visibly by the port rail at the forward edge of the quarterdeck. Neither did his efforts have any effect on the course or speed of the opponent. By the end of twenty minutes, half of Thorngere's arrows were gone, and the galley had halved the distance between them.

"Better arm the men, now, Boltar," he ordered. "And bring me up a jar of lamp oil, a bucket, and a lit candle." Boltar brought them himself and found Thorngere kneeling on the deck, carefully wrapping a thin canvass strip around the tip of an arrow. Several others lay on the deck beside him, already wrapped.

"Isn't that like trying to light a candle by throwing embers at it?"

"Who knows? I'm not going to set it afire by standing here and spitting at it."

"That's true. Or maybe we'll set ourselves afire and deny them the satisfaction of killing us."

"You're such an optimist, Boltar. Here, pour some oil over this." Thorngere held the bound arrow over the bucket while Boltar poured. Another hand lit it with the candle, and Thorngere fired quickly, before any flaming oil could drip on the deck. The arrow arced away like a tiny comet, trailing a plume of black smoke and disappeared over the top of the galley's mast. Another followed it, better aimed this time, and struck the galley's mainsail like a bean bag hitting a pillow. The three archers waited, watching for some sign.

"Went right through," muttered the hand.

"Bounced off," said Boltar.

"Light another," said Thorngere. The third struck the quarterdeck just to the right of the curly headed one, and a man quickly snatched it up and tossed it over the rail. The forth went wide as the Elusive lurched into a wave, then the lookout sang out.

"Deck there! I see smoke at her mast head." And there it was, a definite wisp of smoke curling up and then scattering in the wind. Then, suddenly, a tiny spurt of flame erupted on the sail, just below the yard. Quickly, it started to spread and then, fanned by the wind, the entire sail erupted like a torch in an instant. The galley slewed off course as flaming shards of sail dropped onto the oarsmen below, and many hands dashed to drop the yardarm and toss the flaming remains into the sea.

Aboard the Elusive, the breathless crew cheered and howled. Boltar, forgetting protocol, jumped up and down and pounded Thorngere on the back. "It stuck in the mast, it did," he yelled. "It stuck right in the mast! Took the sail right off 'em, the bastards! Ha ha ha!"

But the galley recovered quickly, and where Thorngere's archery had been a mere annoyance before—indeed, a personal challenge to the real captain, Glaucon, who stood rigidly at his post, his curly hair ruffling in the wind, knowing himself to be the chief target—it had now become worthy of response. With haughty disdain, Glaucon refused Blumholt's request to set a new sail. Instead, he ordered the rowing tempo increased, and sent a half dozen archers of his own into the bows. In seconds, their first volley came clattering aboard the Elusive, or rather, went half aboard, and half into the sea. It drew no blood, but served ample notice that blood was only a matter of time.

Still, the loss of her sail affected the galley's speed, and the increased efforts of the oarsmen only served to tire them quicker. As the archery duel continued—with Thorngere and his mates ducking below the rail every time their opponents loosed (and thankfully, they continued to fire as a group)— it quickly became apparent that while the galley was still gaining, it was definitely not gaining as quickly. How much time it would buy, Thorngere had no time to consider. Rather, he ducked and fired, ducked and fired, and having switched back to tipped arrows to better target the opposing archers, sent Boltar and the spare hand below for lumber to construct a shield to protect the Elusive's own gasping oarsmen.

But that it would not gain them enough time was still very apparent. Looking to the east between volleys, Thorngere could see the cliff face above the cavern passing directly abeam. That meant there was still well over a league to go. Darkness was falling, but the pursuit was so close now and with a clear sky, there was no way it would protect them. No, there was no way. They would never even reach that beach. Thorngere ducked again instinctively as another volley came aboard. An arrow zipped right over his head and thudded into a plank Boltar was holding. He grinned back at Thorngere, but the fear of death was plain on his face.

Then, as Thorngere was about to turn and fire another shot, something in the gathering gloom caught his eye. Something from the direction of the cavern. He took his shot and toppled a fellow overboard who had climbed up onto the galley's bow rail, then looked again. Yes! There it was, another galley shooting out of the lowering darkness, white foam bright under its forefoot. As Thorngere watched, its mast rose up and was set. Then, just behind it, came another galley, and another. All the Elusive's crew saw them now and began to cheer, and behind them, Blumholt's galley sheared off and began pulling away. At its rail, the ramrod figure of Glaucon looked straight across at Thorngere and saluted.

Valerius and Vahla were waiting for Thorngere in Valerius' quarters when he arrived. Concerned

206

that he was overdue from Dulcai, Valerius had ordered lookouts stationed high atop the cliffs behind the city. It was something he had been considering for some time anyway, and while it had taken several days effort, and several near fatal mishaps, to scale the cliffs and rig a series of ladders, lookouts finally took up their stations on the very afternoon Thorngere appeared. Almost immediately, they had seen the two ships approaching from the south west, but were too high and far away to note anything amiss until the trailing ship's sail suddenly burst into flame. They called down the alarm, then, and three swift galleys were dispatched to attempt a rescue.

Word was relayed up immediately when the Elusive emerged from the cavern, safe and apparently unharmed, and Valerius had sent for Vahla to come await Thorngere with him. He was all keyed up and could not sit still. Not only was he anxious to hear the results of Thorngere's mission, upon which so much rested, but he was also antsy as a boy at the end of his lessons to tell Thorngere about his new found sister. They had told no one else, as yet, but had spent considerable time getting to know one another, and had entered into their conspiracy of silence with giddy anticipation. From the awkwardness of their first meeting—he had been suspicious of her motives and she had not known how to approach him—their new relationship had quickly blossomed into one of familial comfort and growing affection.

Valerius saw that in addition to her great beauty (in which he now began to detect a family resemblance) Vahla was possessed of a fine wit and a keen intellect. She was also strong willed and proud as fire, and he no longer had any doubt that she was quite capable of taking a cut at Fantar. In short, his heart went out to her, and as Vahla felt its growing warmth, her own awe turned into adoration. She saw that this huge, dark and forbidding man, this man who was both the heir and image of the high kings of old and of all that was noble, was very much the lonely school boy at times, and her heart, in turn, went out to him. In truth, both had spent much of their formative years alone and cut off from home and family, and their kinship snapped them together like magnets. Then, when Vahla revealed to Valerius the depth of her affection for Thorngere, he had instantly resolved to offer this new and cherished sister to his old and honored friend in marriage. How better, he said, to cement a new union, and reward an old one.

So the two had quite a surprise planned for Thorngere as they waited anxiously for him to make his way up from the river. But the Thorngere who was ushered into their presence did not look like a man in the mood for pleasant surprises. He was exhausted, for one thing, with the strain of the long chase and running battle showing in the haggard lines of his face, and for another, the sight of Vahla and Valerius together, in his apartments, alone, and obviously on very intimate terms, shocked him to his very soul, and he saw them as through a black

208

and lowering cloud. Plus, he did not have good news of his own to bring: Reuters under Fantar's thumb, with his daughter taken and enemy ships occupying his harbor; and now, Glaucon having outrun the Kantaran galleys and their own hidden lair discovered. Thorngere made his report stiffly and formally, even the discovery of The Fortunate Isles and their recent narrow escape failing to lighten his wooden monotone.

Valerius also sobered as he listened, pulling at the long curls of his beard and nodding somberly. It was not good news. Reuters had been their lifeline, their only untainted link with the outside world, the only patch of sunlight to break through the moiling clouds that churned across their landscape. If he was gone, not only were they alone in their struggle, but their backs were unprotected as well. And if their hole had indeed been discovered, then it was only a matter of time before the enemy was at the gate.

When Thorngere finished speaking, he stood at semi-attention, staring over the heads of the two seated figures before him and trying not to look at Vahla, whose eyes beseeched him to do just that. Given the situation, she dared not run to him, but sat with her hands folded stiffly before her. A long silence filled the room, and the only sense of movement was the flickering candle light splashing shadows against the walls. Valerius sat hunched over in thought, softly tapping his knuckle against his chin, his brow furled and forbidding.

"Damn!" he said suddenly, pounding his fist on the table and startling them both. "I was afraid of that. Something in his letters was warning me. But we can't do anything about that tonight, and you look beat, my friend. Here, come sit and have a cup of wine," he said, brightening. "We have some news as well."

"I'm fine, your Majesty," said Thorngere stiffly, his eyes tight.

"What?" Now it was Valerius who was startled. He looked at Thorngere, then at Vahla, then at the room and himself, and suddenly broke into a huge grin. "Ha! Now I see! Oh no, my friend, it's nothing like what you're thinking. This is something much more astounding than that—and something I think will please you very well..." Thorngere's face softened at this and he cocked his head in curiosity. "We have discovered that the lady Vahla here is my sister," said Valerius, rushing his words like a child tearing the wrapping on a present, "and I would very much like the honor of making her your wife!"

Thorngere's face went utterly white with shock and he staggered back a step as if struck hard to the body. He looked from the beaming face of Valerius to the anxious and expectant face of Vahla, and then back, his own face hanging like a wet rag. "Oh, my god," he said softly.

"It's true," Vahla said rising and starting towards him. "I didn't dare tell you before. I didn't dare tell anyone. I didn't know how Valerius would react, or if he would accept me, but I love you Thorngere, I love you!"

Thorngere closed his eyes and leaned up against the door frame, his whole body sagging. "Oh, my god," he said. "Oh, my god. This cannot be."

"Cannot be?" Now Valerius was perplexed. "You do not wish to make her your wife?"

"No, no, my liege, that's not it. You do not understand. I never wanted to tell you before—it would have been too complicated and, I never really knew until... But we, too, are kin, Valerius. I am your brother."

Vahla dropped into her chair like a stone, her face white with astonishment. "But that would mean..."

"Yes, my dear," said Thorngere, his voice harsh with sarcasm. "We are brother and sister," and before Valerius could even open his mouth to protest, he turned and bolted from the room.

Chapter 13
THE MAGE'S LAIR

In the morning, Thorngere and the Elusive were gone. Vahla was devastated and would not leave her bed. Valerius, feeling like a great stone lintel had been mortised onto his shoulders, set out again for the clearing in the forest. He spoke to no one along the road and nodded only slightly to acknowledge the salutes of those who passed. Haradin and his herders he ignored completely as they sat in the morning sun among their charges on the grassy battlements of the old encampment. Along the forest paths he walked, oblivious alike to the fresh pine scented morning air, the brilliant songs of birds in the trees, and the shifting patterns of sunlight on the needle carpeted floor. He walked with his head down, watching his footsteps, and was cognizant only of the great weight that seemed to fill his brain. Against it, he felt wholly inadequate, unable even to make the slightest headway, and unworthy, as a result, to bear the name and symbol that he bore. It seemed to him, in his present depressed state, that all his hopes and plans were about to come tumbling down around him, and he did not know what to do.

In the clearing, the sun was already high overhead. He took position before it and with a silent prayer for guidance, raised the bright red gem to his eye. But it flashed quickly in the sunlight and he jerked his head away, his eye stinging like he had been slapped. Bright red spots swam in it, and he shook his head to dispel them. He tried the Eye again, turning slightly to be out of the direct path of the sun, but saw only murky shadows and distant glimmerings of light.

Was this thing really a fraud, he wondered? Or was he simply so far astray from the intended path that the gods had turned their faces from him? Or was it simply that he did not know how to use it? That, at least he decided, was one thing he could do: he could go and find out. He might find some other answers as well.

Back in Kantar, he ordered pack horses readied with provisions, and the next morning dressed in his old, warrior's battle gear and traveling cloak, and with only a single servant to attend him, left the city again. He forded the river this time, passed the old encampment again, empty of Iblis at this hour, and headed north along a winding forest path towards the mountain gate. If there was anyone living on earth who could help him see through this thicket, it was the Mage, Volkmir, and it was to his lair, high in the mountain fastness to the north, that he bent his way.

He had traveled not more than a mile from the river, however, before he began to sense another presence. The noise of his own passage obstructed hearing, and there was no one behind when he looked back, but several times, between footfalls of horse and man, he was sure he caught a distinct echo of another, more distant footfall from behind.

Gano, the servant, caught it, too, and by quick eye and head signals, they agreed to a plan. As they rounded the next bend in the trail, Valerius slipped off his horse and quickly ducked behind a large boulder. Gano, giving no indication of the move at all, kept on along the trail leading all four animals.

In his hiding place, Valerius readied the small round buckler on his left arm and loosened his great curved falchion in its sheath. As the sounds of Gano and the horses receded, he began to hear definite sounds of pursuit that grew louder as he waited. If it was that bugger Haradin, he thought, he would murder him quick this time and be done with it. But as he listened, he could only detect a single set of footfalls. That did not seem like Haradin, who was very much a coward on his own. Either that, or his companions were exceptionally quiet, which did not seem like Iblis, either—they would more likely be singing and passing a wine jug! As the footsteps neared the bend, he quietly slid his great sword from its sheath and crouched down, ready to spring.

It was Vahla, hurrying along, and still soaking wet from swimming the river. When he stepped out in front of her, she jumped like a startled cat. "Oh, your Majesty!" she said, hand to her pounding heart. "I thought you were one of those horrid Iblis."

"You're lucky I'm not," he said sternly. "What are you doing following me?"

"You're going to Volkmir," she said, meeting his eye defiantly. But then her face crumpled and she burst into tears. "Oh, Valerius!" she sobbed. "My life is ruined. I can't believe it. My own brother!"

"You didn't know," he said.

"What does that matter?" she wailed. "Dead is dead," and she buried her face in her hands and sobbed. "I've lost him and all I'm left with is... is this loathing. I just can't believe I've come all this way to find a family, only to find... that I've lain with my own brother!" She spat this last and was again racked with convulsions.

Valerius took the girl in his arms, but it was lame comfort. She lay against his chest and sobbed uncontrollably. He stroked her sodden black hair and felt her wet body shake against his own. "There, there," he murmured, "it'll be all right," though even as he spoke, he thought it was a silly thing to say, and that it would not be all right. And he thought idly how quickly things can change: how only a few days before he himself had felt desire for this lovely girl; and how utterly those feelings had changed. After a bit her sobs subsided and he heard her sniffle. "How did you know about Volkmir?" he asked.

She shook her head. "I just knew it," she said. "Thorngere told me about him on the boat, and I thought, 'if anyone can make sense of this mess, it's him.' So I followed you."

"Well then, little sister," he said, "you might as well tag along, for we seem to be on the same mission."

215

The mountains around the hidden valley of Kantar extended in an unbroken ring. Rising majestically thousands of feet from the valley floor—often straight up—they presented an impassable barrier that was as effective in keeping the occupants in as it was in keeping foreign adventurers out. Only in two places was this barrier breached: at the cavern where the great river flowed out to sea, and at the Mountain Gate where the northern source of the river tumbled down from the mountains. Here, over the aeons, nature had carved a steep gorge that wound its way down from the vastness of the mountains. At its base, all the material that had been washed away was deposited in a broad alluvial fan, and here one could pick and scramble a second way out of the Hidden Valley.

But it was no easy trek. For a man on foot, it was a long, two day march from Kantar just to get to the gate. After that, it was three or even four more days of hard climbing to make the ascent. Valerius' party had the advantage of sturdy ponies (he had sent Gano back, on the trot, to fetch another mount for Vahla) but still, they were heavily laden and the trail was seldom used. All morning and part of the afternoon it took to pass through the forest and join up again with the north fork of the river. Going was easier along its banks, until late in the afternoon when the land around the river began to undulate in a growing series of ridges and ravines. The river had cut its way through these over time, but its path was more tortured as it wound this way and that, and often back upon itself. Frequently, the banks were choked with boulders and debris, hindering their progress. They camped that night with several miles still to go before the Gate, and after a frugal supper (they were all too bone weary to have much appetite) immediately rolled into their blankets and fell asleep.

Valerius had them off again at dawn, however, and by noon they had mounted the boulder strewn alluvial plain and stopped for lunch before the gate itself. This was nothing more than an immense pillar of stone—a shoulder of the mountains themselves—which had resisted the assaults of the river over the years, and blocked the entrance to the gorge that wound its way upwards behind it. But it had been on this spot, some three years before, that Valerius, with a badly wounded Thorngere at his side, had fought his last battle as Balazar against a troop of Kantaran Guardsmen—the same Guardsmen that Colinus now led—and before they went on, Valerius spent a few moments walking the field and remembering. He had ordered the field cleaned and the remains buried after their return to the valley, so there was nothing to see but lush, unbroken grasses and stunted brush, but he found the remains of the Guardsmen's old fire, and stood once more on the spot just to the west of it where he had challenged them—he, a lone, unwounded warrior against thirty mounted guardsmen. There had been a very brave captain, he remembered, who had died here, one of the last of countless casualties of that long and horrible war.

But his own position had been simple then, he recalled. It was either get past the Guard and leave the valley, or die. There were no other alternatives, and not much time to consider them had there been any. They had eaten little food for days, Thorngere was quickly failing from an inflamed arrow wound, and the new Kantaran King, an evil snake of a man named Cormin, was actively seeking their heads. So Balazar (funny, how he still thought of himself as Balazar then) had boldly marched up to the Guardsmen watching the gate and challenged them to open combat. And with the wounded Thorngere hobbling up to stand by his side, they had fought, and would have died, had they not been rescued by the fortunate arrival of Volkmir's servant, Chad, who by the grace of some god, was an excellent bowman. But Balazar had seen none of that part: brought down by a horse's kick to the head and a spear thrust in the back, he had known nothing more till he awakened several days later in Volkmir's cave.

So he had never really made this ascent, at least not consciously, and as he stood now by the ashes of the dead Guardsmen's fire, and let his eye wander up and up the barren mountain slopes before him, he realized he was not exactly sure of the way. 'How like my life,' he thought: 'standing on a spot where I've fought and almost died before, unsure of how to get to a place I've been before. And I'm supposed to be the great king of the Eye!'

Kicking at the long cold ashes, he had just started back towards his waiting party, when a movement by the gate caught his eye. A mounted figure rounded the shoulder of rock and headed towards them, a small, dark complected man with wiry black hair. It was that same Chad, riding along on one donkey and leading another, as casually as if he was on Main Street. "Master send me," he greeted Valerius placidly. "He not want you get lost in mountains. He say take special care of lady."

Valerius and Vahla exchanged quick glances. "Very perceptive of your master," said Valerius, "to know we were coming in advance."

"Oh, yes," said Chad, beaming. "Master see you in fire, send Chad to help. Chad help before, too, yes?"

"Yes, you were a very great help then. You saved our lives. But how long did it take you to come down the mountain?"

"This third day, Majesty. Chad bring bow, too, but not need now."

"No, not need bow," said Valerius, unconsciously mimicking Chad's stilted speech. "Unless you'd like to shoot us a bird for dinner." And then, under his breath, "Though, since your master knew we were coming before I did, I wouldn't be surprised to find dinner waiting along the way."

Dinner was not waiting along the way, but with Chad in company, it may as well have been. Gano was a very competent servant, and not a bad hand at campfire cooking—he had, after all, been hand-picked by the king—but compared to the culinary marvels Chad performed, Gano was a crude bumbler. While Gano had troubles enough just finding wood to keep the fire going in those rocky mountain wastes, and could proffer little more to eat than dried field rations, Chad produced a succession of exquisite dinners. Shoot a bird he did, within an hour of beginning their ascent, and by the time they stopped for dinner, he had it plucked, stuffed and ready to roast. He gathered wild herbs from cracks in the rocks as they passed, and berries of several types to season his bread stuffing. He found succulent wild potatoes growing in an isolated patch of earth (or had he planted them just for the occasion?), and a form of cabbage as well. From his seemingly meager pack, he pulled enough cooking implements to stock a fair sized kitchen, and in hardly any time at all, had a meal prepared that would have drawn rave reviews at a banquet.

And that was just the beginning. Throughout the three and a half days it took to make the climb— days in which the rare intervals of being able to ride were punctuated by long, grueling hours of ladder-like climbing on foot with calves and thighs screaming in pain—Chad was a marvel of efficiency and inventiveness. Like all good servants, Gano was very possessive of his master, and for some time, Valerius watched the two with amusement, expecting at any moment to see fireworks erupt. But in that he was disappointed. So vast was the gulf in capabilities between them, and so unprepossessing was Chad, that for Gano it was like one of those rare opportunities when a craftsman gets the opportunity to witness a great master tradesman at work, and after an initial flash of hostility, he became Chad's humble devotee, accepting his direction and watching in awe as the master worked.

As for Valerius and Vahla, they had their own concerns which weighed heavily on them. But Chad provided comfort in a degree unexpected, and also a source of instruction and amusement which made the long trip easier to bear. Still, it was a relief when they emerged at last from the twisting, climbing gorge onto a relatively flat and rocky plateau, and after several miles of easy walking (though it was a mystery how any walking could be termed easy with such stiff and blistered limbs as they had), suddenly found themselves at Volkmir's lair. This was a cave, the entrance to which was tucked securely away in a rocky dell, and before which, on a stool and apparently asleep in the afternoon sun, sat the mage himself.

He was an ancient creature, withered and bent. His hair and beard were long and white, and as unkempt as his scruffy gray robe. His hands, which rested in his lap as he leaned back against the rock, were crooked and gnarled like twisted bits of dried root, and his wrists stuck from his sleeves like bleached bones. So still was he as they approached, that Valerius feared for a moment he might actually be dead. Indeed, he looked as though he could have been dead for some time already. But as they stopped before him, he popped open a bright blue eye and raised a shaggy brow.

"You took your time, I see," he croaked. "I expected you yesterday evening."

"Is that any way to greet your king?" Valerius retorted, a half-smile hidden in his beard. "We stopped along the way to enjoy the view. But I take it you also expected Vahla here?"

The mage rose and inspected Vahla as if she were a pony at auction. "Vahla, is it?" he said and traced her cheek with a gnarled knuckle. "Aye, I expected her. She it is I have seen in my visions. You are welcome here, Vahla, my girl—as are you, of course, your Majesty—though why you have come I do not yet know. Maybe together we can divine that fate."

"So, how did you know I was coming?" asked Valerius. They were seated, the three of them, in comfortable chairs before Volkmir's fire in the cave's large, central chamber, the remains of yet another of Chad's delicious meals on the table nearby. The room was large and spacious, one of several in the cave complex, which had been considerably remodeled inside with stone and mortar. It was richly furnished, and the walls were lined with racks of dusty scrolls and manuscripts, and collections of arcane implements. How Volkmir had managed to haul all of these things up a mountain, Valerius had no idea. Probably Chad, he thought.

"It's not polite to ask a Mage 'how' he knows things," Volkmir chirped, "even for a high King. Besides, I don't know how I know. I just do."

Volkmir had aged since last Valerius had seen him. He was more bent and feeble, and his hands, Valerius noticed, had a slight tremor so that he slopped his wine when he raised his cup. He had eaten hardly anything at dinner, and seemed very quarrelsome with Chad. Now, though it was quite warm in the cave—so warm, in fact, that Vahla and Valerius were sweating—he sat wrapped in a woolen shawl and stretched his feet towards the fire.

"Well, since you did know that we were coming, you probably also know why..."

"Who said that?" Volkmir spluttered, rising up in his chair like an angry schoolmaster, which, in Valerius' youth, was exactly what he had been. "What logic says that because I know 'what' I also know 'why'? Did I not teach you better than that, my boy? The trouble with men is not in their brains but in the fact that they refuse to use them! Think, your Majesty! That's how you will solve the riddles you face. Put your thoughts together like the pieces of a puzzle. Study them, look for patterns."

"Well, if you do not know why I'm here," Valerius continued unruffled by his old master's tirade, "then do you know that Vahla here is my sister?"

Volkmir was surprised at this and inspected the girl again, more closely this time. "Your sister, eh? Well, I doubt it not. In fact, I doubt not but that you have quite an extended family, Majesty. Your father was a very active man."

"So I'm beginning to realize. We also just learned that Thorngere has the same connection—which is why Vahla is here."

"Yes, I knew Thorngere was your kin. But he didn't want it known and I respected his wishes. So you were smitten, is that right girl?"

"We were to be married," said Vahla, blushing.

"Ah, I see," said Volkmir and then he cocked his head like a bird and sat utterly still for a time, as if he was listening to something in another room, or as if something had just occurred to him. "Well, I wouldn't worry about it, my dear," he said then. "Time heals all, as they say. Besides, there is more to do in this world than dally among the roses, eh? And if I may twist my metaphor a bit more, something tells me you may also have very useful thorns. But since when, King Valerius, do the broken heart strings of a girl take precedence over the destiny of nations?"

"What destiny has any nation that does not yield to the heart strings of a girl?" Valerius countered.

"Ha! You speak like a poet now, not a king. But seriously, why have you come to seek my council, Valerius Everreigning, High King of Valeria and all the Inland Sea? What would you of Volkmir, Mage of Valeria and your old master of rhetoric and rumor?"

"Your wisdom, old friend," said Valerius, smiling affectionately at the crooked figure before him. Bent and wizened though he was, Volkmir still had a commanding presence. "I have, as you said before, put my thoughts together like the pieces of a puzzle, and I do indeed see patterns there, patterns I do not like. What I do not see is any sign of the light. That is why I come to you, Volkmir." Quickly then, Valerius summarized those pieces: Fantar's growing naval might in the Inland Sea and the difficult situation in the valley; the problem with the cavern and the masts, and the need for a better base; his frustrated hope of cementing a stronger alliance with Dulcai, Fantar's sudden dominance there and taking of Reuters' daughter, and Valerius' own fear of what that might mean for his friend; the recent revelations with Vahla and Thorngere, and finally, his inability to make any use of the Eye. "I fear," he said, "that I may have to make war on Dulcai, though Reuters is the last man I'd want to fight. So I've been hoping for some guidance—a sign—but either the gods have turned away, or I simply do not know how to use this thing," and he held the glittering Eye up by its golden chain.

"Well, at least you believe you should use it," Volkmir replied. "And you try. That's more than your father did. But here, let's see what we can do." Lifting the great stone from Valerius' neck, the Mage held it up by its golden chain and peered at it this way and that in the light of the fire. The stone sparkled and glittered, flashing red across the eyes of the three in the room. "Well, I see nothing wrong with it," said Volkmir at last. "But I have to be very careful with this thing, you know," he said to Vahla. "The last time I tried to play with it, it knocked me off my perch like a bird from the nest, and left me blind for three days! If your friend Thorngere hadn't caught me, I'd have broken my neck like a sparrow! But I'll tell you what," he said, turning back to Valerius, "I still have some old sources I can check, and tomorrow, by the light of the sun, there are some spells we can try. So we will see. But for now, it's late and I am an old man. Chad!" he called, suddenly irritable again. "Are you going to leave me stranded here all night? Come and help an old man to his bed!"

The mage was already up and reading by candle light—and had apparently been up for some time—when Valerius arose before dawn. "You see," he said, looking up from the pile of scrolls on his table, "the problem is two-fold: one, none of your recent ancestors really believed in the Stone, or tried to make any effective use of it; and two, when your earlier ancestors did use it, they tried very assiduously to keep what knowledge they had away from my predecessors. So, I'm afraid I don't know much more about this thing than you do—at least, not much more than I've already shown you."

"But you had the thing for years. You used it yourself."

"Oh, yes, but only in a very limited way. And I never controlled it. It drew me to itself, else I never would have dared even try it—especially after it burned out Fantar's eye—and then it only showed me a bit of what was: never what was to be. I used it, basically, to keep track of you. And then not very often. As I say, it used me more than I it."

"So you're saying you can't help?"

"Well, I didn't say that, exactly. The arcane science is not totally bereft, after all! And I have found a couple mentions here in these old texts. Here's one, for example, of Valerius your great-great-grandfather, 'going up to a high place to see the world in the fresh light of the new day...'"

"First light! I haven't tried that."

"And then, there are, as I say, some waking spells and a couple other things we can try. Perhaps it's just a question of getting the God's attention. But then again, maybe we already have it."

"Well, if first light is an option, let's go for it," said Valerius and together, the massive, black maned king and the wizened, gray mage made their way out of the cave and up a rocky path to a high pinnacle. Valerius had to help Volkmir for most of the way, and when he straightened to look around, the sun was just breaking over the eastern horizon and casting its light like a beacon across the crests of the mountains around him. White peaks leapt out of the night like actors suddenly lit on a stage, while between them, vast valleys and crags lay hidden in blue and black. Valerius, however, ignored this breathtaking vista and quickly positioned himself before the rising sun, and lifted the glittering gem to his eye. Twisting this way and that to catch the light from all angles, he looked long and deep, ignoring the pain of several bright bursts when the stone reflected the light directly through.

But it was the same as before: murky shadows and deep glimmerings, shifting chimeras that approached but never quite materialized into shapes. At one point, red light drifted like a fog across the stone and he thought for a moment that it would part, like a curtain and reveal... But it only moiled and churned and then—he wasn't sure whether he had flinched, or twisted, or if the sun had just risen that precise bit more—it flashed bright like an explosion and he yanked his head away, spots dancing before his eye. He shook his head sadly at the mage's questioning stare.

The two of them went to work on the stone then like a pair of mechanics. They propped it up on a pile of rocks and positioned it this way and that while Volkmir tried some of his waking spells, chanting loud and incomprehensibly in some ancient tongue with his ancient, croaking throat. They took it inside and cleaned it, they boiled it in Volkmir's cauldron while he stirred in pinches of various powders that filled the place with acrid, colored smoke. They heated it in the fire—very carefully, this—and polished it like silver plate. Volkmir tried more spells for waking, spells for joining and growing, summoning spells, even a couple of something spells that seemed very much to Valerius like they were being made up on the spot. And between each of these exercises, Valerius tried the stone again. He tried it by first light and by noon, by firelight and by candle, by the setting sun, and finally, by the light of the rising moon. But it was all to no avail. If there was any presence or vision in the stone, it was withheld from him.

"Are you sure you didn't do something to it?" Volkmir asked for the fifteenth time. Vahla had joined them and the three were again seated before Volkmir's fire, the Eye cast on a low table between them like a broken watch. Valerius was leaning forward on his elbows, chin in his hands, staring morosely at it, and to Volkmir's question, he simply shook his head. "Well, I don't know, then," said the mage. "Sometimes I think my whole craft is just bunk and that we are only given to see what the Gods want us to see. We are their playthings, after all, our lives and struggles but an afternoon's entertainment for them—or perhaps scenes in a larger picture, the scope of which we know not. But I don't know. Whatever is in, or not in that Stone is beyond my poor powers."

Valerius leaned back in his chair then, drained his cup and stroked the long black strands of his beard. "Well, if you cannot advise me from your sight, Volkmir, let me have your thoughts, for I still count you as chief among the wise."

"Valerius, my Liege, you are a kind and gentle man—which is surely the soul of wisdom—and I am just fool enough to believe your words. But I cannot advise you any better than your own heart. All that you say makes sense and Dulcai would seem to be the next logical step. But how you can make war on your friend, the man who succored you, I know not. Necessity is a cruel taskmaster. You should know that above all. But whether you must betray your friend—or whether it would be a betrayal at all—only your heart can tell you."

229

"Aye," said Valerius. "And it would seem that my heart is exactly where the Gods want to leave it." Rising, he grabbed the stone by its golden chain. But as he lifted it from the table, it caught the firelight in a peculiar manner, and seemed to pulse momentarily, and in a brief instant, flashed out a bright red beam, like a laser, that fell directly on Vahla.

Wrapped in her own thoughts, she was sitting, cross-legged in a chair to the right of the two men. But when the light fell upon her, she snapped her head up, and the reflected red from the stone glowed deep in her eyes. She opened her mouth crookedly and in a strange, scratchy voice, chanted, "That which is friend has now become foe. If you want to reach home, away you must go."

It was over in a matter of seconds. The light flashed, the girl spoke, and it was done. But it left a kind of echo, an aftershock that stunned both King and Mage. They looked at each other, then back at the girl who looked at them in surprise. "What?" she asked, as if they had said something she missed.

"Why did you say that?" asked Valerius.

"Say what?" Vahla was clearly bewildered.

"You spoke a prophecy..."

"No, my Liege," said Volkmir, "it was not the girl who spoke. But I do believe I know now why she came."

Chapter 14
EYE TO DULCAI

That same night, along the coast south of Kantar, Glaucon stood at the rail of a swift war galley, peering into the moonlit night at the blank faces of the slowly passing cliffs. They were as close inshore as he dared to sail, pulling quietly with muffled oars, showing not so much as a single lighted candle, and expecting to be attacked at any moment. He had left Dulcai in haste three days before to summon the fleet at Zagorbia. Blumholt was to bring Dulcai's forces north in another few days, and with the combined fleets, Glaucon would crush this rascal pretender, Valerius. If, that was, he could find again that cavern he had seen Thorngere duck into. So with sail, oars, and liberal application of the whip, he had returned to a promontory he had noted just south of the area. There he had pulled in close to avoid the preying eyes of lookouts on the cliff tops and, after the moon rose, slowly made his way northward, all hands who could be spared watching for the cavern or any lurking pirates.

Suddenly, there it was, a large, yawning black hole in the cliff face, the rising tide setting him in towards it. Slowly, with backing oars, he swung around and let the current carry him towards the entrance. Should he slip inside? Would there be a pair of galleys just inside there, waiting to spring? Glaucon could hear the sound of his heart hammering as the ship nosed closer and closer to the black maw. Inside, it was as silent as a tomb and his eyes strained trying to pierce the darkness. Suddenly, a harsh whisper came down from aloft.

"Deck, there! The mast head won't clear!"

"Back all!" Glaucon called, his voice like an explosion in the night, shattering his own nerve. If they were there, surely they would come now. But he didn't wait to see. Swinging his bow around and cracking his whip in the air, he sped off north towards Zagorbia.

Later that night, Volkmir came into Valerius' chamber and spoke to him. "Valerius Everreigning," he said, "Rightful High King of Valeria and all the Inland Sea, why do you lay in your bed asleep while your enemies gather at your gate? Arise, Valerius, and take up your sword! The time has come to strike!" Valerius snapped open his eyes and sat up in bed. The room was empty, but a strong sense of urgency filled him and he roused out the household to prepare to leave at first light.

As he was finishing his packing, Vahla came into his chamber, visibly nervous. "I want to stay here," she said. "I've been thinking about it all night, and I think it's the best solution. You need Thorngere, and if I'm there, I don't think he'll come back. And I'm not sure I could face him if he did. Besides, I think I can be of some use here—not that Chad doesn't do a wonderful job taking care of Volkmir, of course, but I think the place could still

232

use a woman's touch... And I think I could help in other ways... Anyway, Valerius, my King, my... my brother," she pleaded, "something happened to me last night. I don't know what it was, but I just know I was meant to come here."

"Does Volkmir know of this?" Valerius asked.

"Yes, but he told me I must have your blessing first."

"How nice of him to acknowledge the High King," he smiled, then yelled: "Volkmir!" but the shout was unnecessary for the old mage was standing just outside the chamber. As he entered, Valerius assumed his most stern and regal posture. "You knew this all along, didn't you, you sly old weasel?"

"Your Majesty," said Volkmir, "it is impolitic to press a mage about what he knew when..."

"I will be the judge of what is 'impolitic,' Volkmir."

"Well, Chad did happen to have an extra room prepared."

"Did he now? And just what do you intend with this young lady, my sister?"

"I intend—with your blessing, Majesty—to instruct her. With your permission, I will take her as my apprentice."

"A princess of the royal blood, apprenticed to a mage?"

"Majesty, these intentions are not mine but the gods. I am but a facilitator. As you saw last night, she already has the gift."

233

"And," chimed in Vahla, "Apprentice Magician is a step up from tavern dancer... even for one of royal blood!"

"Ha! That I will not dispute," Valerius laughed. "Very well, then, I see I have no choice with you two and the Gods conspiring against me. But hear me, Volkmir, Mage of Valeria," he said, growing serious again. "Though our sister has only lately become known to us, she is all the more dear for that. I charge you to keep her well and treat her kindly."

"It shall be as you command, Majesty," said Volkmir, bowing his balding head.

"And you, Vahla—may you find the meaning here that you seek. But pull gently on these old gray hairs, for the wisdom that is in them is venerable indeed, and highly esteemed by us."

"It will be so, your Majesty."

"Then it is done. Volkmir, the Princess Vahla is yours to command."

Since his earliest youth, Valerius had always been a ponderous thinker. It was not that his mind lacked agility or native wit, but he retained a degree of caution in his thinking and decision making that often forced him to labor exhaustively in his conjecturing far beyond the point where other—and perhaps lesser—men felt their minds were made up. This trait sometimes made him appear slow and indecisive, but such was far from the case as others before now had learned. Once the machinations of his mental machinery were completed and he had weighed all the evidence and opinion down to the finest feather and had come to a conclusion, then would he throw all that weight behind it, and with a purpose as single minded as steel, drive the notion forward to completion.

And now that his mind was set, he drove Gano and their ponies to the point of collapse in his haste to return to Kantar. Absolved of the need to cook by an exquisite supply of ready-to-eat field rations prepared by Chad, Valerius declined even the need for a fire and hardly stopped long enough to light one. On their first day out from Volkmir's lair, he pushed on and on, long past the dinner hour and far into the night. Only when some late night clouds drifted in to obscure the pale light of the moon and make further travel impossible, would he consent to stop. Then, at dawn and after a mere three hours sleep, he kicked an aching Gano from his blanket and drove their bleary eyed ponies on again.

The descent was excruciating at that pace, and as the day wore on, increasingly dangerous to horse and man. Where on the ascent tiring muscles tended to slow one down, on the down slope, cramping thigh muscles made it harder to stop, and before they stumbled gasping out from the gate late that evening, each had had more than one near calamity. Even here Valerius was loath to stop, but after making a three and a half day trek in two, he was as exhausted as Gano and the beasts. He realized, too, that it would be fruitless to press on at night through the black-shadowed forest. Relieved that it was nature stopping him and not his own flagging will, he sank to the rocky ground and slept like a stone until dawn.

The next day there was no stopping, except to let the ponies drink, and it was well after midnight when Valerius entered the gates of Kantar, yelling orders for his captains and commanders to assemble in the palace throne room in one hour. For half of that hour, he allowed himself the luxury of soaking in a hot bath, and for the other half he dressed himself in his most royal robes, and fortified himself with an entire roasted chicken and a carafe of strong wine.

Exact to his time, and announced to a bleary eyed, disheveled, and anxious crowd by blaring trumpets, he marched down the length of the hall and mounted the dais before his throne. There he paused, a huge, black maned man robed in ermine and purple, as stern and kingly as any who had ever born his illustrious name, and looked out over the hushed crowd. Against the gold inlay of his shining breastplate, the bright red Eye of Valeria flickered and glowed in the dancing torch light, and in his dark eyes there glittered a strength and resolve none in that room would ever dare counter. Indeed, though many had known him for years and had accepted him as king for two, none had ever seen him look as regal or impressive as he did at that moment.

They, on the other hand, looked hardly like the champions and commanders of an avenging army. Many had been roused from their beds, others from late night rounds of the cup, and few had the time or inclination to make themselves presentable on what was obviously a formal occasion. Too, they were concerned. Valerius had been gone the better part of a week under mysterious circumstances. Thorngere had come and gone off again, obviously in haste and speaking to no one. Rumors had been afloat about their hiding place being discovered, and about the king seeking visions from his power stone. There was also talk of some magician in the mountains, but nothing was confirmed, nothing was clear except that something was obviously afoot. What that might be, however, none had the slightest idea.

The thirty or so faces standing motionless before Valerius were more familiar than his own. Many he had known his entire adult life; all he had fought beside and would trust with his life. They were the chief captains and commanders of his minuscule army. Each commanded one of the thirty odd war galleys and half dozen transport ships he had managed to assemble over the past two years. The galleys were divided into three flotillas, each under a senior commander chosen from among the older captains. With Thorngere gone, Grumwald was the most senior of these. Though he had only recently joined their force, he had fought against Fantar with Balazar of old for years, and before that had been a captain of the King's Guard in Dunskol. Another was Daemon of Palmania, the second major town sacked by Fantar after Valeria. The third was Eban of Durumkae, whose last sight of his home was charred remains. When Fantar attacked, the defending army marched out beyond the village outskirts to do battle, but as the forces engaged, Fantar sent sappers around behind to set fires among the crowded wooden dwellings. They went up like kindling. Trapped between Fantar's raging hordes to their front and their flaming homes behind, the forces of Durumkae broke in panic and fled. Eban had never seen his wife or newborn babe since, or his aged parents, and presumed them all dead.

Other captains had suffered deeply as well. There was Gainor from Bangorum who had been sent to Durumkae to seek help when Fantar threatened, and who returned with the news that help was on the way, only to discover Fantar's men had already taken the town: the heads of Hamon the king and Hamar his son were impaled on pikes over the gates, and outside the walls a huge pile of bodies—the remains of the city's defenders, among whom were his father and three brothers—was about to be put to the torch.

There was Cristoban of Telos who had gone with his fellows to defend Durumkae and been swept up in the panic that had seized that army, and later watched helpless from the hills as his own town fell; Dimurnal of Dunskol, a dreamy youth when Fantar came, whose father and older brothers had been slain and who, from hiding, had watched helpless as his mother and sister were raped; Zimlait a simple fisherman from Cobanos on the southern coast, who returned from sea to find all he knew and loved swept away. The list went on and on. All were well known to Valerius, and all had their tales of private horror.

Whether Fantar had acted from brilliant strategy or vicious instinct, by striking at Valeria first, he had succeeded in removing the only centralized authority there was in that world, and made it nearly impossible for the rest to mount any coordinated defence. Whether by plan or simple momentum, his forces had rolled on and on, a pack of ravening dogs run wild. Drawing from the lowest elements in a too stratified society, his revolution had spread like fire—had spread with fire—until there was nothing left to destroy. It was a movement based on conflagration, its aims were rape and pillage, its mission to tear down and destroy. Only when the destroying was done, when there was nothing left to conquer, did Fantar give any thought to governing what he had gained. And that's when his own worm began to turn. It was not hard to turn murderers into hangmen, but it was less easy to turn thieves into constables. Starting a fire was easy: controlling a raging inferno was not.

Now Valerius was about to start a fire of his own, and as he surveyed the expectant faces before him, he was struck by a very strong sense of occasion. This was one of those transitional moments, he thought, those small, silent spaces between thought and action that hang suspended in time, the hinges upon which great events turn. He had but a few words to say to the men before him, yet the formation of those words, the decision behind them, had been months in the making, and the actual saying would change all their lives forever. Perhaps even end them. Here they were, he thought, standing silent before him, and would stand so until he spoke. And then? When his words crossed that tiny gap between imagination and reality? Then was in the Gods' hands.

"Men," he said, his voice loud and resonant in the echoing hall, "Here's the situation: first, Fantar has taken control of Dulcai and has our old friend Reuters under his thumb. Second, our hiding place here has been discovered by one of Fantar's minions. So we don't have much time. We must strike quickly, before the forces to our north and south can unite! Rouse up your men now, and divide them into shifts. Work round the clock! We have only two days to prepare, then we leave with the next tide. So let's move! Our time of waiting is done!"

"Where do we strike, Majesty," called a voice from the back.

"We strike south," Valerius yelled, yanking out his jewelled ceremonial sword and stabbing the air in that direction. "We go to free Dulcai!" Thirty other swords flashed out as well, and the hall echoed with cheers.

As the hall emptied, Valerius flopped down on his throne, utterly spent. He had done his bit, had performed that mysterious alchemy that turns ideas into action: he had exercised power. And now the accumulated effects of his trip up the mountain and his mad dash back came rushing down on him and

240

he sagged in his chair, his head lolling. The best thing he could do, he thought, was to get a little rest. There was much to be done in the morning.

"Majesty?" The voice startled him and he sat up quickly, like a kid caught napping in school. It was Colinus, standing hesitantly before him, his hand stretched out to shake the huge king's knee.

"Ah, yes, thank you, Colinus. I must have dozed off," he said and he started to rise.

"Your Majesty," Colinus said. "I have a request."

Valerius sat back down, heavily. "Yes, Colinus? What is it?"

"Well, it's not just from me, Sire. It's from the entire Guard and, well, most of the Kantaran army... We... We'd like to come with you. No, please, your Majesty," he said, holding up his hand as Valerius started to speak, "hear me out. You know our history, Sire, and you know our abilities as fighters, so I wouldn't presume to question your judgment in military matters. But I don't know if you're aware of our situation here... I mean, aware in terms of how we feel."

"Yes, go on," said Valerius, his great weariness held in check like a torrent behind a dam.

"Well, it's two things, Sire," said the diminutive Guard Commander, standing stiffly before the king and launching into a recitation which had obviously been worked out and rehearsed in advance. "We're half breeds, as you know—although we never really knew until the war was over—with Iblian breeder slave fathers and pure bred Kudanim mothers. And

241

that puts us in a very awkward position, what with the Iblis imprisoned in the New City and the pure bred males here breeding sons again. It sort of makes us feel out of place, if you know what I mean. But the worst part is—and I'm not sure you're aware of this, your Majesty, as we've never spoken of it—the worst part is that because of the Rite of the Knife, none of us can have any children of our own. So we feel like total freaks and misfits here, you see, Sire? We don't belong to either group and we can have no families of our own... You're the only one we feel we belong to. You're the one who turned us into men and soldiers. You helped us win our war, Sire, and now we'd like to stay with you—to help you win yours."

For some moments, Valerius sat silent, studying the tiny, yet stalwart man before him, an old saying flickering in his mind like candle light: 'How do you grow hope when the land is barren?'

"Commander Colinus," he said at last, "I appreciate your loyalty, and value it. Indeed, I do, for without it I would have been dead long since! And I appreciate your value as fighters. It's true I do not believe your phalanx could stand up against a charge of full sized warriors—that would be too much to ask—but as mounted archers, you can be superbly effective. So if I have decided not to bring you—and I have decided that—it is not because I doubt your capabilities. The simple fact is, we have not ships enough to carry you and your mounts to Dulcai. But besides that, Commander, you are still very much needed here.

"No," he said as Colinus opened his mouth, "now you hear me out. I can also understand something of how you feel—at least, as much as any man can who has not been through the Rite of the Knife—for I, too, have been without a home. But you are wrong in saying you do not belong here. A home here is your birthright, regardless of who your parents are. And even if that were not the case, you—all of you—have earned a place by right of arms, and you may hold it with honor.

"As for children, I can do nothing about that. There are, as you know, half a thousand or so of your youngsters who have not had the Rite—so there is some hope for your line—but you must understand that the Rite was all part of the pure-breds' defense plan. Without it, and without you, they would have been driven to extinction long ago, and you with them. So while it may not have been fair to you, it was essential to you both. They really had no choice. And remember this, too: you underwent the Rite willingly; you swore your life to the city and to Kala Atar. So fair or no, you are bound by that pledge. If you desert, your lives would be forfeit."

"I hear and will obey, Sire," said the little man, snapping to attention and slapping his fist on his chest in salute.

"Oh, belay that, Colinus. You know I'm not trying to read you regulations. I'm simply trying to talk sense. And one more thing: who would control the Iblis if you and the rest of the Kantaran army sailed away with me? Who would complete the

243

rebuilding? Who would defend Kantar? No, Commander, much as I would love to see your cavalry dashing towards the walls of Dulcai, it would be too much to ask of Queen Salonis that she do without you quite yet. For the next campaign, when we have more ships and are better prepared here... Well, we'll talk. But for now, your duty is here.

"Now, Commander, you really must excuse me. If I don't get upstairs to bed I'm going to fall over right here and you'll have to try and carry me. And great as your heart and courage are, my friend, you are not up to that task!"

But Valerius was not the only one up beyond his time that night. Glaucon, too, was up past midnight, but in his case it was because he couldn't sleep. His ship was nearing the harbor at Zagorbia and he was too keyed up to do anything but pace his narrow stern cabin. Even the two decanters of wine he had drunk since dinner had failed to calm him down, though they had had some effect. In truth, this was a big moment for Glaucon, the opening stage of what would be the crowning achievement of his career: crushing the pretender pirate, Valerius, and securing the entire southern half of the outer sea for the Empire. By this time tomorrow, he would have under his direct command over eighty prime war ships, the largest fleet ever assembled since Fantar's accession. That would make him, Glaucon, the most powerful man in the realm, second only to Fantar. And once he had secured that power, he did not intend to relinquish it.

But would he be able to secure it? That was the question that had him so edgy. Yes, he had orders from Fantar himself to utilize whatever means were required to search out and destroy the pirate, and yes, Tarpon, the military commander of Zagorbia, knew full well the consequences of disregarding instructions from Fantar. But would Tarpon actually hand over his fleet and what amounted to nearly two thirds of his garrison to Glaucon? They had never gotten along, he and Tarpon, had always been rivals in the snake pit that was Fantar's command structure and had hissed and struck at each other several times before this.

And Glaucon knew Tarpon was jealous of this current command. He had as much as said so when they last met, suggesting that the Dulcai situation had been handled badly, that he, Tarpon, would simply have killed Reuters directly and not bothered with all this silly 'influence business' and this taking of hostages. 'A man with a sword between his ribs causes very little trouble' was his opinion. And Tarpon knew full well—as well as he knew Glaucon—that his fleet once taken would never be returned. So would he disobey Fantar? Would he, Glaucon, get a sword between his ribs instead of a fleet?

If Tarpon thought he could get away with it, Glaucon had no doubt that he would. Especially if Tarpon thought he could then crush the rebels and deliver the southern ocean to Fantar. But he could not do that now any more than he could a year ago. Only Glaucon could do that. It was Glaucon who knew the whereabouts of Valerius' hidden hole, and it was only Glaucon who had the girl. Those were the keys. Without the hole, Tarpon would not know where to strike, and without the girl, Duclai would not cooperate, and he would not have the strength to strike. So Glaucon had the edge. But he would have to be careful not to lose it: Tarpon was ever quick with the sword and would kill as readily from anger and frustration as he would from deliberate intent.

The trick was to stay very visible, very public. No closeted meetings here, no confraternity of leaders. No, he had the authority from Fantar to take what he needed, and that was precisely what he must do. He would sail in at dawn, brazenly board the flagship of Tarpon's fleet, and send an emissary with blaring trumpets to Tarpon's hall. There, in public, before all his commanders and magistrates, he would have read aloud his orders from Fantar authorizing him to seize Tarpon's fleet. He would give them twenty-four hours to make ready for sea and then he would be gone. That would give Tarpon no choice but to accede and no chance to do anything else. He, Glaucon would definitely not have dinner with the man—or perhaps he would invite Tarpon to dine with him, aboard his ship— but he would most definitely keep the girl out of sight. One look at her and Tarpon was liable to do anything. Besides, Glaucon had other plans for her.

Reaching for his decanter, Glaucon found it empty and barked angrily for the steward to fetch him another. Then, as an afterthought, he added, "And have the girl brought up here as well." Now that he was satisfied with his scheming, he might as well make the evening's final drink a toast to beauty.

And a beauty indeed was Princess Eomer of Dulcai, daughter of his royal majesty, King Reuters. Even in her present state, disheveled from being roused from her bed and worn from several weeks of close confinement on a ship never designed to provide royal accommodations, even so, hers was a beauty to move the hearts of men. Where her father was rather rotund and of a jovial nature—or, had been until recent events—Eomer had followed her mother, Emma's line. She had been a famous beauty in her time, a princess from the northlands, as fair and supple as a field of ripening grain, who in her youth had made young Reuters the envy of all the Inland Sea when she had consented to follow him to his hot southern home. But she had not adjusted well to the southern clime and had soon left Reuters a widower with a young daughter that was her image and the remaining joy of his father's heart.

Now this Eomer had blossomed into a womanly beauty every bit as legendary as her mother's but with the added spice of having been bred to the southern sun. Tall and stately, with long honey colored tresses, skin a golden, glowing brown, and eyes as deep and blue as the southern sea, she was brought from her cramped quarters below and stood before Glaucon, her fear and distaste for him evident in her eyes. But he was graciousness itself.

"So sorry if I have awakened you, my dear," he purred. "I didn't realize the time. But I thought you might like to know we are just now entering the harbor at Zagorbia and that soon, I hope to provide you with more comfortable quarters. Would you like some wine?"

The girl did not speak, as indeed she had not for several such interviews, ever since the first, when it became apparent she was not to be regarded as a royal guest and that this Glaucon, in fact, had other ideas entirely.

"No? And still not speaking, I see. Well, you will come around, my dear, believe me. When you realize how much better I can make things for you. But you don't mind if I have another cup, do you?" He poured, and full cup in hand, approached the girl. She flinched visibly, but did not try to move away. "You're very beautiful, you know," he said standing close, wine and cheese heavy on his breath. Lifting her hair with his left hand, he lightly traced her cheek with his knuckle. The girl jerked away from his touch and stared at a spot on the wall behind him.

"Ever the royal puss, I see. You know," he breathed, "I could take you right now and none would lift a finger to stop me. In fact, there are many aboard who would even love to watch. Would you like that, my pretty royal kitten? To be strapped down, naked and spread wide to the world before the whole crew? I could even let them have their way with you once I was done. I have a bosun who's hung like a horse... How would that suit your royal prerogative?" And he laughed softly to himself, a heavy, guttural sound deep in his throat. She tried not to react.

"But you needn't worry about that, my dear... There's an easy way to avoid that fate. All you have to do is be nice to me. Wouldn't you like to be nice to me?" And with his left hand, he lightly stroked her breast.

She slapped him hard, then, a resounding crack that knocked him back and made sparks dance before his eyes. His wine slopped all over his toga. "You vixen bitch!" he snarled, his face, already showing the red imprint of her hand, twisting into an ugly rage. He crouched like an animal, ready to spring, but then, with a shudder, mastered himself and straightened, his face resuming its haughty insolence. The girl was too important to harm, just now. But his eyes still snapped with fire. "No," he said, "it won't be that way. You're not worth the risk of damaging. No, my dear, we'll keep you yet awhile... We'll wait until you beg."

She was taken back, then, to her tiny, cramped cabin on the deck below Glaucon's. The door was locked behind her and she could hear the guard resume his seat on the stool just outside. For a long moment she hugged her arms about herself and shuddered, her limbs trembling violently. Calming herself, she lifted the heavy lid on the single porthole in the cabin and secured it by its thong. The night air was cool on her face, like a caressing hand, and away off over the choppy waves, she could see the dim shadow of the land. Carefully, so as not to make even the tiniest sound, she climbed through the porthole and dropped softly into the sea.

Chapter 15
THE RESCUE

Boltar awoke instantly at the soft tap on his door, grabbed his cloak, and went on deck. It was half-way through the midwatch and dawn was still a good three hours off. The sky was dark and overcast with only a faint luminous patch where the moon showed through, and the surrounding forest was black and still. Elusive tugged softly at her lines and swayed ever so slightly as the river current nudged her hull. Ready for instant departure, a full watch stood on her deck and a lookout was perched aloft. The mate approached Boltar and they conversed in hushed tones.

"All quiet?"

"Aye, as the grave. No sign of him yet."

Boltar swore softly and looked out over the rail to where a bare earthen path left the dock and disappeared among the trees. "We'll have to go and fetch him again. Get me a couple reliable hands and an extra cloak. There's a damp chill in the air this night."

"Aye, sir."

"And Dagmar? When's the last time the guard boat circled?"

"Beginning of this watch, sir."

"Send it down to the mouth again and have 'em report back before dawn. We've been here too long already and I'm getting more nervous by the day."

"Aye, sir."

With two men trailing behind, and his own boatcloak wrapped close to keep off the wet from overhanging branches, Boltar made his way carefully along the rutted path. After nearly a mile, he began to hear the sounds of music and rowdy laughter, and in a few moments more the path emerged from behind some screening bushes into the wood yard behind a small roadside tavern. Making his way around front, where noise and bright candle light spilled from curtainless windows, he motioned his two companions to wait, and pushed open the door.

A welcoming smell of strong drink and close-packed, unwashed bodies enveloped him like a fog. It was very late and the tavern showed the effects of thirty or so men who had obviously been at the business of serious drinking for some time. The tables were all awry and some had been knocked over. Empty cups and puddles of ale, and cloaks, and clothes, and not a few of their owners littered the floor, and at the remaining tables, the occupants sat and lolled at all angles, some still clutching mugs, others quietly sleeping. The bartender dozed with his head on his arms while the barmaid earned an extra fee in the back corner, and on a stool by the kitchen, a tired musician strummed listlessly on a lyre. Towards the center of the room, where the candles still burned, a group of three men sat relatively upright, while across the center of the room before them, another group of four played at skittles.

252

Among the latter was Thorngere, looking as wild and disheveled as a mad monk. As Boltar surveyed the room, a fight suddenly erupted among this group and the lot of them tumbled onto a table, swearing, kicking, and flailing. Boltar made his way to the still upright group of three and took a seat next to a large, red-bearded fellow who, with his scarred face and wild appearance, looked as relaxed and comfortable in these surroundings as an otter in a stream. This was Ragnar, leader of the local resistance, and a man whose twin passions in life were good drink and a good fight. Plainly sober after hours of effort and with a glint still in his eye, he nodded to Boltar.

"So, Boltar," he said, "I see you've come to fetch your lad again."

"And I see he's still at it." Both men watched coolly as one of the tousling party staggered past, driven backwards by a blow, blood spurting from his nose. He took several more steps, tangled with a chair and crashed to the floor where he lay, unwilling or unable to rise.

"Wilder than ever," declared Ragnar with a broad grin. "This is about the fifth fight tonight. I've never seen him like this before."

"Has he said anything?"

"Nope, sullen as a priest."

"It's got to be that woman."

"So you've said."

"But you don't believe it."

"Listen," said Ragnar, "I've known Thorngere near twenty years, and if there's one thing he always

253

had, it's women. I just can't imagine him getting upset over one."

"You haven't seen this one... And you didn't see how besotted he was with her. I never saw him like that, either."

"Yeah, well..."

"And he was fine all the way back from Dulcai. Then he goes to the palace and comes back raging like a madman to get underway. All the way here he doesn't come out of his cabin and ever since he's been drunk as Barnabus. What else could it be but that she jumped ship for the King?"

"Well, if so, he'll get over it. One hole's as deep as another—though I'll admit, some smell a tad sweeter," and Ragnar laughed raucously at his own joke. "You just give him his run and he'll come around."

"Easy for you to say. You don't have a ship sitting there in the river waiting for Tarpon to stumble on."

"Boltar, Boltar," said Ragnar, slapping the younger man on the back. "You sound like an old lady! Tarpon's not about to stick his nose up that river. We have an agreement, old Tarpon and I: he leaves us alone here in the delta country, and I don't kill him... At least, not for a while, eh? Ha ha ha! But you want to get your boy home to bed, and I must confess, I could use a bit of sleep myself. This ale wore off two hours ago. Thorngere!" he called, "Your nursemaid's here."

Climbing up from the floor where the fight had devolved into a stagnant wrestling match (one of the combatants had even fallen asleep), Thorngere stumbled over to the table. There was blood on his face and one of his bleary eyes was red and swollen. "Who?" he said, trying to lean on the table, but missing with one hand and almost falling.

"Your nursemaid, you sot," said Ragnar. "He's come to take you to bed."

"Why Boltar," said Thorngere, his hanging face breaking into a sloppy grin, "I never knew you felt that way. I guess I'd better keep my britches up when you're around, eh?"

"It's near dawn," said Boltar. "Don't you think you've had enough?"

"Am I standing?" Thorngere demanded of the room, then more particularly, "Ragnar, am I still standing?"

"Tall as an oak, my friend."

"Well, then, how can I have had enough? Inn keeper!" he yelled, waving his arm towards the kitchen and almost toppling in the process. "More ale here! I'm still standing and old Boltar wants to bugger me. You know, Boltar, I've seen that little rammer of yours. It may not be much of a tool, but you'll have to get me a lot drunker than this before you go trying to poke it up my arse."

Boltar ignored the slur and tried to be jovial in return. "Well, if you pass out here, you're liable to have that Innkeeper's daughter climbing on you, and that could be even worse!"

"Worse!" said Thorngere, looking around for the referenced lady, who was at that moment deftly picking the pocket of her late and now soundly

255

sleeping lover. "Why she's a flower! A verita... A ver... A vegetable flower!" and he headed off to pluck that very bouquet.

Boltar and Ragnar exchanged wry glances. They were obviously going to have to get physical if they wanted Thorngere out of there any time soon. But at that moment, the outside door banged open and three more of Boltar's crewmen entered, leading a wet and bedraggled girl.

"Beg pardon, Cap'n," said the leader, a bare-foot, bandy-legged seaman with arms like an ape, "we found this 'un crawlin' up the river bank and Dagmar said we should bring her right to you. She says she's from Dulcai."

From Dulcai or not, the girl was obviously not of common stock. Even in her current wretched condition—slimy, mud-encrusted, shivering like she had the plague and plainly exhausted—she was still a beauty with long golden tresses, deep blue eyes and a body that was only too visible through her sodden, flimsy clothes. Quickly, Boltar offered her the extra cloak and she wrapped herself in it gratefully.

"What's your name, girl?" he asked.

"Eomer," she said, her eyes calm despite her condition.

"Eomer!" said Thorngere, crossing the room quickly, and sobering visibly with every step. Stopping before her, he peered intently at the girl. "It is you! Well met, my lady," he said, and bowed almost gracefully. "Boltar, how soon can we get under way?"

"As soon as we're aboard, my lord. Why...?

"Because, Boltar, and you, too, Ragnar, I have the honor of presenting you to Her Royal Highness, Eomer, Daughter of King Reuters and Princess of Dulcai!"

Glaucon stood by the rail of the new triple decker, Valadator, flagship of the Zagorbian fleet, sipping wine from a golden goblet and watching her former master, Tarpon, board his gig to be rowed ashore. It was amazing, he thought, how effective a simple bit of parchment and a presumptive air could be. There had not been the slightest hitch in his little scheme, and as evening settled down over the city, he was now the contented master of some forty prime warships and an army of nearly five-thousand men. This and the fleet sailing up from Dulcai would give him overwhelming force, and he would crush this Valerius like a fly.

And it had been so easy!—not that it should not have been; he was duly authorized, after all. But to effect a coup like that! Ah, it was exhilarating. He had simply boarded the Valadator, marched to her quarterdeck, ordered the captain to assemble the crew, and in Fantar's name, read himself in as commander pro tem of the fleet. A copy of his orders, complete with Fantar's official seal, was sent to Tarpon in the palace, along with a note inviting him to dinner aboard the flagship on the night following.

It had been that easy. The dinner was a beastly, frigid affair, of course, as could only be expected when two men in mortal loathing of each other were forced to sit face to face in icy politeness over pate' and roast goose. But that was over now, and the fleet was his. Orders had been issued, and even as darkness grew, torches by the thousands lit up the harbor as the last men and material boarded ship for an early departure.

Yes, thought Glaucon, it had been a most satisfying two days—except for the loss of the girl, which really wouldn't matter now, anyway—and as Tarpon's boat cleared away and began pulling for the shore, Glaucon raised his cup in a silent farewell toast to its chief occupant, then went below to work out his orders for the attack on the hidden cavern.

In the boat, meanwhile, the effectively deposed Tarpon was in an entirely different frame of mind. It had not at all been a satisfying two days for him. As if losing control of one's fleet was not humiliation enough, to have to surrender it to a cowardly lick-spittle like Glaucon was added salt in the wound. Not that there was any choice in the matter. Fantar's orders were clear enough— Glaucon was authorized to use "whatever means" he deemed necessary—and the Emperor's seal was genuine enough—he had gotten several opinions on that. But for the bugger to simply waltz in and take over without so much as a 'by your leave,' and then be required to sit there and make nicy-nice with him over dinner... Garh! It was enough to make a man contemplate murder.

But he was too slick to fall for that, Glaucon was. Too slick for his own fucking good! But this was not over, Tarpon vowed. There would be another day, another opportunity. Glaucon was not the only one with influence at court, not the only one who could use "whatever means." That fleet would have to come back some time.

Frothing inwardly at the bitterness of his humiliation, Tarpon clutched tight to the gunnels of the launch as it danced in the light evening chop of the harbor. He had never been much of a sailor, Tarpon hadn't; had never liked the smell or even the sight of the sea, and even now his stomach was beginning to feel a bit queasy. Of course, that bloody goose didn't help; greasy as a lard bucket and only half cooked... Bah! It was enough to make a man sick. Of course Glaucon probably knew that, the bastard.

So Tarpon was very grateful when the launch finally bumped against the dock and he was free to climb out onto solid ground once more. Still, his stomach would not behave, and as he climbed into his sedan chair, his bowels sent warning that he had better drive his bearers double quick back to the palace if he didn't want to embarrass himself in public. Under the vicious lash of his tongue, they ran more than double quick—which jolted the chair and his stomach something fearful—and when they got to the palace, he ran, too, and barely made it to his private commode before his bowels exploded in a messy, stinking, stomach wrenching bout if diarrhea.

It was not unusual for greasy foods to have such an effect on him, but as the night wore on, the diarrhea and nausea continued. He began to fear he had contracted some other bug, and as he lay sweating and cramping in the dark, he thought he would have to cancel the hunt he had planned for the morrow. Just the thought of jouncing up and down on a horse set him off again and he squatted once more over a chamber pot that had not yet been cleaned from the previous bout.

It was not a good night for Tarpon. The nausea, cramping and sweating grew and as the hours of darkness wore away, the frequency of diarrhea increased. Finally, as it neared dawn and he squatted yet again with trembling limbs and a rectum so sore it bled, the nausea overcame him and he hurled the contents of his stomach all over the floor and down the front of himself. Only then, when he saw to his horror that it was mostly blood, did he realize the truth. Enraged, he crawled to the window, and clinging with slimy, fouled hands to the sill, tried to scream out into the near dawn at the fleet which was even then raising anchor in the harbor. But the blood and bile bubbled up again, choking off his voice, and he gagged and vomited wretchedly, the cramps felling him like a blow. Dropping to his knees, he coughed and gurgled, bright blood drizzling down onto his crooked hands. Then, eyes staring, he pitched forward, dead, his face splashing into his own filthy muck.

By constant attention to the set of his sails, and by putting the crew to their oars the moment the wind slackened, Thorngere made excellent time from Zagorbia. After the second day, his hangover began to dissipate and, except for a dull, sinking feeling at times, and a certain area of thought he would not allow himself to enter, he began to feel some of his former energy return. If he did not think about Vahla, he told himself, everything would be all right. If he saw her there, so be it. It was like death in battle; not a thing one sought, but not always possible to avoid. You simply dealt with the fear and fought on. The rest was in the Gods' hands. That was how a warrior behaved.

But late in the afternoon of the second day, the winds fell completely calm. Thorngere set the men to their oars again, but when it hadn't picked up again by dusk, he let them rest. All through the night the Elusive lay becalmed, drifting aimlessly with the current. In the morning, it remained calm and a light mist clung to the surface of the sea. The sun rose hot and baked the decks as it slowly burned the mist away. Occasionally, little cats' paws of wind would come dancing over the water and Elusive's sail would flutter and fill, and she would start to gather way, only to have the sail flag again and hang as the puff passed by.

Thorngere put the men to their oars, and paced the deck as they forced the ship's bluff bows slowly southwards. It was difficult not to think under such circumstances and he was glad at last when the girl, Eomer, came on deck. It had been some years since he had known her in Dulcai. Then she had been a scrawny child with a yellow braid, racing about the courtyard of her father's palace, and it was surprising how she had matured. She was dressed now in some rough seamen's garb, her own clothes having been ruined, but even so, it was very clear she had become a beautiful woman.

They stood by the rail and chatted idly, waiting for wind. The girl was very reserved—he was not sure she trusted him as yet—and had little to offer in the way of information. Apparently, she had been locked in her cabin most of the time and knew nothing of Glaucon's plans. Of why she jumped in the sea, she wouldn't speak and he didn't press. Some things did not need explaining to be clear. Instead, he told her of the Hidden Valley of Kantar, and of the Kudanim and Queen Salonis, and of course, of Valerius. He did not mention Vahla.

It was pleasant there in the morning sun, under a brilliant blue sky with the last tendrils of mist rising up from the sea and the ship's motion just enough to generate a fresh, salt-scented breeze, and he was glad of her company. There was something soothing about her quiet demeanor, something in her beauty and simple dignity, that took his mind away from that heavy, empty spot inside himself and made it easier not to think, and he was grateful for it. He was not a reflective man, but the contrast of her youth and beauty with the hard experiences of his own life gave him pause. It was not that he felt old next to her, or young either, for that matter; that was not the thing. Rather, he felt stalwart, strong and tested; protective. He had fought long and hard for many years, but in seeing the freshness and vitality of her youth, he began to feel there was a continuity in things, a purpose. In this clear, youthful face, these calm blue-gray eyes, he glimpsed a future—not for himself, that was not it, either—but for everyone. It was as if, embodied in this lovely girl, was that future they were all working for. In her he saw hope, a glimpse of that ideal Valeria that Valerius spoke of.

Or maybe it was just that standing at the rail of a good ship on a sunny morning in the company of a beautiful girl would make even the most decrepit of creatures feel hopeful. In any event, he had mixed feelings when the wind suddenly freshened and put an end to their chat.

But he was not disappointed to be moving again. A sense of urgency had been growing in him since he first saw the girl at the tavern and it now drove him relentlessly. As the wind rose, he kept the men rowing until their oars nearly knocked them from their benches, and later, when the wind rose to a near gale and the spray lifted from the white caps and dashed across the slanting deck, he refused also to reef. The Elusive galloped along under wind torn clouds, her rig strained and bent, her deck rearing, and her bows slamming into the backs of seas and tossing up blizzards of spray. Still, it was not until after dark that he reached the cavern, and with a heavy sea crashing against the base of the cliffs and the tide running against him, he did not dare attempt the entrance and was forced to lay off shore until dawn.

At first glimmer, however, he pushed Elusive's nose into the dark tunnel and with himself holding the lantern in her bows, strained his eyes for the light at the end. But when it came, it brought with it a shock: the river, all the quays along the bank, and the camp beyond were empty. Valerius' fleet was gone. Vaulting from the rail before the ship even touched the dock, Thorngere raced for the palace.

Koltar was having breakfast with Salonis in the sunny morning room next to her private suite in the palace. She had not been well again and was stretched on a small couch by the window, the morning sun spilling over the white shawl that covered her. Koltar sat on a chair beside her, trying to coax her to eat. But she had other things on her mind.

"You'll simply have to face it, you know," she said, her voice strong but raspy.

Koltar put the spoon back in the bowl and set it on the table beside the couch. If she would not eat, there was no making her. "I will agree that it's a theoretical possibility," he replied patiently, "but my dear Salonis, you're a young woman yet."

"Nonsense, Koltar!" the Queen snapped, showing some of her old fire. "I'm old enough to be your mother. In fact, I was older than your mother. And don't patronize me!"

"I apologize... But all I'm saying is that you just need some rest and nourishment. You've been pushing yourself too hard."

"Koltar, I've seen enough death in my time to recognize my own. You're the one who has to face up to the truth: you're going to be king around here before too long."

Koltar looked like he had just been condemned to hang and he shook his head involuntarily. "I'm not sure I can, Salonis... I mean, I know I can. I've known all my life I would have to. But I just can't... I can't be like you."

"You don't have to be like me. You have to be like you."

"That's just the problem, don't you see? I'm... I'm an oddball, Salonis! I've never been comfortable in public and I can't deal with people. I'm a scholar, a loner. I study things and invent things. To be king I have to command people, I have to... I just don't know if I'll be able to do it, that's all."

"Koltar, listen to me," said the Queen. "I have known you since you were a boy, and yes, you are a scholar and an inventor, and yes, you are shy with people. But you are also the most brilliant man of your generation—perhaps of many generations. No one else among our people has invented so much, studied so much. And who was it, Lord Koltar, who marched out between two armies and killed the Iblis, Chubar, in single combat?"

"I fought, yes, but it was the will of Kala Atar that I survived."

"I will not deny the God's will. But my point is that you set your mind to a task and you accomplished it. And I'm telling you that if you will but set your mind to it again, you will be a brilliant king as well. I am sure of it."

Koltar had never in his life heard such praise, especially from such a haughty personage as Queen Salonis. Nor had he ever considered himself as anything other than a recluse, an oddball, one who did what he did not because he was special, but because he could not do other things—like fit in with his fellows. Now, he did not know what to say and looked at her blankly.

At that moment, the door burst open and a breathless Thorngere rushed in, followed closely by the two helpless Guardsmen whose job it was to keep people out.

"Koltar!" Thorngere yelled as he came, but then, seeing the Queen, he became befuddled and began bowing and stammering apologies.

"And good morning to you, Lord Thorngere," returned the Queen. She was delighted at his discomfiture and laughed aloud. "Would you like some breakfast? Here, Koltar, see if you can feed our friend Thorngere some of this ghastly porridge!"

"No. No thank you, Ma'am. I'm sorry. They told me Koltar was here and I didn't realize..."

"Not at all, Thorngere. Not at all. We are delighted to see you again. But you have obviously come on urgent business... Please, tell us what it is."

"The king, Valerius, where is he?"

"You don't know?"

"No, I've been in the north."

"Why, he sailed with his army to attack Dulcai."

266

Forgetting protocol, Thorngere dropped onto a chair like he'd been felled by a blow. "Listen," he said, "I've got Reuters' daughter with me in the Elusive. This fight doesn't have to be! When did they leave?"

"Two days since."

Thorngere groaned ""Oh, Gods! There's no way I can catch them."

"Hold on there, just a minute," said Koltar, speaking up for the first time. "Just how far is it to Dulcai?" His tone was calculating.

"Near a hundred and seventy leagues. Even with a good wind, it takes me four plus days to get there. Valerius will be there by tomorrow."

"Umhmmm," said Koltar, working figures out in his head. "Umhmmm. There may just be something we can do. Would you excuse us, please, Your Majesty? I'd like to show Thorngere a little project I've had in hand down by the river."

267

Chapter 16
THE BATTLE OF DULCAI

Under the hot, forenoon sun, Valerius paced the quarterdeck of Caladon, his flagship. To leeward, he could see Reuters, with Blumholt at his side, standing on his quarterdeck, not more than a hundred yards away. They were that close, and had been for several hours now, yet between them ran two insurmountable barriers. One was the dog-legged sand spit that guarded the entrance to the Bay of Dulcai, and the other was the sudden, yet incontrovertible fact of enmity. Old friends, confidants, and would-be allies, Reuters and Valerius now stood face to face with their fleets arrayed against one another.

This was exactly what Valerius had hoped to avoid. All the way south from the Hidden Valley, he had driven his ships with the hope that matters would not come to a confrontation: that either Thorngere had been wrong in his assessment of Fantar's influence in Dulcai, or that Reuters would rise above personal considerations and join forces with him. But how could he expect a man to sacrifice his daughter on a cause as seemingly hopeless as this? That a motley band of two-thousand odd rebels and a few war galleys could topple Fantar's empire? The very thought was absurd. And for such a price? One's own flesh and blood? Valerius had last seen Reuters' daughter some two years before, a gawky fifteen year-old; bright, vivacious, and obviously adored by her father. She was even then, Reuters said, the very image of her late mother and it was plain to Valerius that her image was all the substance Reuters lived for. If she was in Fantar's hands, was there any doubt of her fate should Reuters join in the rebellion? None whatsoever. So was it any surprise that Reuters, flanked by a dozen or so of Fantar's black hulled galleys, and with Fantar's minion by his side, now stood across that implacable spit of sand, on a hostile deck? Only in the way it happened.

"I'd still like to know what tipped him off," Grumwald growled as Valerius stalked by. They had made excellent time sailing down the coast. While the winds north of the Hidden Valley had been fluky and calm, south of the cavern they had been steady and strong, blowing clean out of the northwest and never slacking from one dawn to the next. The sails of his fleet, once set, were never touched. Nor were the oars as the thirty odd galleys and assorted transports flew along the cliff-backed coast and into the hot, southern waters of Dulcai. But as they came abreast of the bay, with the distant white speck of the city in sight among brown sandy hills, and began traversing the long, ten-mile sand spit that guarded the entrance, they were met by a surprising sight. Just as they approached the channel entrance from the open sea, so, fully manned and under oars, did Reuters' fleet approach from the inside. Both fleets reached the channel at the same moment and here they stood, fully armed and arrayed, yet unable to advance against one another.

Only the channel was open between them, and this was so narrow that it would admit but one ship at a time. For either fleet to try and force the passage and mount an attack in single file would be worse than folly: it would be suicide. So after an initial bristling of spears, a few ineffectual flights of arrows (mostly aimed at Fantar's galleys), and much hurling of threats back and forth across the sand, the two fleets had subsided into a stand-off which had now been grinding on for several hours.

"He probably had lookouts stationed up the coast," Valerius answered on the next turn.

Of the two fleets, Valerius' was in the far more precarious position. While Reuters was in an ideal defensive position—in protected waters and in his own front yard to boot—Valerius was anchored in open sea, off a lee shore, and was some five hundred miles from his base of operations. The wind had only to blow a bit harder to make his position untenable. Had he been able to reach the protection of the bay, he would have been able to control events: Reuters would either have had to attack to drive him out, or negotiate. As it was now, however, Valerius' hand was forced: he must either attack, or sail ignominiously away.

"What we ought to do, then," said Grumwald, "is sail up the coast, take out those lookouts, then sneak back at night."

"That's a thought," said Valerius, still pacing. "But I doubt it would gain us much." There were probably several posts, he thought, and if they didn't see any on the way down, how would they find them all on the way back? And if he knew Reuters, he would wait for an all clear signal before standing down from the channel. So a sail up the coast would probably find them right back here on the morrow, in exactly the same position. Except that maybe a storm would blow in by then and beach them all.

"How about landing a force on the south shore and marching on the city overland?" Grumwald was persistent. As Valerius paced, he stood spread-legged on the rolling deck, his battle cap tucked under his arm and his wild gray hair blowing about his face.

"Well, that has more possibilities," said Valerius, stopping at last to discuss the matter and regretting he did not have Colinus and his swift horse archers, "but I'm afraid it still won't do. It would only send a weaker force to do what we brought an army for. And it wouldn't help us force the channel. That's our main problem: we can't stay here. Do you suppose there's any way we could get two ships through the channel abreast?"

"At high tide, maybe. But now, with the ebb running like this, the current would knock 'em about and they'd run afoul of each other. That would be worse than running 'em through one at a time."

"Ummm, you're right. But if we wait till this afternoon's flood, we'll have wind and tide working with us and against them..."

"Aye. We can bunch the fleet like a ram and smash our way through!"

"Can you think of any other options?"

"Unless you want to send a party out to dig a new harbor, the only spot to land along this coast is right through that channel."

"Then that is where we will go."

Through the rest of the morning the two fleets faced each other in eerie silence. And as if melded with their wooden timbers, the fleets' principals faced each other, too. Valerius, flanked by Grumwald, stood his deck, and Reuters, with the obese Blumholt at his side like a great black sheep dog, stood on his. The four faced each other, silent, grim-faced, and immobile, staring at each other as the long minutes ticked by and the tide slowly drained from the bay. At last, slack tide came and the sand spit stood high between them like a wall. Noon came and went. Then, ever so slowly, the reeds along the southern, inner shore began to twitch and bend towards the east. In another hour, the flood was streaming strong back into the bay, and the wind, which had been steady all morning, began its afternoon rise. White caps flecked the deep blue of the sea and beyond the spit, wavelets ruffled the bay.

"We'll take the van, Grumwald." Valerius announced, resuming motion like a statue suddenly imbued with life. "Signal the fleet to close tight behind us."

"Aye sir."

One by one, Valerius' ships hoisted their great stone anchors, and under oars alone, backed away from the beach to begin forming a long double line behind the king. On his side, Reuters, too, began shifting his fleet to meet the imminent and obvious attack. His ships, with his own foremost, were arrayed in groups of three—each pair from Dulcai shepherded by one of Fantar—and poised like wedges to drive into the flank of Valerius' line as it cleared the channel.

But all this took time—there being nothing hasty about ancient naval warfare, except death when it came—and it was nearly another hour before the players were all in place and the stage set. The flood was running strong now and Valerius stood just outside the channel, his crew backing oars continually to hold position while the fleet lined up behind. To his left and just a half ship's length behind, was Christoban of Telos. Behind him and to his right was Zimlait of Cobanos, and then Gainor and Dimurnal. Behind them came the second group under Daemon of Palmania and the third under Eban of Durumkae. In the rear, carrying extra troops, siege equipment and supplies, were the transports. Together, they were all that was left of an old order, and if they survived, would provide the seeds for a new.

Valerius stood with his arm poised above his head and his eye on the lookout perched aloft. As soon as the line was complete, he would drop his arm, signalling the advance. Sails would drop from their yards, oars would churn and the attack would begin. But it was not yet. The last few ships were still jostling for position and the rest were holding their collective breath when, suddenly, the lookout glanced to the north and sang out. "Deck there. Sail ho."

It was Thorngere, soaring down the wind like a falcon. Soaking wet from flying spray, he stood at the tiller of Koltar's latest contraption. High on the windward rail, three equally wet Kantaran crewmen sat with their feet hanging over the side, and beside him, braced against the jolting waves and with her long, honey-colored hair plastered to her head and shoulders, stood Eomer, daughter of Dulcai.

It had been a wild ride. Koltar's solution to the stability problem with this fore and aft rig had been to widen the boat. He had done this in a peculiar but highly serendipitous manner by taking two smaller, fully enclosed hull forms—pontoons, actually—and building a bridge deck across them. He had also thought to lengthen the flow path of the wind on the sail by extending his gaff and sail forward and down till it nearly touched the deck forward. Experiment showed that with this configuration, the lower boom was unnecessary (in fact, it constrained the natural, wind-formed shape of the sail) so he ended with a large, loose-footed lateen sail suspended from the long sloping yard.

Though he had no inkling beforehand, the result of these experiments was a sailing craft that could outrun a horse and was, in all probability, the fastest means of transportation mankind had yet devised. On it, Thorngere and crew had made the near five-hundred mile trip from the Hidden Valley to Dulcai in just under thirty hours, reaching speeds unheard of in that age. Unlike normal craft which sat deep in the water and effectively plowed their way through it when sailing, this kattumaram design, as Koltar called it, skimmed across the top of the water. Thus there was no impediment to its ultimate speed, and with its new, more efficient rig, it fairly flew.

But it was not a comfortable ride. Koltar's kattumaram was only a small prototype, less than twenty feet in length and totally open on deck. There was nowhere to hide from the spray which continually flew across the deck, nowhere to sleep without risk of being suddenly tossed overboard as the craft bounced from wave to wave, nowhere to cook, and nowhere to secure even the slightest amount of privacy. So it was a wet, beaten, and bedraggled crew that soared down with the wind, and by the time they reached the upper end of the Bay, Thorngere was near collapse. As the afternoon winds had increased, the strange craft had lifted its windward pontoon right out of the water and accelerated to even greater speeds than before. Even with his sheet eased and the weight of his three crewmen to counterbalance the wind, it was all Thorngere could do to keep the thing upright and under control. The sight of the two fleets braced him, however, and as they careened towards them, he gritted his teeth in a broad grin.

Valerius stood open-mouthed, watching the strange craft approach, his arm still suspended in the air. The eyes of both fleets were on it, in fact, as it tore across the sea. Never had they seen anything of man sail so fast! It moved like a gull that swoops down from the sky and skims across the wave tops, looking for fish. Down the wind it tore, travelling at three, even four times the speed of a normal craft, and tossing up sheet upon sheet of spray like a stone sent skipping across the sea. From the time it was first spotted as a small white dot on the horizon it was only a few minutes until it was hull up, and then a few more until the figures on deck began to resolve from the spray.

As he recognized Thorngere, Valerius moved to the rail and waved. Thorngere waved back, wildly, but did not steer towards Valerius' ship. Straight towards the channel he ran, right for the slot between the two fleets poised for slaughter. Valerius looked, then looked again, at the girl clinging to Thorngere's arm. Soaking wet, with her tangled hair lashing about, and her rough sailor's clothes flapping about like wet drapes, she looked familiar to him and yet not. Either way, he thought her the most beautiful woman he had ever seen.

For his part, Reuters had no trouble recognizing the girl. Turning immediately, he drew a short sword from his belt and drove it up into Blumholt's throat. The blade ripped through the man's vocal cords, then severed his brain stem, and like a puppet whose strings have been suddenly snipped, the big man collapsed in a heap, his venting lungs spraying the air with blood.

"Rally to me!" Reuters shouted, waving his bloody sword in the air. "Rally to me! Dulcai to Valeria! Dulcai to Valeria!" And ordering his ship spun around, he rammed the galley of Fantar on his beam. Reacting quickly to this unmistakable signal, his other captains moved to attack their unwelcome guests, and in moments those fierce guard dogs turned into yelping curs.

When Valerius saw Blumholt fall, he too signalled the attack. As one, thirty sails sprouted from their yards, and as one, six-hundred pairs of oars dug into the sea, and for the first time in a generation, a battle fleet under the flag of Valeria drove into the fray. Aided by wind and tide, they burst through the channel and quickly meshed with the opposing fleet. But it was no longer Reuters' ships that were the object of attack. In that instant of recognition, the sides had shifted. Near enemies were now allies again, and the forces of Fantar, so confident in their numbers and position only moments before, now turned and fled for their lives.

But it was no contest. Outnumbered now by more than four to one, Fantar's squadron's only thought was escape. Half of their number were rammed or boarded immediately by ships closing in from both sides, but still, another half-dozen broke free and raced off in the only direction open to them: back towards Dulcai. Sensing their intent, but with his own ship still engaged, Reuters pointed and yelled to the passing Valerius, "Don't let them reach the city! They'll barricade themselves in the palace and we'll pay hell to get them out!"

"Good to see you again, Reuters!" Valerius yelled back and the two men exchanged broad grins before he raced on in pursuit of the black hulled interlopers.

Though they lived under an oppressive regime and worked essentially as slaves, the shipwrights of Palmeria were still masters of their trade. And when Fantar sent this squadron south under Glaucon, he picked for it his newest and fastest ships. So by the time Valerius and a dozen of his ships were able to dodge and swerve their way through the melee to begin their pursuit in earnest, their foe had already put a mile of clear water between them. It was a ten mile run up the bay to Dulcai, and though Grumwald stormed and swore, and the men pulled for all they were worth, it soon became apparent to Valerius that he would not close the gap before Fantar's ships reached the city. Truth be told, the gap was even getting wider. But he did not speak aloud of this. Rather, he paced his deck and summoned to mind the layout of Reuters' palace and the lay of every street leading up to it.

He had quite forgotten Thorngere and his strange craft, when the white flash of its triangular sail suddenly caught his eye as it zipped by. Thorngere was still at the helm with the girl beside him (straining forward intently, their yellow hair bright against the blue of the bay, they looked like twin statues carved of gold), but the three crewmen had now clustered their weight as far aft as possible as the thing skittered along before the wind like a stick flung onto a frozen pond. Valerius stood at the rail and watched them pass. His own ship, he reckoned, was moving at a good ten knots. Thorngere had to be moving at twice that speed, so quickly did he cross Valerius' stern and dash off in a wide arc around the northern flank of the fleeing enemy. But where was he going? In moments, the odd little boat was reduced to a white speck heading for the upper reaches of the bay and Valerius, feeling suddenly very slow and stodgy on his proud flagship, was left with only his thoughts.

Even with the tide pushing him, it took the better part of an hour for Valerius' leading ships to reach the city. And as he rounded the spit of land that provided a breakwater for Duclai's inner harbor, he fully expected to find Fantar's galleys secured to the town docks and their crew in possession of Reuters' fortress like palace. But that was not the case at all. He saw Fantar's ships all right, but they were not docked and they were not what first caught his eye. What he first saw was the little white, triangular sail of Thorngere's kattumaram flapping unattended as the tiny boat bobbed against a pier, and behind it, a black, roiling mass of townspeople, armed with forks, sticks, rocks, and spears—whatever came to hand—surging against the docks and preventing Fantar's men from landing. At their forefront, his own sword glinting in the sun and with the brilliant blond girl at his side, stood Thorngere himself.

Fantar's ships had apparently already tried to force a landing and had been beaten off, as they were now beginning to pull away from the docks, leaving the waters around them flecked with bodies. But not even the master shipwrights of Palmeria could save them now. Valerius' little battle fleet quickly cut off any possibility of escape, then moved in to board.

Valerius' own Caladon, with the Royal banner of Valeria fluttering at its peak, was first to grapple with an enemy. The two ships ground together, the grapnels were thrown and with a great shout the King himself, the brilliant red Eye glittering on his chest, leapt with his boarding party across the midships rail and onto the enemy's catwalk. But here was a curious thing: there was no one to fight. To be sure, the decks were crowded with armed warriors and below, the benches were crammed with chained and gasping slaves, but no one offered any resistance. As Valerius stormed up the catwalk, a raging Grumwald at his side, the enemy laid their swords on the deck in submission.

It was the last thing he expected. Still, giving quarter in that age was a thing unknown, especially among enemies as bitter as these. When you fought, you won, you fled, or you died. It was as simple as that. But now, raising his sword to strike a man down, he caught sight of the fellow's face and froze in mid stroke. He was a young man, hardly more than a boy from Valerius' perspective, and though he was plainly terrified, he made no move to resist or avoid his fate. Rather, he knelt trembling, his eyes shut tight and his head bowed, his lips mouthing a silent prayer. This was an enemy? Valerius lowered his sword. He could not strike. Nor did those around him, and in moments, fighting stopped on the other ships as well. After the crash and roar of the ships' joining, and the screams of attacking foes, a sudden silence descended on the scene. Even the townspeople, crowding the docks and cheering like mad spectators at the cockpits, fell suddenly still and stared at this strange tableau.

Recovering his wits, Valerius pushed past the young crewman and moved on towards the ship's quarterdeck. As he went, man after man knelt before him until he reached the ship's captain, a grizzled, professional veteran. This man still held his sword and Valerius tightened his grip on his own. But the man offered it out, hilt first, and knelt before him.

"Majesty," the man said, "I have done my duty as my lord commanded. Now all hope is gone and we give ourselves up to you. If you are the great Valerius, scion of that ancient name, I ask that you grant us your mercy."

Valerius looked about at the kneeling figures around him and for the first time in the near twenty years which had passed since the fall of Valeria, saw a different face on his enemy. These were not the brigands and bandits that had burned their way around the Inland Sea. These were the sons of those towns, conscripted or simply serving their state.

Always before he had seen Fantar's face in every man he fought. Now he saw a new face, a new generation, and understood for the first time what Volkmir meant when he said the tide had turned. He meant the tide of time. Taking the proffered sword from the kneeling captain, Valerius bade him rise, and the crowds on the nearby docks burst into cheers.

The tangled ships were soon warped alongside the docks and a gangplank was laid. With due pomp, and attended by Grumwald and an honor guard, Valerius stepped ashore. This was a strange and heady thing for him, to play for the first time the role of royal conqueror. He had trod this very dockside many times before, as the warrior, Balazar, and even as an untried, unrecognized King Valerius, seeking succor from Reuters. But never had he landed as Valerius, High King, and never had the people, like his enemies, knelt down before him. He stood totally overwhelmed for several seconds, then rushed over to Thorngere and raised him up.

"Thorngere, my brother, never this! It is I who should be kneeling before you after that little rescue. Where did you get that craft? Never mind, I can already guess the answer to that. But tell me, who is this young lady whose mere appearance can change the fate of nations?"

"Your Majesty," said Thorngere, "allow me to present Eomer, Princess of Dulcai."

282

"Surely," said Valerius, though he knew full well the answer to the question he was about to ask, "this is not the same Eomer I last saw chasing a hoop in her father's courtyard?"

The girl blushed deeply and dropped her eyes, but Thorngere continued, "And if any rescuing was done, it was she who did it. She rallied the people here. I merely provided the means of transportation."

"Then, Princess Eomer of Dulcai," said Valerius, looking down at the girl, "Valeria is in your debt."

"It was your name," the girl said softly.

"I beg your pardon?"

"It was your name that rallied the people, Your Majesty," she said looking up at him with eyes so clear and deep that his own lost focus for a moment and felt a rush of dizziness. The noise of the crowd fell away and for a time—he could never say how long—there were only those eyes, holding his. "They knew me, but it was you they followed."

"Oh, I don't know about that, Princess," said Valerius. "I think I'd fight through fifty ships to know you better." Then, realizing what he had said, he flushed deeply and looked quickly about for something to cover his embarrassment.

Fortunately, at that moment, Reuters was hurrying along the dock from where his own ship had just landed. Rushing up to them, he snatched his daughter up, and with exclamations of joy, gave her a huge hug. Turning to Thorngere, he shook his hand vigorously, then gave him a hug, too. "My friend," he said, tears streaming down his cheeks, "you have given me back my life!"

Thorngere grinned awkwardly, but said nothing and in the sudden silence, Reuters seemed to realize that Valerius was standing there, looking suddenly very solemn and very stern. He turned to him and met his eye, then looked away, then forced himself to meet his eye again. "What can I say to you, my friend?" he said, "except that I was very glad to stick that pig Blumholt when I did."

"I think you may say," said Valerius, "that it was the strongest blow yet struck on behalf of the new Valeria."

"Then I am doubly glad of it," said King Reuters, "for it was struck on behalf of Dulcai."

"Is that not the crux of a true alliance?" asked Valerius, his eye beginning to twinkle.

"It is, indeed," said Reuters, and breaking into broad grins, the two men clasped hands and the crowd once more broke into cheers.

"But tell me, Reuters, how did you manage to man your fleet so quickly as to meet us at the channel? You had us in a real tricky spot there."

Suddenly the smile dropped from Reuters' face. "I did not man my fleet to meet you, Valerius," he said, "at least not at the channel. We were sailing north to join Glaucon and attack you in your lair."

Chapter 17
THE WALLS OF KANTAR

Valadator had a very uneasy motion in the swell and Glaucon, along with a large number of her military contingent, was feeling the effects. He and his fleet had been standing hove to outside the Hidden Cavern, waiting for Reuters, since late the previous afternoon and during the night, a long greasy swell had set in from the west—no doubt the remains of some distant storm at sea—and having no way on to steady her, and with her huge mast unstepped and lashed along her deck the night before, the ship had taken on a slow, corkscrewing motion which had sent even some of her blue-water crewmen to hang over the rail. Now, as a grey, sunless dawn filtered down from the towering cliffs and there was still no sign of Reuters coming up from the south, Glaucon faced a decision: he could continue to wait, or he could attack with the forces he had.

If he had not been so sick, waiting would have been the favored choice. Though he was fairly confident of superiority, he really had no idea what he would have to face once inside that cavern, and above all, he had a mortal dread of sailing into that black maw. Since his earliest youth he had had a terror of confined spaces and the thought of crawling in under all those thousands of feet of solid rock made his knees weak and his bowels churn. If

Reuters were here, he would at least be able to send him in first—the honor of the point, and all that—but without him, that honor belonged to no one but himself, and he really feared he might embarrass himself in the process.

But how long could he wait? If the other ships were anything like this, his army was getting sicker and weaker by the minute and already some of the men were looking questioningly in his direction. How long before those looks turned into questioning words? How long before they began to question his courage? He was, after all, an unknown entity to most of them. What would happen if he lost their trust? And finally, how long would the sea let him wait? As the day lightened, it was clear that the remains of the distant storm were neither distant nor remnant. Dark, solid masses of cloud were filling in from the west, and the wind was beginning to gust up in fearful little rips. A storm on this coast and with no sea room under his lee could put his whole fleet on the rocks, and with it, his own vain dreams.

No, he thought, studying that lowering sky, Reuters or no, cavern or no, he really had no choice. He had to attack.

But the decision was not the real obstacle. As Valadator neared the cavern entrance, and Glaucon's throat constricted tighter and tighter, it became apparent there might be another problem. His ship might not fit. He had sent one of the smaller craft inshore the night before to measure the cavern and they had reported there was breadth and

286

height enough for Valadator. But now, as the great ship edged in against the outflowing tide, and with Glaucon running from side to side and her helmsmen working constantly to steady the ship against the following sea, it suddenly became clear they had reckoned without her sweeps. Her hull would fit, yes, but her oars would be pinned to her sides like the wings of a dragonfly.

"All back! Oars aback!" Glaucon screamed just as the first bank was about to strike. Like clockwork, all three tiers—one hundred and eighty oars in all—reversed direction and dug hard into the tide churned sea. The ship halted in her course and then, imperceptibly at first, began to back away. But just as her great thrusting beak was clearing the entrance, a rogue wave rose up astern and slapped hard on her blunt transom. A ton of cold seawater sluiced over the rail, soaking Glaucon, and for just the briefest moment, knocking the steersman off balance. He lost his grip and the rudder slammed back hard against the ship. This was unfortunate, for with the tide pushing the bow out and the sea pushing the stern in, the ship suddenly slewed around broadside to the sea and the next wave lifted her up and slammed her against the rocks directly across the cavern mouth.

Nor was this all. Caught unawares, and propelled by the same forces, the next ship in line bore down on Valadator and only just swerved aside in time, her wicked, bronze-sheathed ram just grazing Valadator's exposed belly. This ship, too, then broached in the following sea and was thrown broadside against her huge consort, grinding the oars between the two hulls to splinters.

Miraculously, neither ship was seriously damaged. Floating free on the outflowing tide and quickly putting some sea room between themselves and the cliffs, a quick inspection showed only minor damage to Valadator's stern castle and a few galley slaves killed or maimed by their oar looms. Glaucon, however, was seriously shaken, and it was some time before he was again able to summon the courage to order his ship back into the cavern. And when he did, it was under tow with two galleys in line before him and a third to guide his stern from behind. Still, as the blackness of the cavern closed about him (with that wet, slimy ceiling so close over his head) he had the thought that perhaps this was not the lair of Valerius at all, but the road to hell.

That Koltar was aware of this approaching fleet was little comfort. No sooner had Boltar and the Elusive disappeared southward in Thorngere's wake than the lookouts on the cliffs spotted the fleet's approach. For a time they hoped vainly that it would pass by, and when it didn't, they sent the word down. And they had counted them, too, several times during the evening and morning that followed, and Koltar had done the arithmetic in his head and knew he was facing a force his tiny people could not possibly cope with. The question was— and he put it so to the high council which was convened that evening in the great hall—should they try?

Valencius, the grizzled commander of the army, rose to answer. "My Lord," he said, "We have fought our entire lives to regain this city, and I believe I can speak for all here when I say that we would rather die now than surrender it again."

"Hear, hear!" said the room, and Koltar nodded in assent.

"Furthermore, My Lord," Valencius continued, "these are not just our enemies. They are the enemies of King Valerius, and I, for one, would rather die than forsake him!"

"Hear, hear," said the room, louder than before.

"And finally, My Lord, I submit that we are not helpless. Our stature is small, but our swords and spears are sharp, and our phalanx—that Valerius himself taught us—is strong. I say we fight!"

The room cheered loudly now, and Koltar felt his own face twisting up into a wide, tooth-bearing grin, though some little voice in a corner of his brain said he was a fool for doing so. Then he stood and signalled for quiet.

"Thank you Valencius. You have uttered my sentiments and, obviously, those of all the men here. We will fight this invader..." again the room erupted in cheers and it was some moments before Koltar could continue. "The question is, how do we fight them?"

The discussion then became general with a number of proposals being put forward, and before long, various factions forming to press for one or another. The main controversy revolved around whether or not they should attack this fleet inside the cavern, or wait until they emerged before the city. Valencius' faction held that the enemy would be most vulnerable inside the cavern. But Colinus' group contended that the Kantaran's greatest strength against such an enemy was archery and mobility, neither of which could be brought to bear effectively inside the cavern. "What matter those strengths," countered Valencius, "if we can apply others?"

"How would you attack them?" Colinus demanded.

"With fire!"

"Yes, and just how would you propose to do that?"

"Simple. We'll load some small boats with straw, set 'em afire and let 'em drift down with the tide onto their ships."

"And if they come in with the rising tide?"

"Then we'll send those vaunted archers of yours down the cavern road and shoot flaming arrows into 'em."

"No," said Koltar, entering the discussion for the first time, "I like it not. First—with all deference, Valencius—I think they would have to be fools not to enter with the tide. Second, I fear archers with flaming arrows along the cavern road would be more visible than their enemy and would only succeed in showing them the road is there. And third, the cavern is far too important for us to risk it. What would happen to those crystalline sections of the ceiling if an entire ship were to catch fire beneath them? Can any of us guarantee they would not crack from the heat and cause a cave in?" There were some startled looks and nods of concern at this: a collapse in the cavern would turn their Hidden Valley into a lake.

"But even if it didn't," Koltar continued, "several burned hulks sunk in the channel could just as easily damn up the water enough to flood our fields. And at the very least, it would lock us in and Valerius out—and I don't think any of us want to be locked in here, cut off from the rest of the world again. But even aside from all that, I don't think they're most vulnerable in the cavern anyway. I think they're most vulnerable when they try to land. Think about it! That's when our archery can be most effective."

"What about fire?" someone called out.

"Well,..." said Koltar. "I'm not really sure it would be the best thing for us to destroy these fellow's means of transportation, do you? I mean, I think we'd be better off convincing them to leave!"

This got a bit of a laugh and with his main points carried, Koltar left the details to the professionals, and went upstairs to fill Salonis in on the plan. It was quite late by then and he found her sleeping soundly. Not wishing to wake her, he tiptoed out and went back to his own chambers where he sat at his work table and fiddled aimlessly with his papers. He was much too wrought up to sleep, though his thoughts were no longer forming consistent patterns. It was here, with his head down on the desk, that a messenger found him next morning when he came to report the enemy fleet was moving in towards the cavern entrance.

Rising quickly, Koltar went immediately to tell Salonis. But as he stepped quietly inside her door he found her awake and looking at him strangely. "Good morning, Your Majesty," he said, bowing his head and averting his eyes as he approached the bed. Even for him it was not meet to look directly back at the Queen. "I trust you slept well?"

But Salonis did not answer and after a moment's hesitation, Koltar raised his eyes and looked at her. She was staring as before but now, as he stood close by her side, it was plain why the look had seemed so peculiar: Salonis was dead.

The blackness of the cavern seemed to go on forever and Glaucon stood amidships on Valadator where her great mast lay with its end resting on her rail, and hugged tightly to its comforting girth. Forward in the inky blackness, flashes of yellow lantern light twisted and danced as the two galley tugs felt their way along, and from behind, similar flashes from the forty trailing ships played about the walls and ceiling. But where he stood, it was totally dark. He feared the darkness, but would have feared the light more. The dark was at least limitless, and as long as he hugged to his mast he could sense there was a before and after in the void around him. But the light would define boundaries, would reveal the slimy black walls closing in, the dank ceiling pressing down. No, in this kind of blackness, it was better not to see.

When it seemed to Glaucon that the morning must surely have passed completely away, (though it had only been a couple hours) word was passed back that there was light ahead. Glaucon could not yet see it for a time, but when he did, it was a small white dot of light, daylight. He hugged tighter to his mast to keep himself from running forward, focused on his breathing, and watched the light grow.

Then, with a suddenness which surprised him, the light ceased to be a disk ringed by blackness and became a blinding brilliance of sun. He squeezed his eyes tight shut against the glare, and bit by bit, opened them again as they adjusted to the light. It was then that he became aware of Valadator's captain, and several of the officers and men, staring at him. He was still hugging tight to the mast, and suddenly realized he had also been hiding his face in the crook of his arm.

Recovering himself quickly, he strode to the rail to see in what disposition Valerius had arranged his forces. But here was another surprise. Ahead of him stretched only an empty river. There were no pirate galleys, no enemy battle fleet, only along the banks, a few ramshackle docks and abandoned hutments. But there, over there on his right hand, rose the stern gray walls of a city, and before it, spread across the plain along the river, and arrayed rank upon rank in line of battle with shining armor and flags fluttering, stood an army of several thousand. But here was another deception—or the blackness of the cavern had affected his ability to gauge distances—for the army seemed to be composed entirely of children!

For a long moment, Glaucon's brain refused to process the information presented to it by his senses and he stood there at the rail, staring blankly. He was aware that the captain and his mates were standing by his side, awaiting his orders, but that part of his mind which formulated such things was momentarily inoperable. It could not be an army of children. Or could it? This Valerius was not here. Could he and his bandits have sired so many bastards, then slipped away and left them alone to face an invasion? No, they could not be children. Surely, they were just very tiny men. Look at them, the logical part of his brain insisted; they are all of a height, in disciplined ranks. And look there! Several of the smaller leaders even had beards! This awareness came flooding in as a great relief and Glaucon was about to laugh aloud when the first rank of archers rose up from behind the docks and loosed a volley.

An officer beside Glaucon grunted and toppled over backwards, a shaft protruding from his right eye. Glaucon stared at him in shock until a second volley came aboard, then suddenly, he was galvanized into action.

The combined fleets of Valerius and Reuters—totalling some sixty war galleys—reached the Hidden Valley late on their fourth day out from Dulcai. The lead ship, with Valerius himself at the helm, quickly unstepped its mast and without

294

opposition, slipped into the cavern. One by one, the rest followed suit. The trip north had not been nearly as quick as the one south and Valerius had been in an extreme state of agitation and unable to sleep for most of it. They had stayed in Dulcai just long enough to take on water and re-man the Palmerian galleys (as usual, the galley slaves proved ready volunteers). But the winds, while still strong, stayed just that much north of west that he was forced to tack the entire way, and wished mightily for Koltar's fore and aft rig. As it was, he led his ships inshore as far as he dared on the long northeastward tacks, then, rather than lose some of that ground on the opposite tack, put his men to the oars and pulled off shore to the northwest. Only when they were about to fall off their benches would he come about and set sail to the northeast again. And still, it was only when he was steering the ship with his own hands that he felt they were actually getting anywhere.

In his quieter moments, he was surprised at just how strong his reaction was. During all his time in the Hidden Valley he had always considered the place as a kind of gaol and spent most of his energies planning ways to get out of there. Now, with the news that this Glaucon was attacking, and may by now have even taken Kantar, Valerius realized just how strong an attachment he had formed for the place and its people.

He was expecting to see something as they approached the cavern. He was hoping it would be the Zagorbian fleet, not yet having entered. But when he saw nothing, he did not know whether to be relieved or even more anxious. This Glaucon could have been delayed. Reuters had been. But then, by his own admission, Reuters had wanted to be. On the other hand, that same fleet had been in Zagorbia for over a year now and the local commander, Tarpon, had yet to send it south in any kind of force. So, maybe the two of them were still there, in Zagorbia, wrangling over who controlled what. That would not be unlike Fantar's minions. Then again, maybe not. Maybe they were, at this very moment, drinking wine in his own hall in Kantar.

He also expected some sign when they entered the cavern. It did not seem possible that a hostile fleet could have passed through without leaving some trace, or at least a rear guard. Yet there was nothing. The rearing cliffs looked the same, the dark, welcoming hole looked the same, and as they felt their way along in the blackness, the shaft from a lantern forward flickering along the walls, it all seemed the same. It felt like home. Yet as they slipped quietly along under muffled oars, speaking only in whispers, his heart hammered in his chest.

He was very surprised, however, when about three quarters of the way through, a blue light suddenly flashed ahead of them. Then a green one. A lantern was quickly shown forward to reveal three figures standing on the wet cavern road that, ages since, had been carved from the solid rock along the banks of the river. It was Volkmir, along with Vahla and the ubiquitous Chad. Valerius steered in towards the bank, and as his men leapt ashore with lines and grapnels to secure the ship, Volkmir fired off a pink flare just for the doing of it.

"I don't suppose I need to ask how you got here?" Valerius greeted him.

"No, but there's much else I could tell, if you had a mind to listen."

Valerius, with Thorngere and Grumwald, lead the three of them down to his cabin. In a few moments, Reuters, too, came hurrying along the cavern road from his ship. They all squeezed around a small table, hunched shoulder to shoulder over the light of a single candle, while Volkmir filled them in on the situation. Glaucon, with a fleet of some forty ships and a force of about five-thousand had invested the town three days since, he told them. The Kantarans had made a determined stand, and their archers had wreaked havoc on Glaucon's men as they came ashore, but their battle lines simply could not hold against opponents so much larger than themselves. They were driven steadily back and finally, after much stubborn fighting, forced to retreat behind their walls. Here, however, their industry in rebuilding the town had stood them in good stead, for with sturdy walls all about and archers lining the battlements, Glaucon had yet to force a breech. Nor, said Volkmir, did he seem particularly inclined to force one, so viciously were his troops stung every time they approached the walls. For the past two days, then, he had contented himself with brief sorties, and put most of his troops to building siege engines.

"Then the town stands!" said Valerius, a grin spreading across his face and relief flooding through him like a breath of spring air. "And their ranks didn't break under the onslaught?" It was he and Thorngere who taught them how to fight in phalanx.

"No, they were overpowered, clearly, but their shield wall held and they gave a very good account of themselves. Thorngere, you would no doubt have been proud to see how many of Glaucon's troops will not be siring children as a result of that 'spear high, stab low' trick you taught the Kantaran."

Thorngere grinned quickly, but in a very distracted fashion. His emotions were in tumult. Vahla was directly across from him, and he could not stop looking at her. But neither could he meet her eye.

"Well," said Valerius, "the question then is how best to launch our own attack," and he proceeded to question Volkmir in detail about the disposition of Glaucon's forces. With his finger, Volkmir sketched out the town and river on the table top and indicated Glaucon's concentrations. He had made a fairly immediate and straightforward attack, leaving the bulk of his ships quite close to the cavern entrance, rafted two and three deep along the docks. He had struck directly towards the main gate then, only extending his left flank around the Kantaran right as he gained ground and they began to pull back. They had not strayed perceptibly from these positions since, which left a considerable section of the plain open between the city and Valerius' former encampment, and a wide section of river bank open by which they could reach it.

Valerius, studied the invisible tracings on the table top as if they were a detailed map. "My first thought was to attack across their decks and capture their fleet. But since they are already bunched in here between the walls and the cliffs, and since I think we have a slight numerical advantage—significant if you count the Kantaran—I think we should try a two-pronged attack."

"Split our forces?" Reuters sounded dubious.

"In an assault like this, the trick is to bring the greatest number of troops to bear in the shortest amount of time. Look at the pickle you had us in there at the channel. But look here," he said, pointing to the invisible cluster of Glaucon's ships on the table top, "if we attack over his decks, we'll just end up choking the river with our own ships, and only be able to fight on a fairly narrow front."

"Well," said Reuters, "you say there's room up river. Let's just push on past their ships and all go ashore there."

"That would get us all in the field, all right, but it would also leave the front door open for them to escape. I want to bag this whole bunch," said Valerius, his eyes going hard. "And I want those ships.

"Now, here's what I propose: Thorngere, my brother, you stay here in the cavern with Reuters' men. I'll take our ships and push on up river, like Reuters said, and attack from that flank. Then, while they're facing about to deal with us, you strike from the cavern along the river and cut them off from their ships."

Thorngere and Grumwald nodded in agreement, their eyes following the intended movements on the table. But Reuters was still skeptical. "How will we coordinate our attacks?"

Valerius pondered the problem for a few moments, then acting on a sudden inspiration, lifted the Eye and its golden chain from his neck and handed it to Vahla. "There is a place very near the cavern on the opposite side of the river where you can climb part way up the inner cliffs," he said. "There you can command a view of the cavern entrance and the entire plain about the city. Go there with Volkmir, my sister, and stand ready. We will sail up river just before dawn and when the first shafts of the morning sun strike the cliffs, you hold high the Eye so that it flashes in the sun. That will be our signal to attack. Thereafter, Chad will relay messages between you, Reuters and Thorngere, and you will be able to flash them to us using the old Valerian signal code. You remember it, Volkmir?"

"I devised it," said the Mage shortly. There was a foreboding tone to his voice and a discouraging look in his eye, but Valerius did not heed it. Thorngere was more direct.

"Do you think it wise to give up the Eye?"

"I'm not giving it up. I'm just trying to find a way to make it useful. Vahla is our sister, after all. And besides, the Eye will be much more visible up there on the cliff than around my neck. And if Volkmir can add some of his scintillating

300

pyrotechnics, I think it may very well help overawe our enemy. Any more discussion?"

There was none, though neither Volkmir nor Thorngere were entirely convinced.

"Good. Then, let's get a little rest while we can, and may the Gods be with us."

As the group broke up and left the cabin, Thorngere started to reach for Vahla's arm, then dropped his hand and tried to speak. But no words would come. For an instant she faced him and their eyes locked, jolting him like he had been struck. Then, the great Eye Stone of Valeria dangling from her clutched fist like a fish on a string, she turned and hurried out behind Volkmir. 'If I die tomorrow,' Thorngere thought, 'it will not be too soon.'

Chapter 18
THE BATTLE FOR KANTAR

It was that time between darkness and dawn when the world is a grey shadow and it is said that the demons of the night grow weary of their haunts and slip, like mist, back to their lairs. Valerius stood in the forepeak of his ship, Caladon, and watched a mist begin to rise from the river. He had been up most of the night, briefing his commanders, and had just sent Volkmir and Vahla off to scale their perch on the cliffs. He could see them still, their little boat with Chad at the oars, pulling quietly across the river, the shadows of the mist enveloping them. His ships had been hauled up close to the cavern entrance and he now stood just inside, looking east towards the dawn. Ahead, he could see the dark, clustered shapes of Glaucon's ships, secured three and four deep to the docks, and from the land beyond, came the first signs of life in the enemy camp. A fire was stoked up over by the shipyard, and from somewhere came the echoing clatter of metal, though of arms or cooking pots, he could not tell.

In a few moments now, as soon as there was light enough to see his course, he would give the order to advance, and he spent the remaining time going over the plan once more. Had he forgotten anything? Did everybody understand their parts? Had he made the right decision to take the ships in first and not lead with Thorngere's attack from the cavern? One more time he considered the reasoning: Thorngere and Reuters would be attacking from a very narrow portal and while they would certainly gain more surprise attacking first, his own advance should draw the bulk of the enemy away from the cavern. Thorngere's attack then should actually be a greater surprise as it would catch the enemy in the rear. If they each drove along the river bank, they should very quickly establish contact, and if things did go wrong, they could always jump aboard Glaucon's ships.

Yes, Valerius thought, the plan made sense as it was. He would have room to maneuver, and if the Kantaran could sortie with their archers, that would put pressure on three sides of the enemy. Glaucon would have nowhere to go but up the cliffs. And if he could scale those, he was welcome to the view!

Absently, Valerius reached for the red gem which normally hung on his chest, and his hand started when it was gone. Thorngere had not been pleased to see him hand the Stone to Vahla. Neither had Volkmir. Had he made a blunder? Had he, like his father before the battle for Valeria, refused to see? Would he end this day like his father had ended that? He did not think so. Rather, he felt the decision to give Vahla the Eye was inspired by the god. Nearby, just beyond the first docks, he could see group of figures, stoking up another cooking fire. He shifted his heavy breastplate, checked his helmet strap, and felt his stomach churn. It was almost time, he thought, and time, as always, would tell.

In his great cabin on Valadator, Glaucon dreamed of a maiden, an elusive maiden whose features he could not quite distinguish but whom he wanted very badly. She was sitting close beside him on a couch and he could see her breasts through the fabric of her top and the long lines of her thighs below. They were drinking wine and laughing, but she managed always to keep the cup between herself and his questing lips. She was being coy with him. He detected a hint of mockery in her mirth and felt his anger rise with his passion. He would show her, he thought...

But suddenly, he felt himself being rudely shaken, and opened his eyes to the hairy face of his servant bending over him. "Master, master," the man said. "Ships are entering the river. Many ships!"

"Reuters at last!" Glaucon exclaimed and leapt from his bed. Hastily donning a tunic and downing a swallow of wine, he hurried on deck. It was just first light and the world was still pale and dripping from the dew. A mist stood on the river and the plain before the city was still deep in shadow. Moving upriver from the cavern was a long line of ships, stepping their masts in succession as they cleared the cliffs, and unfolding their rigs like great frigate birds. This puzzled Glaucon. Valadator's rig—indeed, the rigs of all his ships—still lay lashed along the deck. In the flurry of the attack, they had not even thought to raise them. So why would Reuters...?

The lead ship pulled abreast of Valadator just then, and Glaucon looked across the narrow strip of water between them and directly into the eyes of Valerius. The sight shocked him so that for an instant his knees buckled and his heart stopped, then thundered in his ears like a blow. He had to grab on the rail to keep from falling. The face was that of a young Fantar! But with both eyes intact, and without that habitual scowl. It was a large, powerful face and the eyes struck him with an almost physical force. And in that instant he realized, first, that these were not Reuters' ships at all, and second, that it was not, as he had been claiming all along, an imposter or a pretender he had to deal with, but Valerius Everreigning himself.

From her perch on the cliff, with Volkmir and the ever attentive Chad at her side, Vahla watched the dawn unveil the panorama of the Hidden Valley from the dark cavern entrance all the way up the misty ribbon of the river to the distant hills in the east and dense forests of the north. Close at hand, as the rising light lifted the shadows, she could see the walled town of Kantar and before it, still wrapped in slumber, the sprawled camp of the enemy with their ships lining the river.

With a mixture of awe and dread, she watched as the stately procession of Valerius' ships moved silently up the river. She saw Valerius at the helm of the lead ship, glorious in his war gear, and was

305

surprised at the seeming lack of reaction in the camp. Then she saw a curly headed figure emerge from the cabin of the huge three decker. She saw him move to the rail just as Valerius passed, saw him pause, then spin about and begin madly waving his arms. In a few seconds, she heard his distant shout, and in that instant felt her stomach flip and her knees go weak, for she knew, even before the clamor of the alarm reached her ears, that it had begun.

Instinctively, she reached up and grasped the large, red gemstone that hung about her neck, the fabled Eye of Valeria. Her heart was pounding but in her mind's eye, another face lingered before her, and silently, she prayed for his safety.

Thorngere stood just inside the cavern entrance, his back pressed against the wall, and watched the last of Valerius' ships disappear beyond the nearby bulk of Glaucon's docked transports. Beside him, also pressed against the rock, was Reuters, and behind them, stretching away into the quickly coalescing blackness along the cavern road, against which their bobbing ships were docked, were some two-thousand armed fighters of Dulcai.

From his position, Thorngere's visibility was limited. He could see up river to the beginning of the docks, and he could see a good stretch of forested land across the river, but without exposing himself in the open, he could not see anything of the enemy camp. Neither could he see the small shelf of rock on which Vahla and Volkmir were supposed

306

to be perched. This was not quite according to plan. For years there had been a small bit of woods along the scree at the bottom of the cliffs that screened the cavern entrance, and Thorngere had assumed he would be able to use this for cover. But that assumption was rash, as Glaucon's men had quickly stripped the woods bare for firewood.

"How are we supposed to see the signal?" Reuters whispered, echoing Thorngere's own concern.

"I don't know. We could put a man in the river..."

"I think we ought to attack right now. There will never be a better time, and..." Reuters was interrupted by the sound of a shout from up river and then the blare of trumpets sounding the alarm. In moments, the enemy camp was alive with sound, some very close by.

"I'm going out and take a look," said Thorngere.

Events now began to unfold with a majestic deliberation and a seeming will of their own. While Valerius and his half of the fleet continued their stately course up the river, Glaucon's camp erupted in wild activity. Men shouted and leapt for their arms. Those still sleeping were kicked viciously from their beds, and all streamed towards their standards. Reacting like a dog whose territory has been threatened, and knowing from bitter experience that his enemy would be weakest as he tried to come ashore, Glaucon ordered an immediate

307

attack. Like a tide, his army surged eastward along the plain, following the progress of Valerius's ships, and striving to meet them the moment they stepped ashore.

From her cliff-side perch, Vahla watched this foot race of men against ships. She could see Glaucon, sitting astride a horse now amidst a sea of men, shouting and gesticulating while his servants tried still to put his armor on. Then, from the corner of her eye she saw another figure dart from the cavern and her heart skipped as she recognized the golden mane. He looked up and for an instant their eyes met across the distance. Then he was spotted by those who had not yet left the camp. An officer shouted and several men rushed Thorngere, brandishing swords. Reuters and several of his men came to his defence. Seeing this melee, Glaucon ordered more men from the camp and in moments, a tiny battle was in full swing about the mouth of the cavern.

In his planning, Valerius had assumed there would be time to land and form his troops before the enemy could react. He didn't get it. Glaucon's men were no green recruits, no undisciplined rabble. The core of this army contained the very men who were in the van of Fantar's conquests. They were veterans, hardened by years of war. Not a few of the older ones had fought before Valeria itself, and with Fantar personally at their head, had circled the Inland Sea, only ending their conquests at Zagorbia.

They were men Valerius's troops had fought before, and had never beaten.

Even now, as his prow ground into the soft bank just below the ford, the first of the enemy were racing towards them, urged on by a wildly shouting Glaucon. Vaulting the rail with Grumwald at his side, and trusting his ship to grapnels thrown quickly ashore, Valerius and his fellows barely had time to brace themselves before the first wave of Glaucon's men were on them and they were fighting for their lives in a vicious skirmish.

But it was not the full force of Glaucon's army, nor was his attack particularly coordinated, else Valerius would have ended his quest right there. Winded after a near mile run, they arrived, not in battle line, but in a ragged trickle. Many had dashed off to fight barely awake and half armed, and without even having had time to take care of essential morning business. And as the fastest were not usually the largest nor most powerful fighters, many died that way, their bowels and bladders voiding only in the slackness of death.

What saved Valerius was simple mathematics: his troops were landing at a slightly faster rate than Glaucon's were arriving, and for a time, he achieved numerical superiority at the point of contact. His men were also fresh and fully prepared for the action that awaited them, so while his landing did not go precisely as planned, he was soon able to advance and solidify his front. Recognizing that his chance to repulse the landing had been thwarted and that he was only wasting men in this sporadic effort,

Glaucon sounded a recall and the bleeding lines fell apart.

Panting himself and leaning for support on his bloody falchion, Valerius stood at the forefront of his own line and watched grimly as a fallen enemy writhed in pain on the ground before him. The man's stomach had been slashed open and his intestines had spilled out, entangling his legs. A few moments before he had been a lusty warrior, screaming his battle cry and attempting to remove Valerius' head. Now he was a pitiful thing, his eyes glazed from the shock of his wound and his life quickly ebbing. Stepping forward, Valerius drove his sword into the man's chest, ending his misery. Then yanking it free, he waved it high in the signal for the general advance. The killing for this day had only just begun.

The signal was repeated by flag from Caladon, but there was little Vahla could do when she saw it: the fight at the cavern was already underway and it was not going as planned. Rather than surprise the enemy in their rear, Thorngere and Reuters' forces had themselves been surprised and were now penned in the cavern, fighting furiously to get out. But of their two-thousand men, no more than a half dozen could actually come to grips with the enemy and they were being held at bay by fewer than fifty opponents. Helpless at the sight, Vahla turned to Volkmir.

"Don't look at me, girl!" he snapped, working furiously with flint and steel. "I didn't come up with

310

this cockamamie plan. Just stand there and wave that stone around and let's see if we can't make some sort of a show!"

Vahla did as she was told, holding the great Eye aloft by its golden chain and waving it this way and that. But the day had dawned overcast and the magic gem remained mute. Behind her, Volkmir set off a succession of green and pink flares, but the only attention these seemed to draw were a few flights of arrows from the enemy camp, all of which fell considerably short. Beyond this, they might as well not even have been there.

His troops reformed around their standards and recovered a bit from their mile run, Glaucon launched another assault on Valerius' advancing forces. With a roar and clash that sounded to Vahla like a distant winter storm, the two lines met head on and the serious fighting of the day began. Valerius held a shallow crescent of the river bank around his ships, an area perhaps a quarter mile long and no more than a hundred yards deep at its thickest point. His plan had been to push west along the river and south towards the city, hitting the enemy on his flank driving them towards the pocket formed by the city walls and the inner cliffs. But in his very quick countermeasures, Glaucon had shifted his troops around to his right so the bulk of them now faced Valerius from the south.

This left Valerius in a very difficult position. He could not shift to his right along the river without stretching his line and endangering his own ships, and being outnumbered now by nearly two to one, he found he could not advance against the enemy's front either. Very quickly, he saw his line begin to contract into a defensive posture and then slowly start to give ground. Valerius and his small personal guard ravened up and down the line, shouting encouragement to his men, and here and there, rushing boldly against the foe. Where he fought, the line advanced. But when he moved on to the next group, it stopped.

And where were Reuters and Thorngere, he wondered? Their attack should have been drawing off some of these men. Yet from his position, he could see nothing of the cavern entrance, and other than some colored flares there were no signals coming from the cliff.

Thorngere and Reuters were fighting for their lives. Locked in the cavern like wine corked in a bottle, they hacked and slashed vainly for room to maneuver. Again and again, Thorngere hurled himself at the enemy, screaming his battle cry and beating down their shields. At least a half dozen men had gone down before him, dead or seriously wounded. Yet their comrades simply dragged them out of the way while others stepped forward to take their places, and the square foot of ground just won had to be won yet again.

But if they could not advance, neither could they be driven back. Cork and wine were in equilibrium, force and resistance balancing in that narrow neck. Stepping back among their fellows to catch their breath, the two leaders conferred hastily.

"This is stupid," said Reuters. "We'll never dislodge them this way. Let me get a crew back aboard and flank them from the river."

"Good," said Thorngere, gasping. "You do that, and I'll keep pushing." And with that, he turned and leapt back into the fray.

Vahla felt like a wooden doll on a shelf at a fair. Standing there on the cliff, the great magic gem dangling useless from her outstretched arm like a toy bauble, she felt more helpless and frustrated than she did when Fantar had dragged her off by the hair. Below, the battle was obviously not going well and there was nothing she could do but watch. She could not even not watch, so ominous and compelling were the scenes unfolding before her. To her left she could see Valerius' bold assault being pushed back step by step, the troops constricting into a tighter and tighter ring around their ships. To her right, Thorngere's furious but futile fight before the cavern where a handful of Glaucon's men blocked half an army. She saw Reuters and Thorngere fall back, saw them talking, and then saw Reuters work his way back into the cavern. But the instant he was lost to sight, he was lost to mind as well for her heart leapt afresh as she saw Thorngere lunge desperately back at the foe.

She saw him strike down a man in front of him and leap over his body at the man behind. And she saw the man to his right raise his sword like a bat.

She screamed a warning but whether it was ever heard she never knew for the man swung that sword and Thorngere's head, or his helmet—the distance was too great to tell—flew off like a ball, and his body dropped like a rock. Vahla staggered as if struck, and would also have fallen, had not the ever attentive Chad been at her side.

Back up river, Valerius was growing desperate. Throwing himself back into the fray at the center of his line, he managed to rally the troops and advance a few paces. But the fighting was hard and brutal with quarter neither asked nor given. They had been at it for well over an hour now and sweat streamed from Valerius' body. His sword arm ached and his voice was hoarse, his breathing heavy. Around him, good men were falling by the score, their battle cries turning to screams of pain. As he watched, Grumwald took a vicious cut on the hip and fell back, gushing blood. Rax, the great wrestling champion and a whirlwind in battle, went down to a thrown spear. Zimlait, the simple fisherman from Cobanos who rose to captain one of Valerius' galleys, tasted death from a sword thrust. Even Valerius himself, reacting a fraction of a second too late, caught a nasty, glancing blow on the helm that sliced off part of his crest and left his head ringing. Few there were who were not bruised or bloodied, and no relief was in sight.

What was in sight, however, was Glaucon himself. His battle organization seemingly well in hand, he had dismounted now, and with his personal guard and standard bearer close about him, was making his way through the ranks directly for Valerius and the faltering banner of Valeria. Every time Valerius looked up, that hated standard with the twisted Falcon emblem of Fantar, was closer. And once or twice, over the heads of the crouching fighters, he could see Glaucon himself, his lips bared in a ferocious grin and his eyes glowing with blood lust. He had his quarry nearly at bay now and while he would not dare fight Valerius man to man, he would wait till he was down, then move in for the kill, an event that did not appear long in coming.

Koltar meanwhile had not been idle. Aware from his lookouts the evening before that Valerius was approaching with a fleet, his preparations were well in hand and he stood now atop the highest rampart of the eastern wall, awaiting the right moment to attack. Below him, clustered about inside the gates and ranged in well-ordered ranks which stretched up several streets, stood some four thousand tiny Kudanim warriors. Their arms burnished to a high sheen, their diminutive forms rigid with martial ardor, they waited with their shields slung on their backs, their swords at their sides, and short, powerful bows gripped in their hands.

But Koltar was confused. He knew from the count of ships his lookout had provided that not all of Valerius forces were engaged. He could also plainly see that the forces that were engaged—and Valerius himself—were outnumbered and very hard pressed. But where were the reserves? Why were they not being brought in? This was why he hesitated. He wanted, as best he could, to coordinate his attack with whatever plan Valerius had. But not knowing that plan, and seeing strange things, he had held back.

Now, something caught his eye from the cavern. It was a ship, then another. This must be it, he thought, the second phase. Barking an order to the signalman beside him, he raced down the steps, yelling for the gates to be opened. Behind him, the signalman stood facing due east and waved high a bright red flag with the leaping panther emblem of Kantar.

To Vahla, it was like the doors and shutters of a darkened room were suddenly thrown open, filling the place with light. That quickly, it seemed, did the battle scene before her change from desperation to jubilation. It happened like this. Reuters and two ships rowed up river, landing beyond the small knot of enemy blocking the cavern. These men turned and fled, unleashing the entire Dulcai contingent which then streamed through the enemy camp and onto the battlefield, striking Glaucon's left flank. At the same time, Koltar's brave warriors attacked from the city. They formed their line in a semi-circle around Glaucon's rear and poured volley after volley of killing archery into his ranks. Then, in a total surprise, the hills to the east erupted with mounted cavalry, led by Colinus and supported by

316

several thousand Iblis with the former butcher, Haradin, at their head.

And as if to add the Gods' blessing to this sudden turn of events, the morning clouds suddenly parted, bathing the whole scene in glorious sunlight. In her hand, the great red Gem suddenly came alive, refracting the rays and shooting off cartwheels of flashing light like Volkmir's powders exploding in a bonfire.

For Valerius, relief came almost too late. Pushed back right to the river banks on each flank and with Glaucon himself bearing down on his center, Valerius could feel the resistance of his men begin to flag. Aggressive determination was turning to fear and arms that thought of nothing but the sword, now hung behind shields. The will to win was fading, and when fear turns to desperation, death can take on the guise of a beckoning handmaiden, promising warmth and security.

Pushed back himself, recognizing those first signs of defeat, and struggling against them in his own mind as well, his heart leapt as he heard fresh war cries on his right, then saw the first flight of arrows plunge like falcons into Glaucon's rear. Confusion rippled through the opposing ranks like wind through a field of wheat. Men hesitated and looked about, orders rang out to shift fronts, and in that briefest of intervals, Valerius' men regained their hearts. The tide of the battle turned right then. Ferocious once more they went back on the attack. Now it was Valerius and his standard driving towards Glaucon, and now it was Glaucon who felt the tremblings of fear in his ranks.

It was then, when the Iblis host smashed into his right and the sweeping cavalry was nipping at his wings, that the sun suddenly burst forth, illuminating the scene like a carving in bold high relief. And at that moment, just at Glaucon turned to shout an order to an aide, a single red beam shot from the distant gemstone and struck him square in the face. It was possibly an accident, a random occurrence. Hanging there in the direct sun, the stone was flashing out thousands of beams. It is highly likely that many men were struck by them without even noticing. But Glaucon caught the flash directly in his eyes. Glaucon knew its source. Glaucon understood what it meant.

In that instant, all the fight went out of him and he stopped dead in his tracks, his sword hanging from a nerveless hand. And in that instant as well, Valerius' contingent broke through the ring of defenders surrounding Glaucon, and without even realizing what had happened to the man, Valerius lunged and drove his sword upwards at the man's unprotected throat. Glaucon saw the blade coming, saw again that face so like that other face, but it was as if he was already dead and saw his mutilation from beyond himself. He saw the hilt of the sword and the powerful, hairy arm driving it. He tasted the cold, bitter steel as it tore through his throat and knew he was dead. But he felt nothing.

Chapter 19
THE KING OF KANTAR

Even with numerical and tactical superiority, it was several hours before the final remnants of Glaucon's force threw down their arms and begged for mercy. No quarter had been given during the fighting, but Valerius could not countenance the slaughter of unresisting men. Utterly blown himself by this time, and bleeding from a dozen cuts, he granted their plea, and under a hot noon sun, watched as the victors cheered and the vanquished were stripped of their arms and marched off to the Iblis' cattle pen across the river. Of Glaucon's original four thousand, fewer than five hundred remained alive and walking. The rest lay sprawled about the field, dead or too hurt to move, in a scene of unrivaled gore. Among them lay not a few of their attackers.

Valerius had won a great victory, he knew, yet he felt no sense of elation. Rather, surveying the butchery around him—the empty faces of the dead, the agony of the only wounded—he felt a deep sadness, a weariness of the soul. He had felt this way before—many times, in fact—but had always attributed it to the exhaustion of battle, or to the fact that his side had usually lost. Yet here he had won, and the feeling was still there, and he realized now just how much he hated war. Odd feeling, he thought, for a man who had spent so much of his life making war, and had so much war yet to make.

Picking his way back along the bloody path of his own advance, Valerius found the body of Glaucon, pale and stiff now, drained of blood, but still bearing an expression of distant surprise about its marbled eyes. He motioned for his attendants to strip the valuable armor off the corpse, then hoisted it up by the hair and tried to hack off the head. But the blade of his great falchion was dull from fighting and would not cut: the corpse just shuddered as he whacked at it. Pulling Glaucon's own sword from its scabbard, he hacked through the final bit of gristle and bone and handed the thing to Gano. "Have it pickled," he said. "I think we'll send it as a present to his master."

"My congratulations, Your Majesty!" called Reuters, as he and his personal guard picked their way among the bodies towards Valerius.

"Well met!" Valerius called back. "And congratulations to Your Majesty as well." Meeting, the two kings clasped hands warmly. "Though I thought for a while there you had decided to go back to Dulcai."

"No, no," said Reuters. He was blood spattered, but apparently unscathed, and bore a broad grin on his plump face. "I wouldn't miss the chance of watching you hack off Glaucon's head for all the world! But we did have a bit of trouble getting out of that cavern."

"Speaking of which, where's that other rapscallion, Thorngere?"

Reuters looked about as if expecting Thorngere to step out of the crowd at any moment, but he did not. "Why, I don't know," he said. Then one of his aides whispered in his ear and his face blanched. "I'm told he fell by the cavern entrance."

"Dead?" Valerius' face, too, went ashen.

"I don't know." Together, they hurried through the remains of Glaucon's camp, where soldiers from both attacking forces were busy plundering, and found Thorngere in the midst of a small cluster of people, Volkmir, Boltar and Chad among them. He had been arranged comfortably on the ground near where he fell and Vahla, her face stricken and tears streaming down her cheeks, was sitting beside him. His eyes were closed and his hair and tunic were soaked in blood, but Valerius could see from his faint breathing that there was life still in him.

Vahla moved aside as Valerius knelt to examine his friend. It was said the hands of the king were healing hands. Thorngere's limbs were warm and despite loss of blood, still retained good color. That was a good sign. His breathing was easy, also a good sign. Gently, Valerius rolled him to his side, being careful to support his head. On the back of his head, just above the neckline, was an ugly gash from which hung a large flap of scalp. "His helmet must have taken most of the blow," said Valerius, "else we'd be finding his head somewhere else."

321

"Aye," said Volkmir, who had crouched down to look over Valerius' shoulder. "But it'll mend. Chad...," he started to call, but Chad was already there, medicinal kit in hand.

The king's hands might have the healing power, but Chad's had the ingredients. While Valerius held Thorngere steady, Chad quickly cleansed the wound with water, stitched the skin back in place, and deftly bandaged it with healing herbs. "He be fine," he pronounced, probing for a moment along the side of Thorngere's neck with his index finger . "His heart still strong."

"Good," said Valerius. "And I think we can make ample use of your talents elsewhere today as well. Volkmir, could you and Chad set up shop in one of Glaucon's tents there?"

"Certainly, your Majesty. That's precisely what I intended."

Valerius rose and turned to leave but found Vahla standing before him. She was still pale and trembling and he caught her arms for fear she might fall. "He'll be fine, little sister," he said softly.

"I know," she said, shaking her head slowly. "It's not that. It's just the whole thing. I thought you were all going to die...!" she sobbed, falling against his chest, tears flooding her eyes afresh.

"Battle is not a pretty thing," he said, holding her gently and patting her back. "And there are never any guarantees."

"I know," she said, straightening quickly and wiping her eyes with the back of her hand. "I'm sorry. I just never saw a battle before. I'll go help

Volkmir and Chad now. But here," she said, lifting the heavy red stone from her neck. "I think this is much better left in your care."

"I think you may be right," said Valerius, and as he settled the heavy chain about his own neck he felt a sudden lift, like a cool breeze on a sweltering day, and with it a sense of strength and vigor. It was such a definite and immediate sensation that he caught his breath and looked down at his hands and flexed them into fists. There was power there. And on his chest, the light in the stone rippled a deep russet red.

A litter was fashioned for Thorngere and as they bore him off towards a nearby tent, they were met by Koltar and his Guard, still under their battle flag and marching in formation. Many of their quivers, however, were empty. Valerius greeted them warmly, but Koltar was very formal in his reply. "Your Majesty, Valerius, High King of Valeria and over all the Inland Sea," he said, standing stiff and seeming quite nervous, "Before we speak, I have other news—sad news—which I must now make public: Her Majesty, Queen Salonis of Kantar, is dead."

In the midst of so much death, could the news of one more be so telling? Indeed, it could, for Queen Salonis had been many things to Valerius: his enemy, his kidnapper, his attempted assassin, his ally, host, and for these past two years, a most dear and respected friend. He took the news of her death like a blow and staggered back from it, his mouth slack with surprise. It was not until Koltar filled in the details—that she had known she was dying for some time but had hidden the seriousness of her illness, that she had gone peacefully in her sleep with all her affairs in order, and that she had confirmed Koltar as her successor—that Valerius could bring himself to respond.

"Then she has made one of her wisest decisions at the end," he said. "Though I mourn the loss of this great, guiding spirit of your people, I honor and congratulate you, King Koltar, on your ascendancy."

Somewhere, among the crowd of soldiers which had gathered about the leaders, a voice sang out. "Long live the King!" Instantly, it was taken up by others until all over that hard won field, thousands of throats rang with the cheer. "Long live the King! Long live the King of Kantar!"

Among the crowd was Colinus, arriving on horseback, with the Iblis leader, Haradin, by his side. On hearing the news, the sturdy little commander quickly dismounted, and with the other nearby Kantaran, knelt in obeisance before his new sovereign. Then he rose and knelt before the High King.

"Colinus, my friend!" said Valerius raising him up. "I am delighted to see you safe—though I must say I was even more delighted to see you arrive a while ago! I owe you—we all owe you—our thanks."

Embarrassed by the praise, Colinus started to mumble something about Koltar's orders, but Valerius turned his attention to the Iblis. "And you, Haradin, my thanks to you as well. If anyone had asked me beforehand who would have lead such a rescue, young Colinus here would have been my first guess. You, I confess, would have been the last. Nonetheless, your people have helped us achieve a great victory here and you have earned our gratitude. But how came you here?"

"It was Lord Koltar—I mean His Majesty Koltar, your Majesty," said Colinus, not to be denied his lines. "When these outlanders besieged us, he sent me out through the old tunnels..."

"Aye," said Koltar, "but it was only to fetch the troops who were guarding the New City, not the Iblis. Any enlistment of new allies must stand to his own credit, Your Majesty."

"Is this true, Colinus?" said Valerius, eyeing the little man before him as a school master might eye a mischievous but doughty boy.

"Yes, your majesty," said Colinus, not quite knowing whether he had done well or ill.

"And what say you, Haradin? What induced your people to come to our aide? We have none of us been friends to you."

"Ah, Your Majesty," said Haradin, his face a mask of humility. "Is not a friend the enemy of one's enemy? From what the Commander here said, it was clear who the real enemies were: we simply did what we could."

325

The man was lying, of course. A quick look at his eye told Valerius that. The 'enemy of one's enemy' bit was too rehearsed, and clearly, it cut both ways. Besides, this was far from the first time Haradin had tried to cheat him. And Haradin knew that Valerius knew. Yet he was bold-faced in his tale and spoke, no doubt, from a perfectly clear conscience. All he had done was seize an opportunity to arm his people. That they had fought against Glaucon and not with him, was due purely to the direction the battle was taking the moment they arrived.

So it had been a very close thing, Valerius thought. Yet could the man be blamed for seeking freedom for his people? What was his lot—their lot—otherwise? Perpetual servitude, most of them locked away in New Kantar, no doubt suffering the same malady the Kantaran had suffered when they lived there: a diminution in male offspring which would lead to an eventual and inevitable extinction. So could he be blamed for a would-be betrayal when both his aims and actions were in the interests of his people? It was a question of perspective.

"Haradin," said Valerius, his eyes going hard. "I have often wondered why I did not have you killed a score of times before this. You and I both know there has been provocation enough. Now I see your life must be a lesson to me... Or at least, a perpetual question. By your actions, I would like to reward you. Yet I fear that if we turn you loose, you will slit our throats. The only thing I can trust in you, Haradin, is that you will work to your own purposes. So what are we to do with you?"

"I think I may have an idea," said a weak and raspy voice. It was Thorngere, awake and listening on his litter. "There is a place I know, an island..."

The grim task of collecting the wounded and burying the dead consumed the better part of two days. The prisoners were rearmed with picks and shovels and a huge mound was raised to cover the remains. Friend and foe were laid side by side, the only difference being that the victors were buried with their arms, while the vanquished, who would be their slaves in the afterworld, were buried naked. A great mound of war gear was raised, too, and with Glaucon's fleet now under his control and the addition of the many galley slaves who instantly offered their allegiance, Valerius had become a force to be reckoned with.

But not without cost. Many were the prominent names and capable leaders laid among the rows of dead in that mound. Chief among the Kantarans lost was Valencius himself, Chief of the army. An axe, hurled in desperation at the stinging archers, caught him flush in the face, splitting his nose and skull. Among Valerius' forces, Eban of Durumkae, whose last sight of his home had been smoke and flames, went down to death never knowing the fate of his wife and newborn babe. Christoban of Telos, too, fell, he who had watched helpless from the hills as Fantar sacked his town. He was leading his men in the charge when a thrown spear brought death hurtling and the black mist covered his eyes. Cedric and Moromar fell, warriors who, like Valerius himself, had survived the fall of Valeria. Others, too numerous to mention, also tasted of death that day, and many more besides felt the searing bite of steel.

In their tent within the former enemy camp, a group led by Vahla, Volkmir and Chad worked without rest to succor the wounded. For many, there was little they could do. Any wound in that age was life-threatening, but the loss of a limb or an open belly wound were almost certainly fatal. And when treatment was unavailable for several hours because of the sheer volume of wounded, many others who might have healed, died from loss of blood, or later from fever born of infection. So the trio worked as quickly as they could, staunching, binding and stitching where they could, trying to offer some comfort where they could not.

Of the three, it must be noted that Chad was by far the most proficient. Though he had learned his skills from his master, and while the master could still claim more formal knowledge, Chad had an instinctive efficiency about his methods and a manual dexterity that far exceeded his teacher. He did, however, have one habit that annoyed Volkmir no end, but which probably saved more lives than anything else that was done save cauterizing itself: from some stubborn well of instinct or innate observation, he had gotten the notion that wounds must be washed clean before they were bound and as Volkmir pointed out numerous times, this delayed proceedings unconscionably. But he would not be deterred. Despite Volkmir's grumblings, curses and even cuffs, Chad was there with every patient, tenderly cutting away soiled clothing, washing away dirt and gore from the severed flesh. It was only because Vahla insisted (she noticed how the cool water and gentle ministrations tended to ease the patients), and because they so badly needed the help that Volkmir suffered him to continue.

Valerius offered what comfort and encouragement he could but, of course, there were many other demands on his time. There were also concerns weighing on his mind that he needed to work through, but it was not until the second day, after Salonis had been laid to rest in the sacred grove of Kantaran Monarchs—the first in several generations to be so honored—that he got the chance to break away from his advisors and find a place to think. He had lingered behind the procession at Salonis' tomb to offer a private word of encouragement to Koltar, who appeared quite lost as the body was entombed, and then walked down to a wooded spot by the river behind his old encampment and sat on the bank to think.

The question, of course, was 'what next?' He had eliminated the immediate threat to Dulcai and Kantar, but if he did nothing more, or even waited too long, that threat would recur. And besides, his objective had never been to simply remove the threat. His objective was to remove Fantar and that did not require defense, but offense. Offense he still

329

could not see his way clear to launch. Yes, he had doubled the size of his fleet. Yes, he had secured the support of Reuters. Yes, Kantar was still a safe haven, and if something could be done with the Iblis it would be safer still, but compared to the might of Fantar, his own was like that of a child taunting a bear.

Well, maybe not quite. Children don't send bears the heads of their minions. And in terms of sheer military capability, he had, after all, just defeated the very army that had taken Zagorbia...

Suddenly, Valerius sat bolt upright, the answer perfectly clear. For days something about this situation had been subtly nagging at him and now, suddenly, it was so obvious he felt stupid for not having thought of it before. If the army from Zagorbia had come here, who was there? What was next? Zagorbia was next! Leaping to his feet, Valerius hurried off towards camp, his mind already formulating orders.

He had not gone a hundred yards, however, when he came upon Reuters' daughter, Eomer, with several of her attendants. She had been helping with the wounded and now that the worst was over, had also sought a secluded spot upstream to bathe. She had just donned a simple shift and was having her long hair combed out. Valerius had not even realized she had accompanied Reuters from Dulcai.

"What are you doing here?" he blurted as he blundered into their little encampment, startling the girl.

330

"Why?" she exclaimed looking about as if she expected the enemy to leap from the trees. "Is it not safe to be here?"

"Oh, no, I didn't mean that," he said, feeling suddenly awkward and uncouth. "It's safe. Yes, perfectly safe—and I'm sorry if I startled you. I just meant I didn't realize you were here in Kantar."

"And where else would I be, your Majesty?" said the girl rising now to curtsey before him and casting him a sidelong glance. He was struck again at how tall and stately she was. Her limbs were long and slim, and yet there was a suppleness about her, a natural grace. She was very beautiful.

"I had assumed," he said, still flustered, "that you were in Dulcai where you would be safe."

"I thank your Majesty for his concern. But does he not think my father is capable of protecting me?" asked the girl, an eyebrow raised.

Valerius caught the quick glint in her eye, and realized she was teasing him. A smile cracked his own lips beneath his beard. "Did the Princess perhaps not realize there was a war going on here?"

Suddenly her eyes went somber. "Very much, your Majesty. I have been helping to tend the wounded. I did not mean to make light of their suffering."

"Oh, I don't think you did. I'm sure you were a great comfort to them."

"Thank you." She looked up at him for a long moment and he could see that she, too, had suffered from the experience. "Is it always this bad? War, I mean?"

"Well, this was a particularly bloody fight, but it is seldom pleasant."

"I wanted to be here to see Glaucon fall," she said, "after the way... after the way he treated my father. But when I saw all those poor men," and here she shook her head sadly. "I don't know, I felt like I was wrong to want revenge."

"There is a difference between justice and revenge," Valerius said. "Glaucon got what he deserved. And it was because of him, and his Master, that this war started in the first place."

"Do you ever get hardened to it?"

Now it was Valerius' turn to shake his head sadly. "I thought I was once," he said. "But no more."

"Good," said Eomer. "I would not like to think of you like that."

The directness of this remark startled him and he looked at her in surprise. Her eyes smiled back at him and he felt the smile go way deep inside, then return and break out on his own face. It felt very warm.

"What will you do next?" she asked.

"Well if I may," he said, still smiling, "I would like the honor of escorting you back to the safety of that vaunted father of yours."

"It is I who would be honored, your Majesty," and she offered him her arm.

The next day, an official coronation ceremony was held for King Koltar. A procession of dignitaries was formed on Valerius' new flagship,

Valadator, and then, with Koltar in the center, paraded through all the ranks of the armies, then through the gates of the city and up to the palace. Thorngere's wound prevented him from marching, but Vahla walked along in the van beside Volkmir and noticed this time, that the streets were thronged with men, women and children, and that their smiles were bright enough to light up the very cavern. In the palace, Valerius and Reuters mounted to thrones on the dias, Valerius in the center and Reuters on the left, while Koltar, resplendent in his coronation robes, knelt before his own throne on the right. The old blind singer, Teukonis, recited a long ode in honor of the occasion and then Volkmir, acting as high priest, sanctified the crown and gave it to the high king. Valerius held the crown high over the tiny man's head and pronounced the words of coronation.

"Lord Koltar, son of Kam, rightful heir to Her Late Majesty, Salonis, Queen of Kantar, I Valerius Everreigning, rightful High King of Valeria and all the Inland Sea, do hereby proclaim you King and rightful ruler of Kantar." And with that, he placed the crown, so long dreaded, onto Koltar's head. King Koltar rose and mounted to his throne and the assembly started to cheer. Those outside began to cheer as well, as did those in the city, and the army outside: even the Iblis cheered until it seemed every living soul in that valley was yelling his heart out. The noise swelled up into the heavens so the Gods would take note and look down and see what a momentous thing had occurred on earth.

Then the room hushed and His Majesty, King Koltar spoke. Regal in his robes and crown as he came to the front of the dias, he looked every inch the king despite the huge outlanders seated behind him. Koltar thanked the gods, his royal confederates, all the leaders and dignitaries there assembled, and promised to faithfully discharge the royal duties incumbent upon him and to always be faithful to the true interests of his people and his city. To that end, he went on to name some new officials for his administration and some new officers to fill recent vacancies in the army. Chief among these, was Colinus, Commander of the late Queen's Royal Guard, whom Koltar now elevated to Commander in Chief of the Kantaran army. A stunned Colinus beamed and winked at Vahla as he accepted the insignia of his new rank.

"But there is one other thing I must address," said the new king when the appointments were completed. "This is now the second time we in Kantar have become indebted to King Valerius for our freedom. Were it not for him, and King Reuters and these other valiant souls here, both living and now lying dead, we would be in thrall to another power, one perhaps even more insidious than that which we fought for so many years.

"There is no way to adequately discharge such a debt except by providing service in kind. Therefore, as King of Kantar, I Koltar, son of Kam, do freely and without reservation pledge my fealty, and that of my people, to Valerius, Rightful King Everreigning of Valeria and all the Inland Sea."

With this, Koltar turned and knelt before Valerius and all his people in the hall did likewise.

"Thank you, Koltar," said Valerius, his booming voice echoing in the audience chamber. "That which you have freely offered I most gratefully accept. Arise! And be one with the people of Valeria." For the second time, cheers swept out of the hall and into the streets.

"But speaking of such things," Valerius continued when the noise subsided, "there are a couple other points of business we must attend to. Bring forth Haradin of the Iblis.

"Haradin," he said when the swarthy, former butcher was brought before him, "long have I puzzled how to deal justly with your people. You have been an insidious, despicable lot, and the crimes you have committed against the Kantaran people have been unspeakable. For this, you have been kept under confinement these two years past in the new city of Kantar. In itself, this is not an onerous punishment. Indeed, it is probably much less than you deserve. But I am told you have already begun to suffer the strange malady of the waters which afflicted the Kantaran when they lived there and that the number of male children born to you has already diminished greatly. As this will eventually lead to the extinction of your race—a punishment I think too severe—I have long sought an alternative. I also feel some obligation, since, as the Kantaran Chronicles show, it was because of my ancestor that you came to the Hidden Valley in the first place. Lastly, your recent help against Glaucon has made finding some alternative even more imperative.

"But what is to be done? If we release you, you and I both know you will simply go back to your old crimes. Then what? Thus, with the advice of King Koltar, I have decided upon a different course, which we will undertake if you and your people join as willing parties to it. In his recent voyage back from Dulcai, Lord Thorngere and Captain Boltar discovered a group of islands off shore which show every indication of being very hospitable. In fact, Lord Thorngere has named them the Fortunate Isles. If you will agree to it, we will board you and all your people on the fleet here assembled and, with suitable provisions—including livestock—transport you hither and help you establish a new settlement. If you succeed and prosper there, the land will be yours forever and you yourself shall reign as King over it. So say I, Valerius, Rightful King Everreigning of Valeria and all the Inland Sea. What say you, Haradin of the Iblis?"

Haradin shifted from side to side, his eyes darting warily over the assembled Lords. This news came to him as a complete surprise "What guarantees does Your Majesty offer?" he countered.

"Haradin," Valerius sighed, "you may take as a guarantee that I have not killed you before now."

"I see," said Haradin. "Then I say that your Majesty is most just and generous indeed! I and my people will participate in this venture—though we have no truck with the sea—and will most happily see the last of this cursed valley which has brought us nothing but war and suffering for generations."

"Boltar," said the King. "Do you think you can find these islands again without Thorngere?"

"Without a doubt, your Majesty."

"So be it, then. Grumwald, as Lord Thorngere is still recovering, I will entrust you with the command of this venture. Take all the ships and as many men as you need. And make haste for while you are gone, the rest of us will begin gathering provisions and preparing for the next step on our road back to Valeria: As soon as you have returned, we will all board and set sail for Zagorbia!"

Here a great cheer broke out, even louder than the ones preceding it, and spread out from the hall throughout the Hidden Valley. And once again, the gods were forced to look down and note the stirrings of destiny on earth.

"Your Majesty!" called Koltar when order had been somewhat restored. "With the Iblis no longer a threat here, I beg you will accept the aide of our Kantaran army under the command of its new Chief, Colinus."

"And I, too," said Reuters, "beg leave to accompany you with the fleet of Dulcai. It is clear to me now that our strength and our hope is in union. That is the way we must proceed."

"Thank you King Koltar, and King Reuters. Both of your offers are most gratefully accepted. However," said Valerius, his face and voice going stern, "there is one other matter, King Reuters, on which you and I must treat. Bring forth the lady, Princess Eomer!"

Eomer was escorted to the dais by two of Valerius' personal guards and stood quietly before the three seated kings. She was wearing a long, simple gown of white and her golden hair was drawn back behind her head and bound up in a bun. At her temple was a fresh sprig of laurel. She stood with her eyes lowered and her hands folded quietly before her. Reuters looked quickly from his daughter to Valerius and back, sudden suspicion etching furrows across his brow.

"Reuters," said Valerius, his voice still harsh and commanding, "we have known each other for many years. You have been my friend, my supporter, and my ally. I have trusted you with my life, and would do so again. Yet, when we sailed south recently to enlist your aide and strengthen our alliance, you met me with open defiance, your fleet set in line of battle against me. This was, I am told, because of this girl.

"Now, understand me clearly here," he went on, holding up his hand to prevent Reuters from interrupting, "as a man I can appreciate your feelings towards your child, and I am also very grateful that trouble was averted between us. However, I would not be doing my duty as King if, before we accept your continued support, I did not address this potential threat to our alliance."

At the word 'threat' the furrows on Reuters' brow deepened and his eyes began to flash angrily.

He started to speak, but Valerius rose up, and holding up his hand, commanded him to silence.

"I do not doubt your honor, King Reuters, but I also know you to be a man who is ruled by his heart.   And against that heart, I must defend. Therefore, as is my right as High King, I claim as hostage the Princess Eomer,"—and here, Reuters leapt to his feet, his hand reaching for his sword— "to abide with me as my wife and my Queen."

As these last words sank in, Reuters stopped still, his sword half drawn, his face stupid with surprise.   Then, seeing the broad grins on the faces of Valerius and Eomer, he realized he had been had. Not to be outdone, however, he stood his ground and shot back, "If you think to take my daughter through threats and royal perogatives, King Valerius, you had best draw that great sword of yours and we'll make an end of this discussion right here!"

"All right, Reuters," said Valerius, his dark face softening with a warm smile, "how about I ask the hand of your daughter for the love I bear her?"

"And what say you, my daughter, to this mad and scurrilous proposal?"

"I say, my lord," said Eomer, her eyes rising up to meet those of the High King, "that it is my most heartfelt wish come true."

"Ha!" said Reuters, slapping his sword back into his scabbard. "Then it shall be so."

339

Chapter 20
VALERIUS THE KING

It took several days to move the Iblis and all their goods from New Kantar, which was located in an adjacent valley some ten leagues to the east, and load them aboard the waiting fleet. The Iblis were not water people and many did not want to go. They feared the whole plan was a trick, and that once at sea they would be cast overboard, or at best, be left stranded on some barren rock of an island, and there was much crying and lamentation as the long lines of women and children were herded aboard to find places between the men who, for security's sake, had already been chained to the oars.

With a population nearing seven thousand, it took more than half the fleet to transport them and a goodly number of troops to guard and keep them in line. In recognition of his exalted status, Haradin and a few of his closest advisors were not chained to benches, but were lodged in some state in the junior officers cabin aboard a limping Grumwald's flagship. Haradin gloried in his elevation from herdsman to Lawgiver, the Iblis term for their sovereign, and was not long (less than two days, in fact) in earning Grumwald's wrath over some petty thievery which, when he stood accused, Haradin interpreted as a slight to his new found dignity. However, hobbling around with a wounded leg and playing nursemaid to seven odd thousand screaming, seasick Iblis had not put Grumwald in the most tolerant of moods, and he soon had Haradin triced up spread-eagled from a deck beam and threatened to roast his testicles with an oil lamp if he did not mend his ways. Having singed enough hair off the referenced articles to make his point, Grumwald dumped the howling Lawgiver unceremoniously into his tiny cubby hole of a cabin and the rest of the voyage passed uneventfully.

Boltar had no trouble navigating his way back to the Fortunate Isles, and the weather remained steady and mild the entire way. The isles themselves proved as welcoming and hospitable as promised, and as the long suffering Iblis were turned loose ashore, they gamboled about like children. Grumwald's men spent another few days unloading stores and tools, and helping the new natives fashion rough shelters for themselves (which shelters, much tattered and worn, they would still be living in two years hence), before the considerably lightened and now undermanned fleet upped anchor and set sail for the east.

As the last ship rounded the point which enclosed the bay and squared away for the open sea, Haradin ran down onto the beach from the trees, where he had been watching, and hurled a rock after the distant vessel. It fell well short of its intended target, however, and in a second effort he pulled down his breeches, and urinated at them with a penis still red and swollen from its recent scorching. Finally satisfied he had fully enunciated his parting thoughts, he spat by way of punctuation and turned back to shepherd his people.

Thorngere, meanwhile, was mending very slowly from his wound. The cut on the back of his head had healed quickly enough, thanks to the deft ministrations of Chad, but the inside of his head was a different story. Though he tried to joke and make light of it in his better moments—saying this was the first time he ever had evidence of anything actually being in there—Thorngere continued to suffer from excruciating headaches, blurred vision, and nausea. Food would often not lie in his stomach and, after two weeks, his great frame had considerably wasted, and whenever he tried to stand, he was felled by dizziness and pain.

Still, he was making some progress. The headaches were lessening in severity and more nourishment was staying down than coming up, so that by the end of the second week—about the time Haradin was bidding Grumwald's fleet farewell—he was able to sit up comfortably in a chair by the window of his chamber. It was here that Vahla found him when she came to say goodbye.

He was dozing when she entered, and for several moments she stood in the open doorway, uncertain whether to stay. She could see how wasted he was and for an instant her mind flashed back to the image of him that first morning after she had entered his camp, when she saw him wading in the river with his fishing spear, and how the morning sun played on his golden hair and the taut, massive muscles of his back and shoulders. Then she saw him again as he emerged naked and dripping from the stream, a fish wriggling on the spear and his manhood pendulous before her. As she had then, she gasped at the sight, but this time it was as much from shame and confusion as from passion. Hurriedly, she turned to go, but Thorngere's voice stopped her.

"Vahla?" It sounded weak and tremulous, not at all the vibrant tenor that was so much like music to her. The sound of it tore at her heart and she went to him.

Thorngere was still not seeing clearly, and when he woke to see the form of the female in the doorway, she seemed surrounded by a glowing nimbus. For an instant he thought her a spirit from another world, a vision, or a hallucination. Then he recognized her and his heart leapt, only to plummet again as that other, ironical side of his brain hissed that she might as well be a spirit, might as well live in another world, for all she could live with him.

She sat on a chair beside him and reached out to touch his hand, then drew back. They looked at each other, then away. "I... I came to say goodbye," she said finally. "I'm leaving with Volkmir this afternoon."

"You're going to stay with him?" His voice was flat and forced.

"Yes. He's getting on and needs help. And he's been teaching me things. He says I have the sight and am to be his apprentice. He said it was foretold I would come to him."

"And Valerius gave you the Eye during the battle."

"Yes, but I don't think that was right. I held it like he told me, but..." and here she stopped and shook her head, "but it was not meant that I should. It felt like I was holding a serpent."

Silence fell between them then, like a sudden fork in a turbulent river. Their eyes swam with emotion they could not speak. Finally, Thorngere blurted the question which had been plaguing him: "Why didn't you tell me you were his sister?" he demanded.

"And why didn't you tell me you were his brother?" She shot back. Then the silence again fell between them. The answers would not make any difference.

After a time, he spoke once more, his voice quieter, more resigned. "It is good you are going with Volkmir. It will be a place for you."

"And you?"

"Me? I am what I have been—a creature of the King. I will bide or do battle as I am bidden."

"Thorngere," she said, her own voice growing strong with urgency, "you must promise me not to seek your death in battle."

"Seek my death?" Fiercely, his eyes slashed into her face. "You think I did this on purpose?"

"I think you have a will of steel, Thorngere of Thuringia," she said, her eyes holding his, "and I think you would walk face first into death and not blink if you thought it would serve. But you also grow as hot as molten iron and I would not see you cast away foolishly. I know not why the gods have seen fit to play with us so, and cast us aside like shattered ingots, but I do feel there is a purpose here, and... and...," here her prophetic resolve broke down and she buried her face in her hands. "Oh, Thorngere," she wailed. "Do promise me! I could not bear it if I felt you had thrown your life away. No matter what we are, you are still precious to me!"

Thorngere squeezed his own eyes shut as two tears trickle down his cheeks and melted into his beard. Pulling her hands away from her face and seeking her eyes once more, he said, "For that, I will promise, Vahla, Princess of Valeria. For that, I will promise."

It took the better part of another week after Grumwald's return for the fleet to be scoured out (the Iblis had not demonstrated a great deal of appreciation for toilet etiquette), re-provisioned and loaded for the trip north. Kantaran armories were emptied of their thousands of bows and arrows, stables were constructed on the crowded lower decks to house their terrified mounts, and even the siege towers, catapults, and mangonels Glaucon had begun constructing were dismantled and loaded aboard. With Thorngere still too weak to join the expedition, (though by now it was clear he would recover) the bulk of the work fell to Grumwald who, as the King's official Flag Captain, took charge like a bosun and worked the men till they were ready to drop. None resented this, however, but worked all the more willingly because first, Grumwald was very able and the men knew matters were being managed with a practical efficiency; second, the army was buoyed by a tremendous sense of confidence and optimism after their victory, and by the belief that, at last, the tide of events was turning their way; and third, because the High King was closeted away in the palace with his new Queen, and none wanted to face him if any problems they caused forced him to emerge.

On the day they were to leave, however, Valerius' presence was required whether he would or no, and early that morning, he slipped carefully from his bed, so as not to awaken the sleeping Eomer, and tiptoed out onto the balcony off his sleeping chamber. It was still very early. There was not a breath of air and the first shafts of sunlight were slanting through the mist rising up over the river. Somewhere overhead, on the palace roof, some birds had started chirping. Valerius stretched luxuriously and leaned on the rail. This was his favorite time of day, when everything seemed fresh scrubbed and clean and the world held promise of being a better place.

And it did. Valerius had never felt so happy or confident, both in his life and his future. Down on the river, a great fleet of ships crowded along the bank, in places rafted three deep, and aboard rested an army of near ten thousand men ready for the trip north. It was not yet a force to topple an empire, but it should do for Zagorbia, and beyond that, well, he would see what Zagorbia would bring. For years he had wondered how Fantar had managed to conquer the Inland Sea as he did. Starting in the mountains with a small band of rebels, he had soon grown to become a veritable hurricane, sweeping away the old order with an incredible violence. Now Valerius was beginning to see that success in war multiplied strength. He had always thought arithmetically, 'if I have a hundred men and lose ten in battle, I will only have ninety for the next battle, and so on until, if I survive, I will stand alone at the beginning of the tenth battle.' But it didn't work that way. Success generated, rather than depleted, resources. He was beginning to see now that, so long as he won, the ten men lost would be replaced by fifty or sixty gained and if this held true, there was indeed a chance for him to regain his throne. And the chance was sitting there in that river, waiting for the tide, and for him to come aboard.

Still, he was reluctant to leave. The past few days, while he had left the work of manning the fleet to others for a change, he had discovered another source of strength and contentment he had not really believed could exist. At least, not for him. She was sleeping there in the other room, and the mere thought of her brought a smile to his lips. Such a slender, wisp of a girl, yet so strong in herself! So wise, and so loving. And so passionate! Valerius looked down at his great beefy hands, at the bristly black hairs on his wrists and knuckles, the cracked, sword-worn callouses on his palms, and wondered how such a marvelous creature as she could abide one such as himself. He felt like an ancient rock by the side of the sea, weed and barnacle encrusted, beaten for ages by the pounding surf, and she a lovely gull, as slender and light as the air itself, a creature of the sun and sky come to nest on his hoary, salt stained back. And he felt blessed by that, deeply contented, and bent all his rock-like thoughts to securing her comfort, protecting her from the storm. For the first time in his five and thirty years, Valerius was deeply in love.

Yet, he was not a rock. In fact, he was a storm maker, and to do so, he must leave this love. Lightly, he cupped the red gem of the Eye on his palm and watched the morning sun glitter on its face and ripple through its amber depths. This too, was not unlike Eomer, and he wondered should he be using it more? Perhaps instead of playing the gawky bridegroom, he should have been out in the hills, seeking the Eye? No, he didn't think so. Somehow, he was beginning to feel that the Eye communicated to him in other ways, that it was not always required, or even desired, that he search its depths directly. It was as if there was a kind of music, a harmony in the world that the stone allowed him to feel and he knew when he was in tune with it. And he was in tune now. Zagorbia was part of the tune and he was right now in going there.

And go he must, before the sun rose too much higher. Turning, he was startled to see Eomer standing in the doorway, watching him. She was naked but for a shift held up to cover her breasts, and she was smiling. "Good morning, my Lord," she said.

"Good morning, my Lady," said he and thought that the rising sun might just go hang for a little while longer.

The weather was too calm on the trip north. Summer was drawing to a close and it was that still period of warm, breathless days and cool nights when the sun's heat was just beginning to fade, but before the storms of fall. After five days at sea—gorgeous, blue sky days in which there was just enough wind to fill the sails, yet hardly enough to move the ships—they were still shy of their objective. That afternoon, when it became clear they would not make it before dark, Valerius decided to lay off and make their landing as early as possible in the morning.

He summoned all his group captains for a final meeting and afterwards, as their various gigs scattered across the flat sea to their own ships, he stood at the rail and watched darkness draw its curtain of shadow over the distant land. His plan was to sail in under Glaucon's flag in hopes of catching Tarpon off guard until they could get ashore and establish contact with Ragnar's resistance forces, and he was wondering about the likelihood of Tarpon and Glaucon having established private recognition signals to clear his return. Somehow, he doubted it. From what he had heard—and seen—of those two, he did not think the former would be cooperative enough to arrange signals after his fleet had been 'borrowed', or that the latter would have condescended to needing them. Still, missing signals could change the game completely and he would have to be on his guard that he was not the one walking into a trap.

Grumwald came up to report all the captains departed and the gangway secured, and Valerius asked his opinion. "You spent a bit of time with the fleet," he said, "do you think it likely Glaucon and Tarpon would have private recognition signals?"

"Oh, I spent time with the fleet, all right... Two fucking years I spent—begging your Majesty's pardon—thanks to that faithless bastard, but I had no knowledge of signals of any sort. All I heard of Tarpon was that he was a murdering sodomite."

"Hmmm," said Valerius. "So that's why you were so grateful to be rescued!"

"Ha! One whiff of my smelly old arse and he'd have opted for murder, sure." The two men laughed, then lapsed into silence as the quiet waters whispered around the hull, and the distant shore slipped into total blackness, unbroken by even a single light. Soon they would have to start the last ten mile pull so as to reach the Bay of Zagorbia by dawn.

"But I was grateful indeed to see old Thorngere that day," Grumwald went on. "And when I heard you had become King—I mean that you were Valerius, not Balazar—well, I near fell overboard again."

350

"Why?" asked Valerius, seriously curious now. "Did you not think Balazar would have made a good king? I'm still the same man, you know."

"Aye," said Grumwald, "on the inside, I'm sure. But from the outside, there's a definite difference. The Valerius I see now is not the Balazar of old, if you don't mind me saying so, your Majesty..."

"No, no, Grumwald, speak your mind. We've known each other too many years to dissemble. Besides, I find this very curious."

"Well, I don't know if I can explain it, but I've seen it, and others have, too. The old Balazar, he was one of the best fighters I ever saw. Whenever we went into battle, I always tried to stay close to him. In fact, he saved my hide any number of times, as you well know. He was a great warrior, but he was always just that, a warrior. I don't know how it is, but you, Valerius, are become a king."

First light found them positioned off the harbor entrance, about four miles from shore, in exactly the spot one would expect a friendly fleet to wait if it did not want to navigate the crowded anchorage in the dark. With a perversity men have long claimed intentional, the wind, which had been dull and fluky for so many days, suddenly piped up, blowing fresh from the northwest, and with Glaucon's gaudy banner fluttering from the masthead of Valadator, and with the other ships of his former fleet similarly attired, the grand procession got underway. Row by row, the ships set their sturdy square sails, and foam

351

began to boil in their wakes as they formed into a long column of threes and headed for the town.

The harbor of Zagorbia was an open dish, protected from the west and south by a high rocky point, but open to the northwest, and on days like this, it was a very lumpy and uncomfortable anchorage. The town itself was built on a rising slope along the northeast shore, and was crowned by a large, fortified palace. Several stone piers stretched along the waterfront and between these and the rising ground which led to the point lay a long, crescent shaped beach of fine, grainy sand. It was here that most of the town's smaller fishing craft were drawn up out of the weather, and it was here that the bulk of Valerius' fleet aimed their prows, while Valadator and several of the other larger galleys, headed for the piers. If the flag ruse worked, there would be no immediate resistance and the two attacking groups would join and deploy through the city. If the ruse did not work and they were met on the beaches, Valerius had issued firm instructions to fight towards each other and join forces as quickly as possible. He wanted no repetition of the attack on Kantar.

Being the largest ship in the fleet, Valadator quickly drew ahead of her fellows and as she neared the inner harbor Valerius ordered the sheets eased and the lines readied for docking. Dressed in his best armor and wearing a new battle helm with a golden crown affixed that had been a parting gift from King Koltar, he mounted the high poop and intently surveyed the town. It was quiet. Too quiet for this hour. The streets were empty of peddlars and pedestrians, the houses were all shuttered, and atop the broad avenue which lead to the palace, the huge bronze gates were shut tight. A precaution? An ambush? As Valadator swung to come alongside the pier and her crew crouched behind the bulwarks, ready to spring ashore, Valerius scanned every street and alley, looking for some sign of activity or intent.

At the last moment, just before the ship touched the dock, Glaucon's banner was dropped to the deck, and the white, red and gold standard of Valeria was raised in its place. With a jolt, the great ship bumped against the dock, and before the dock lines were even secured, Valerius and two hundred armed men leapt ashore.

More followed in a rush as first the larger ships came alongside—all now carrying Valerian colors—and then the smaller ones grounded on the beach, their crews vaulting from the decks and wading ashore. In moments there were a thousand men ashore, then two thousand, then four, and still there was no sign of welcome or of hostility from fortress or town. Taking no chances, Valerius spread his men quickly to join with those on the beach, and very soon he stood before a solid, formidable battle line. And still the town was quiet.

Suddenly there came the sound of a shout from the palace. Then another, then a rising tumult of voices. The gates swung open and Valerius tensed and adjusted his grip on his great falchion as a swarm of men burst forth and charged down the hill, all yelling and waving their swords. But then he relaxed and began yelling himself, for in their lead was none other than a grinning, cheering Ragnar.

Epilogue

It was nearing harvest time in Valeria when a dilapidated trading scow drifted into the harbor, loaded to the gunwales with wine casks. She carried the flag of Zagorbia at her single masthead, but other than the cloth of this emblem, the neat, newly coopered casks on her decks and the freshly painted name across her transom—Effusive—she hardly looked as though she could have braved the voyage across the Inland Sea. Her yellow, salt-stained sail was tattered with patch upon patch, her rigging had so stretched that her mast slopped about when she rolled like a stick in a cup, mud and rank weed clung to her sides, and neither her deck nor her crew had felt the effects of a scrub brush in some time. Still, the practiced eye could tell she was not an unsound craft, and as she tied up at the dock and her hands began rolling their cargo ashore, there were more than a couple along the waterfront who gave her a second, sidelong glance.

But Valeria in those days was not a town in which to remark such things, much less comment upon them, and while Effusive completed her unloading, her skipper—a dapper young fellow who, despite his frayed apparel, seemed incongruous himself on such a vessel—left the ship, and headed through the sprawling, ramshackle, waterfront streets towards the main gate of the city.

Attending him were two seamen bearing a small cask

It was his first visit to storied Valeria, court of the Empire, and as he passed through the gates unchallenged, he was surprised at what he saw. That Valeria had been the site of a great battle—the last fought by the old High King—and an even greater conflagration set by its then conqueror and now chief resident, Fantar, was the stuff of legend. But those events had also been near a generation ago, and he did not expect to find evidence of them so plain. Yet there it was: inside the towering, well-mended walls was a curious conglomeration of newly built and rebuilt edifices side by side with charred ruins. Nor were there even any shops or street vendors. All that—the common and commercial—lay outside the walls. Inside were the grand, palatial homes of the new military aristocracy and, while they had to clear rubble to build, they cleared it only where they built.

So it was a curious sight—quite literally a new city rising among the ashes of the old—and it spoke loudly about the man who ruled the place. Plainly, he was a man who would not bother to bury his dead. And it was to pay his respects to this very man that was the errand of the Effusive's captain.

The palace was not hard to find, but sat, a fortress within a fortress, on a high outcropping of rock in the city's northeast quadrant. At its gate, he was challenged, but when it was reported he brought gifts and news from the south, he was not kept waiting long before he was ushered into the audience chamber of Fantar himself. This was a long, rectangular room with barren rock walls and lined with tables still cluttered from the previous night's feasting. At the far end, upon a raised dais lit by windows in the vaulted ceiling above, sat the Emperor's gilded throne, and upon it, the Emperor himself.

The captain started involuntarily at his first sight of this august and powerful personage, for he was plainly a man far gone from the effects of drink and debauchery. His once mighty frame had slumped and settled, the bulk accumulating around his middle like melted wax, his greying hair and beard matted and thin, and his head with the famous eye patch so plain, seemed unsteady on his neck and twitched involuntarily. But when he got close, after he dropped to his knees and was bidden to rise from this deep obeisance, then did he see Fantar's real power. It shown in his eye, an eye that flashed like a burning coal, an eye that was as brilliant as it was calculating, and as mad as it was both. With that eye alone, and in spite of his other infirmities, Fantar ruled an empire.

"You have brought news," the Emperor growled, his voice grating, impatient.

"And gifts, your Majesty," said the captain trying, in contrast, to make his own voice sound light and happy.

"Who are you?"

"My name is Boltar, Your Highness. I work a small trader on the southern shore. I have been sent to present your Majesty with this well-aged cask of

357

scented brandy, compliments of your most devoted servant Glaucon, and to inform your Majesty that the pretender is dead, and all is well in Zagorbia and Dulcai."

"Ah, that is excellent news, indeed! Scented brandy, you say?"

"Yes, your Majesty. It's quite a delicacy along the southern coast—aged with special herbs and spices. I believe you will find it most palatable."

"And all is really well?"

"All is very well, your Majesty."

"Ah!" said Fantar, his countenance visibly relieved. He continued on, muttering something incomprehensible, then dismissed Boltar abruptly. "Hie you back immediately, Captain Boltar, and give Glaucon my compliments. Tell him he has earned the gratitude of his Emperor."

It was not until very much later that evening, after a wild, celebratory feast in which the heady brandy was shared among all his closest advisors, and until the small spigot in the cask became plugged by something, that Fantar learned the truth. Picking up the near empty cask, which was considerably heavier than it looked, he felt something go bump inside. Shaking it, he felt it again, and suddenly enraged, smashed the cask down upon the floor. It burst, spraying the remains of the brandy about the room, but as it did, a large ball shaped object wrapped in cloth—a corner of which it was had blocked the bung—rolled out across the floor, unravelling as it went. The room fell totally silent as, fascinated and at the same time horror stricken, Fantar watched the white and red banner of Royal Valeria unroll, revealing its golden lion, and at its end, unveil the sodden, severed head of Glaucon.

With a cat-like agility few would have guessed he possessed, Fantar pounced upon the head and lifted it up by its dripping hair. "Your compliments, eh?" he snarled, addressing the ghastly, pickled face, his own eye glittering with madness. "I'll give you 'compliments' as I gave you my royal stud, you arse wriggling sycophant!" and he flung the head the full length of the hall where it smacked against the hard stone of the wall. "And as for you, Valerius Everreigning," Fantar shouted, slurring the name and addressing the world at large, "I'll give you such compliments as you'll never forget. You think to make war? I will show you war! I will show you war such as you have never seen! I'll..." And here he stopped in mid shout, a sour, wretched expression consuming his face. Arching his body sideways, he vomited, spewing forth a horrible stream of Glaucon tainted bile.

Finis

End of Volume Two